Con

&

Vist

Book 2 in the Vist series

By Anka B. Troitsky

February 2022

CONSTRUCT & VIST

NSBN: 978-1-7391959-1-5

Dedication to those friends
who didn't make it.

References

This book contains the quotes of the following authors:

Charles Darwin

Mary Shelley

Jane Howard

"I say there have never been populations of either mermaids or centaurs because I can't see how they would copulate with their kind. And hybrids are, by definition, sterile."
From a GCSE school homework

Contents

I am grateful to all my dear friends who supported me and encouraged me in my writing journey.
Also, to my editor Andy Hodges,
The Narrative Craft.

Epigraphica, offering to temple of O'Teka J-67985

Humanity has an enemy. It is a very talented one in its evil. It works slowly, without much thinking, acting mostly on instinct. This instinct is never wrong, but without a reasonable frame, it sometimes fails. It is in that failure that the enemy causes the most damage. Much more so than in success. With a lack of careful strategy or tactics, that evil could bring more devastation and pain because, having abandoned reasoning, it cannot revoke itself. Even without any special plan, this enemy has poisoned, destroyed and slowed down humanity ever since people walked the Earth ... or any other planet. It is hard to recognise. It always has the best intentions in its heart ... And that is probably why it is so powerful ... This evil does not know what it is doing. If cunning men decide to help it, it is even more destructive. And it kills more. And if you come to identify your enemy by its true name, what do you do then?

Do we treat it kindly and show mercy? Otherwise, how are we any different from evil? Good question. How are we better than evil if we help it?"

Sullivan D'Archly, Our Path, 2nd edition – year AC301

Chapter 1. Andrea

Andrea Hesley was the first to finish the test. She checked it twice and looked at the timer. As she had twelve minutes to spare, Andrea closed her silverish eyes. She tried to recite a newly learned prayer but could not concentrate on a single line. So instead, Andrea looked out through the classroom window at the long, thin spear of the O'Teka temple.

The skylight, filtered by the protective field, appeared blue, like the sky on Earth. At least the bible's texts and icons describe it that way. They also said that generations ago, the Earth was swallowed by a red giant that used to be the ancestors' Vitr. Andrea could not help but feel happy about Vitr being such a young star. It would take trillions of generations before Vitr even sped up its fusion. Then, life on Noverca beside a white dwarf would be impossible to maintain, even with all the protective field technology.

Two bureaus away from Andrea, a young man had also finished checking his work and made a quiet clicking noise with his tongue. Andrea turned to him and smiled affectionately. Her brother, Timofey Hesley, had recently dyed his curly hair the same colour as his skin – mauve, a slightly darker tone than Andrea's.

He spoke in sign language to her in the silence of the classroom, "How did you do?"

Andrea shrugged and made a face that signed, "Fine, how else?"

Timofey asked again, "Are we still going to the craft market? Maxin and Iris said there are fashion makers from White City and earthling game traders."

Andrea lifted her hands off the keyboard and replied, "Of course. It'll be fun. What time do you finish your shift tonight?"

"At seven."

"I'll be working until six, but I must also clean up. Let's go right after dinner."

"I thought you left the egg farm last week. Why are you still there? It is not your purpose."

"I know, but I have been working there since I was nine. I missed those cute baby chicks and went back yesterday to make sure that the new girls are managing. They will be fine, I think. An extra apprentice is always a good thing," said Andrea with a sigh.

"I always said that you were obsessed with those birds," said Timofey, rolling his eyes. Andrea was about to give him a worthy reply

3

when the bell forced everyone to upload their tests and vacate the room for the next group.

Forty-three students logged off from their bureaus and activated their amulets. Timofey wore his amulet under the poncho he had bought from the earthlings at the market.

He stopped outside, cleared his throat, and said aloud, "The best teacher in the world is a need, and the best pupil is purple!"

"Tim, rephrasing classics is an offence to O'Teka. Where are you off to now?"

"To the temple, where else?"

"And he accuses me of obsession!"

Her twin brother was obsessed with something bigger than birds and newts. Their great-grandfather, who died in a fire on one of the farms before he was fifty, left his sons a riddle in the form of a very old bible he had inherited from his mother. Neither Andrea's grandfather, grandmother, nor Andrea's dad had been able to solve it, and now Timofey would spend at least three hours in the Temple of O'Teka every cycle, digging into the archives.

"Good luck!" said Andrea, then she waved goodbye to her brother and went to the narrow street between the town wall and Flower Park.

She sat on the bench by a smoke tree and placed her amulet on her left palm. She once again repeated the prayer she wanted to memorise. The first lines were particularly hard because they mentioned strange things from the ancient alien past:

I feared that summer would end

Now at the end of autumn

I welcome the blessing of winter

The girl already knew that on Earth, different seasons used to replace each other across most of the surface, but she left the rest to the poor translation from the dead language. She could not even imagine such a thing as autumn, but winter is called a blessing quite rightfully. There is nothing but death in Noverca's nightside. And that is where her love went to search for lost Earth evacuation pods. Is that why this short poem made her feel so acutely, strongly sad and wishful? Had she become weak? Was he still alive?

Andrea searched her amulet for messages. Nothing new. His last message had come through almost four cycles ago. She had replied immediately, but now she felt a corrosive desire to write to him again. She had promised to wait for at least a week if this happened. She must fight the temptation.

Once again, she prayed and remembered the last few words of his most recent message, "And if I feel too cold, the thoughts of you will warm me up. I have to go now. Vist is waiting. See you at the harvesting festival. Love you! Yours. Nat."

There was something different and particularly nice about how these earthlings expressed their feelings. No one else in Andrea's circle of young men could say things like that. Now she understood why he insisted on writing messages instead of recording voice messages. Written words can reach your mind with a new tone every time you read them. Also, where he is, the sudden noise coming from his amulet could potentially put him in danger. How clever was her most beloved man in the universe! Andrea felt a little better, but her resentment of Vist strengthened. If it wasn't for Vist, Nat would have been here. But then again, if it was not for Vist, Nat would never have come to Noverca. Still, someone else could have looked for those pod-fliers. Andrea cared about missing lives, but not as much as she cared about herself and Nat.

Andrea got up and slowly walked towards the gates to the industrial district. She must not think about her worries until the work was done. She would try and enjoy herself tonight too. Maybe she would even buy a new dress from the Fashion Earth craftsmen to wear on the cycle of Nat's return. A lovely dark-green dress – he loves green.

The amulet beeped briefly with a new notification. Andrea stopped, and her heart seemed to stop too for a second. It was a conv-call. She activated the communicator, then forgot to breathe in haste. Unfortunately, it was only her mother. A small holo-screen – the size of a saucer – appeared in the air above the amulet.

In the middle of the circle, the three-dimensional round face smiled expectedly. "Andrea, honey, how did it go? Do you know the result yet?"

"Yes, mum, I know I have done it all right. The results for the basic exam came through as soon as I uploaded my answers. But the project still needs to be analysed by the master for the final exam mark of Perspective.

"Have you made up your mind then? Nobody had to choose their purpose a second time in our family."

"Mum, I have narrowed it down from four to two options. Although it was hard to let go of the bird- and newt-egg farm."

"And music. Honey, I had my hopes for that one."

"I know. But choosing between protection technology and heat-suit engineering will be much harder. I don't want my future to be influenced by Nat's choice of activity after the rescue mission is over, but if he leaves Altyn I want to be able to do it too. We might both go to the White Capital."

"Oh, did you check the news? They have found more missing earthlings ... have a look when we are done talking."

"Okay, mum ... do you mind if we ... you know ..."

The face on the screen smiled again, "I guess we are done talking. I'll see you at dinner."

The holographic face disappeared and was replaced with a news report. The temple broadcast that the medical transport had just brought in four survivors from the North East Nightland of the continent. The pod had been found about fifteen hundred kilometres from the shore, buried in the ocean ice. The rescue team melted an ice well almost fifty metres deep to recover the bio-sleep tanks. They tried to salvage the pod's equipment, but the chances of brining it all up were small. The tanks were delivered to the Nguyen Medical Centre, where an attempt would be made to recover the evacuees from Earth or preserve their genetic material.

Andrea skipped over the information about the pod content impatiently and viewed it again when the rescue team was mentioned. There was no bad news about any death or injury, and so she sighed with relief. This explained why Nat hadn't written anything for so long.

Andrea looked away from the screen. Next to her on the bench, a small emerald grasshopper landed and cleaned its tiny antennae. She decided not to go to the farm and messaged the owner, Mr Kuan-yu Liamson. She explained that she needed to take care of a personal matter. This time she had quit for real and wished him and his family all the best. Then Andrea turned around and rushed across Flower Park towards the train station. All she wanted was to feel closer to Nat tonight.

Half an hour later, she stood in the middle of Nat's living room and looked at the wall covered in icons. Nat had them permanently projected from the data storage into flat, thin plastic sheets. Apparently, on Earth they would have been dye-printed on something called paper – a brittle and flammable cellulose product that earthlings made bibles out of in the past.

Some icons were as small as Andrea's hand, and some were as large as a tabletop. She loved studying them one by one, over and over again ... Their landscapes were unimaginable.

Nat had admitted to her that it looked very different when he left Earth. But when he was a child, he described seeing the blue colour above his head, giant trees with green leaves, colourful meadows and vast rivers. There were flowers and dark forests on the continent of Gera too, but the light – you could easily see things even in the shadows – that's how bright their Vitr used to be. Andrea couldn't stop wondering how earthlings could see anything with their unmodified eyes in such brightness.

Nat had said that some icons captured the images of something called a "sunset" and a "sunrise." Andrea failed to see the difference. Nevertheless, Earth looked more like Gera outside the protective dome on those projections. The trees looked dark, and the sky was red. Their star, called the Sun, looked more like Vitr, only smaller. Andrea perfectly understood the principles of day and night, of seasonal changes and shadow movements, but she found it extremely difficult to imagine. Some earthlings had brought a collection of screen flicks and 3D visors to experience such sensations, but Andrea preferred Nat's verbal descriptions of the effect. She liked the way his face changed every time he did it.

Some icons had animals on them – the predecessors of the animals of Gera, without radiation-reflecting fur or scales. Their eyes looked wrong and deep, and their size made them look completely unrelated.

And, of course, there were people on those icons. Not even one of them was purple, scaly or furry. She saw brown skin, like Doctor Zina's, white, like Nat's, and even a few people with long hair and bushy beards of various colours. But everybody's skin looked unnaturally smooth and unhealthy. One icon was a projection of Nat in the company of the earthlings she had never met. A girl with orange hair and a young man with dark curls. The girl's freckles were brown instead of violet. Behind them was a saddled beast, the size of a *horse*, cloned in farms on Noverca, but it resembled a dog with black-and-white fur. Nat always spoke about his friends with deep sadness. He said they had died before he came to Noverca, but at least they grew old together. On that icon, Nat looked younger. His eyes used to be blue before the operations, and his internal organs had not been replaced yet. He looked so vulnerable and fragile. She missed him so much.

Here was an icon of their holiday together on Pettogreco Island. This island was discovered a couple of generations ago, seven hundred kilometres from Gera, and it turned out to be quite suitable for life. It, too, lay within Noverca's habitable belt and was slightly larger than its town. The climate there was temperate, with a scattering of small islands and shallow waters that had become home to genetically adapted fish and arthropods from Earth. The island especially attracted earthlings. For some reason, they loved the yellow sand found there, and the opportunity to grow groves of carapalm trees and tall grasses. The fourth city, Carib, was founded there, now inhabited equally by genetically adapted earthlings and Uzhans of Noverca – an artificial race of people tolerant to extra heat. They spent more time bathing under the filtered rays of Vitricus during that trip. Nat's skin darkened, and he looked almost as dark as Doctor Zina on that image.

Andrea sat down and frowned at the picture of Nat with five earthmen, two women and a strange person in a long dark robe. Andrea could not tell if it was a man or a woman. She was not even sure if it was a human. It was a loader. A technologically enhances earthling. The girl knew only the name and that although Vist had come with the others from Earth, he or she was devoted to O'Teka more than all her priests, many generations before. Nat told her that Vist had visited Noverca in the past, a long time ago, when Andrea's great-grandfather was still a schoolboy, but she could not comprehend how that was possible. Now this loader carries a title even greater than Grand. An architexter.

She never studied wormhole transportation. This was Timofey's purpose. He tried to explain to her that this group, including Nat, were the first ones to leave the Earth but the last ones to arrive at Noverca. Tim was sure that Architexter Vist was the man who had found a way to meddle with wormholes, so that the travellers' ship could go very close to one of those black holes, where time slows down. Then the wormhole was activated again – the only way to escape the great gravity – and the ship *shifted* to Noverca, its crew jumping a few generations into the future as if they had travelled in a time machine. This would make Nat almost as old as her great-grandfather. That was too much not only to comprehend but also to imagine.

Andrea spun the chair around to face another Earth construction that Nat had built in his house – a fireplace. It looked as if no fire had been lit for years, although the smell of pink wax was hard to get rid of. Above the fireplace, there was a crossbow on the wall. A weapon nobody used on Gera. Apart from a small data storage device, this was the only thing Nat brought with him from Earth.

Andrea looked at the strange item and found the old music track on her amulet's playlist. It wasn't a new thing bought off the Earth evacuees. They had never heard of it. It was a song from the collection of the very first priests of O'Teka. Andrea recognised only a few words, but the melody was magical. She hummed it, as she had done many times before, intentionally skipping the unknown words, "Hmm-hmm to celebrate ... Mmm-hmm-hmm ... Hmm-hmm-hmm to give away ..."

A few minutes later, she was asleep in the chair, her mind at peace. The window glass darkened, imitating late twilight with a couple of stars in the unfamiliar inky sky. She had missed out on dinner at home and a market trip with her twin brother that night.

Chapter 2. The Branch

I love nights. At night my body is vigorous, and my brain is sharp. I'm sleepy and dumb during the day by comparison, but Bebia insists on me working those hours. She doesn't understand. Since I was a kid, everything that I could read, I remembered and learned while she was sleeping.

She was a little aloof and slow today. When I asked her what was wrong, she shed tears and replied that she loved me and wanted me to live a long and happy life. I didn't answer, but I think she had made up her mind. Up until now, she had rejected offers to assign a free transport unit for her – out of respect for her services. Today she agreed. But not only that! She will take me with her. Apparently, she allowed her friends to equip the prototype model and assign a number to it because of me. Otherwise, they said that it would be recycled too. I didn't even know they had one spare just in case she came to her senses. Perfect. Although I am the only one who did not believe her sweet words. She just decided to leave but realised she could not manage without me. She needs my help.

I am on my way to the laboratory tonight. Once upon a time, it was hard to turn around in here because of all the equipment, tables and tools. It's almost empty now; everything is either packed or recycled for materials. And this is the last facility on the station that was taken away for scrap because people needed medical help until the very end.

Just last week, I helped her with heart transplant surgery on that man – here, in this compartment. But now, no electrical wires remain in the walls, and all the floor tiles have been lifted for their aluminium joints. She let precious metals be evacuated! Anything else but me ... Up to this moment, she was sure we didn't deserve to go with the others. No one even thought of asking me what I wanted. I don't understand this. Only yesterday, I was convinced I would have to kill someone to save my life. But today, that need has vanished. I'm a little disappointed. I, somewhere deep inside, anticipated such an act. I excitedly made plans: on a similar late night, I would make my way into the launching dock and do it. Although it would almost certainly end in exposure and serious consequences. (I hate the word "consequences"! It hurts.) Each vessel is programmed to respond to the owner, but it doesn't matter anymore. We are going too. And I will have my own transport. Thanks to her sentiments.

Of those few thousand people, no one cares about what happens to me. They didn't even talk to me. They never looked me in the eye. They accepted me as a part of her being, not even her child ... more like her pet. Bebia stopped telling me years ago that I am just like everyone else or maybe better. I think they are all nothing but cowards, so keen to escape death that they practically reside in their transport units with their most precious possessions. Everything else is recycled. All other stations are disassembled – even the waste section and medical facilities here are gone. What is left of KOSI will be abandoned as soon as the last transport has gone.

The wormhole opening mechanisms will disengage and shut down. Eventually, the station will run out of energy and freeze on the inside. As Jupiter's gravity shifts again, it will pull KOSI off orbit. The station will melt on its way to the liquid core as it passes through the outer and inner atmosphere, before melting in the fluid layer. I wonder why Bebia wanted to stay and watch this happen. Most likely, she would be dead by then anyway. She would die first, and I would be alone because I could survive a little longer in the low temperature. I don't mind being alone. I just don't want to die. Why did everyone accept that I must stay behind? What's wrong with me? And why did she change her mind? I see only one reason. She wants to carry on using me ... as she always did.

Chapter 3. Search

Rod was very tired when he entered the common room, so he poured himself the largest-possible mug of coffee. The coffee pot was cold by that time. Steven closed the cake jar and shook a few crumbs off his front. He was working his way through Marta's homemade biscuits. "Have you checked the KOSI update on this one?"

"Yes." Rod finished his coffee and checked the pot for more.

"Anything useful there?"

"Nothing of what Vist wants ... yet ..."

"Hey, Rod."

"Mm?"

"Last time, you said that after the fifth hour of pod launches, only one more party was getting ready to go. And then Vist said that none of the pods numbered above 600 had crashed. Maybe this is it? This is truly the last one. There will be no more pods to find."

"SD-211 is still missing, though. The important one."

"But it was lost for much longer than the others. Surely there will be no one left alive. Is it worth risking so much for a few genes and bits of scrap?"

"Steven, are you going to eat Marta's cakes all by yourself?"

"No," answered Steven, "but they are almost as good as those my German grandma used to make."

He pushed the jar back on the magnetic shelf, walked across the small room and sat next to his friend on the stool fixed to the floor. Everything was fixed to the floor on this huge cargo avion.

"If the bio-sleep tank is not damaged, Selest could still be alive," said Rod. "Bloody hell, man, I am so dehydrated!"

"But it landed forty years ago. The newest emergency landing tanks couldn't sustain you for more than forty years."

"It was thirty-nine years and eight months. We still have four months of hope."

"You need four months of ZPE-converter charge in that tank," said Steven, pulling the bottle of carrot juice from the fridge next to him then placing it on the table in front of Rod.

Rod emptied it in a few long and heavy gulps and sighed, "That too. Anyway, it is not up to us. Vist will decide. Don't you think Tolyan and I wouldn't rather go home to the kids? But Selest's vessel is more important than any others we recovered since the KOSI station went down."

"What happened to KOSI? Was the station melting or something?"

"Sort of. The Sun's gravity has changed too much. The last seven people left when it was about to go off orbit, and every school kid on Gera now knows their names."

"Are you still writing your book about the evacuation for the temple?"

"*The Summary*? Yes. Some pods we found had their own account of the events. Very interesting."

"What does Vist think about it?"

"She doesn't, not yet anyway. But she hopes that one of the pods we find will lead us to Selest," said Rod. He rubbed his eyes, pulled his eyelids, and then carefully removed his night-vision lenses.

"That old woman's? But why? She will be what ... over 150? She might not have survived the bio-sleep, let alone the landing. Why is Vist so sure her pod didn't get lost on the way here? Hundreds did."

"Every pod had a unique introduction signal as it entered the atmosphere. Vist spent ages in O'Teka's temple looking through the records. She is certain that SD-211 is here somewhere."

"I don't know. We looked in chronological order. This pod here truly has to be the last. Didn't we give up on SD ages ago?"

"We did, but Vist and Nat didn't." Rod closed his eyes and sighed again.

"It's late, Rod. Go to sleep," said Steven, putting his large hand on Rod's skinny shoulder.

"I am not done there yet. As soon as I remove anything readable from the scrap, you and Tolyan can melt it down ... tomorrow."

"Well, I am done. Good night." Steven got up and made for the door.

Rod got up but only repositioned himself in a comfortable chair by the wall.

"And if you see Mrs Darkwood anywhere, tell her I need something stronger than caffeine. We are running out of time," Rod said loudly, throwing his head back on the chair's soft fabric.

He noticed how Steven stiffened his shoulders at these words on his way out. Rod closed his eyes. He almost fell asleep. Then Vist's voice made him jump. Rod grabbed the amulet on his chest and activated the response mechanism.

"Mr Baker-Green, are you there? Rod?"

The slightly metallic voice was neither female nor male, distorted by a device in Vist's larynx.

Rod stared intensely at the loader's face on the holo-screen. "Baker is here, Sir ... Ma'am. What's the news? Do we have it?"

"Yes."

Rod always thought that when he heard Vist say this word, there would be more excitement in his or her tone. But he was wrong.

The voice was still melodic, calm and annoyingly levelled. "Rod, how long until we finish working with LU-569?"

"Tomorrow, the equipment will be ready to go by noon. Anything valuable will take no time to extract. You have already uploaded the data, and successfully, by the sounds of it." Rod could not contain his yawn. "Mik and Steven will melt the scrap down in less than six hours if we don't faff around. Things cool down quickly here, and I say we can leave by tea time."

"I don't need to wait that long. We will split the team tomorrow morning. Do not rush, and when you are done – go home. Tom and you can fly the avion, am I right?"

"Who will you go with then? How far?"

"Not too far ... That's why I can't wait. We were lucky. Every time we recover another lost evacuee, I hope it might be someone who knew Selest personally, and their tracker was programmed to watch out for her. I have the latitude right, but SD-211 has landed one-third of the meridian away from the target. I want Marta to fly the *Wasp* spaceship and Nat to back her up and be the muscle. The rest of you must finish the job and regroup on Gera."

"Why can't we all go? We can come back and pick what is left of the LU pod later. It's not like someone would pass by and nick the avion."

"Don't forget our business commitment, Rod. I assume you want to get paid for this one. We are already two cycles behind schedule. Also, there will not be enough food for the next week if we all go. Mr Baker-Green, I don't think we will recover the pod itself, and I will explain why later."

After Vist disengaged, Rod sat back and thought for a moment. Then he activated his amulet again and made a new entry in the log file. Soon, his *Summary of the Earth Evacuation* would reach its last chapter. His first book, or a bible, as Novercians call it. Fighting the desire to close his eyes for a few hours, he checked the paragraphs containing information downloaded from the pods, or as the evacuees called them, the "transport units."

Vist's team had found and brought in twenty-eight pods to the capital. For some reason, the loader could not find one particular pod. It was a very important one. Not everyone understood why, but they knew that a very old woman from Earth, who had known Vist from childhood, must have arrived in it. But something in the identification signal was wrong. Something bothered the loader. Vist had tracked down every successful pod that left Earth on the same day in the year 3465.

That year the human population in the solar system was fewer than 2,000. That is much fewer than all humanity at the end of the last ice age. Although a little greater than during the mythical great flood of any version. And, of course, far less than they all hoped for. Even Vist was unable to predict the many natural disasters and new diseases that took away millions of lives in the last few decades of the Object mission.

No one had explained why what was supposed to happen five billion years later started so early and progressed so fast. The Sun swelled up, turning into a red giant. The water on Earth evaporated. Some water was saved in relatively small, recycled amounts that were technologically preserved on the Moon, on Mars and on space stations around Jupiter. The biggest part of Earth was stripped of life by the intense heat and radiation. Those last surviving occupants of the planet did just that when they decided to die at home in the underground settlements.

No children have been born in the solar system since 3441, apart from those few cases within the religious groups that initially refused to participate in the Object mission, instead attempting an alternative plan. That plan, which involved drifting off on the Moon, seemed more desirable for most people, who just prayed and hoped to be taken care of. Their leaders made many promises, frightening everyone who would listen with terrible consequences if they did not believe in salvation by the Lord and did not do what they were told. They asked people to trust them and misled them into thinking that the Object mission had failed. This persuasion worked until Object started successful relocations from Earth to Mars and then to Jupiter's orbital stations twenty years later. It was too late to change their minds then. Rod could only guess how many who did not care even for selves became Moon-dust fossils. That is, assuming the Moon wasn't enveloped by a red giant and instead drifted away into space. Just as the believers hoped it would.

A few weeks later, the wormhole opened, and the transport units went to the System of Vitricus, a hundred every hour with six parties in total. But they began arriving in the Noverca system in intervals separated by a few years, one party at a time. They fell from the sky like death bombs. The colony received a sign of the wormhole opening a month before the first signals came through. To protect the colonists and incoming travellers, the pod navigators had to accept the coordinates for the softest possible landing and provide enough space. The Novercians prepared the landing polygon over a shallow ocean region west of Gera and called it the "chessboard" because it was divided into squares.

According to the plans left for Object by Vist, the pod computers were already programmed to understand Noverca's geography and its system of coordinates, register a given square, and navigate a good few hundred metres away from each other. The accuracy was not perfect, but the number of pods that missed their target a little was negligible. The number of those pods that completely failed to accept the landing instructions was devastating. The first party lost almost a quarter of the pods before entering the Vitricus system. Of the ninety-four who survived the journey, only seventy-two landed according to the instructions. The rest crashed as they decided to land by themselves.

Those who landed successfully trusted the loader's advice and calculations. They accepted them as fact. Careful analysis probably revealed a lack of perfectly conclusive information but not a single contradiction or blind guess. Some of them had clever theories, but they did not contradict Vist's.

The others used a loader's blueprints, but because they did not like certain aspects and found them too hard or too expensive to implement, they came up with self-inflicted doubts. They concluded that the only way of learning dependable life skills was in a constructive way.

Rod tapped the command "Dictate," and he said in the voice he used when reading books to his daughters, "Never mind that you could be easily biased by the others' authoritative or majority opinions, or suffer from a lack of rational thinking or any illogical convictions. From your perspective, triumph appears very flattering, but unlike any humanitarian subjects, science and maths demand that your new ideas and earlier-discovered facts have to integrate as precisely as the instruments of a well-tuned orchestra. You can pay a high price for your whim if you only have a one-way ticket."

Chapter 4. The Branch

We are going to be launched with the second party of evacuees. They will be sending the first four hundred units through the hole all morning. This last hour, I have been feeling anxious and even scared. Bebia still does not let me talk to the others, although they have started to acknowledge my existence, since I have become an evacuee. That young woman, Kaila, the daughter of our last patient, didn't turn away when I waved hello to her.

I am so hungry. I understand we shouldn't eat for ten hours before bio-sleep, but this is a very unpleasant ten hours. I dislike all these people even more now. Towards *her* ... I feel something I can call *hate*, and I must control myself. Indeed, if it's true that we are going to the planet's surface, we won't have to live so near to each other any longer. Some people claim to remember life under the planet's surface and even on the surface, and they describe something they call "personal space." A comforting concept. Maybe I will finally find my own place and my own way.

It is time. We are getting into our transport and setting Bebia's hand case between two brackets on the wall. The shape of the bio-sleep tanks inside the unit makes me think of breakfast eggs on a saucer, but when I open the lid of one of them, the base looks like a giant spoon. With such rusty joints, it will be harder for her to assume an embryo position.

She swallows a dose of serum, and I help her into the bio-sleep tank, then close the transparent lid and release the Kyros foam. She is trying to tell me something as it envelops her body, but I don't need to hear her out. The last thing I want is to feel that weakness again. I felt it all the time when I was a child because she was nice to me. She even tried to arrange birthday parties for me. Once a year, she would make a blood cake, candles and gifts, like in those flicks from the past. But there were no other kids on the station to come to my party, and after my fifteenth birthday, she stopped the tradition. If she was a real mother, she wouldn't have stopped it. But I am grateful for the access to those flicks. They explained a few things about my childhood that I did not understand before.

For example, there was a time when I could not understand why everyone was much bigger than me. But ever so slowly, they shrank to my size and became even smaller. I realised what I had been deprived of all my life. The kids of the past were spoiled. They had fun, toys, games and parties. They were loved and kissed, but here no one wanted to touch me. Even she stopped hugging me some time ago. All I had was education and work. She stopped the games, too, and forced me to study far too early. I am aware of it now. I was the only child here, not born but created to be a backup for her. She never really loved me. She never gave me what I wanted. Especially the food I craved. I hated her food ... more since there have been no more chickens on board. The only tasty thing I ever had were those tiny grey creatures in the waste block. At nights I could catch them with no effort until they were all gone. By then, I was old enough to help her clean up after the organ transplants, and I was often lucky to find an extra snack for myself left by the patients in the lab.

I hear two men sealing our transport and moving it to a starting platform with launching guns. I am not taking serum as I have no intention of sleeping yet. I want to watch the launch. I check her for the last time to ensure she is asleep. Under the lid, her face has sunk into the Kyros foam, which has already started to crystallise. I remove her case from its brackets on the wall, taking out the small personal terminal and telling the central computer to connect it to the outer cameras. They were installed for orientation when landing. The main computer gives me control over them, and I activate the holographic screen. I feel the vibration of the conveyor. This means they have started feeding transport units into the launching guns – one by one.

The units all vary inside. They have different numbers and contents, painted in different colours, decorated with blazons, names, messages and slogans. Still, they all have the same shape – a bullet shape of identical size and weight. This shape is compulsory, as they are to be launched from those eight guns that will send them inside the wormhole at a certain speed. On that journey, they will separate more, the gap between them will somehow grow, and they will arrive days apart. The next party to launch just a couple of hours later will arrive a few years after us. I can feel my transport charging into the gun. I am taking the risk of staying awake. She told me that I may not survive the launch, as it is quite a shock to the system. I drop the terminal, rush back to my bio-sleep tank under its lid, and press myself into the Kyros foam. I shut the lid when I feel it – I think my guts are getting all mashed up, and I am losing consciousness.

Not for long, though, because the foam solidified only on the surface when I opened my eyes again. It is no harder than caramel. I kick the lid open and try to sit up, scattering the shards of foam. The gravity compensator is working, and we are moving at a constant speed. I feel fine, save for a headache. I scan my vitals, and apart from a few ruptured capillaries, everything is in order. She told me that I heal even quicker than the modified others, so I will be okay soon. I fall out of the tank and shift back to the shiny terminal holo-screen on the floor. I can see several other units around mine that look like they are suspended in space. But we are moving ... we are on our way to the hole. There are dozens ahead of me and dozens behind. They said this journey would take about a week. At last – my personal space. I wonder how it will feel to be finally alone here, awaiting not my death but my freedom and a life of my own.

I can't see the mouth of the wormhole, and apparently, it is not as big as the ones they opened up before I was born. All I can see on the screen is a slowly growing area of the sky with no stars. It took another hour for this darkness to surround us completely. The glowing reflection of the enormous red sun we left behind slowly slides off the transport units, and even with my nocturnal eyes, I find myself in complete darkness and complete silence.

Chapter 5. Zina and Tom

"Can you hear me? Can you understand me? Can you see me?"

The man's eyes focused on Zina's face with effort. His mouth opened and he exhaled, but the noise it made didn't sound like a voice.

Zina smiled encouragingly and said loudly, "If you understand me, blink twice."

The man on the medical bed squinted then shut his eyes tight, but when he opened them again, he just stared.

"It's okay," said Zina to a short young assistant standing next to her. "He probably can't count yet. Scarlett, wait for a minute and try again. Call out when you see the first sign of cognition."

She walked to another bed, where a skinny woman sat shaking and sweating.

"Better?" Zina asked her.

"Yes, thank you. Is he ... going to be alright?"

"Your husband? He looks very promising."

"Doctor, but he will be fine, right? Tell me he will be fine ... you must ... just say it!"

The woman shook even more in what seemed to be violent, hysteric convulsions. She didn't cry but held her breath while making a high-pitched whine.

Zina took her by both hands and looked into her eyes, "Breathe slowly, please. Breathe with me. That's it. In ... and out. In ... and out. I can tell you that your husband – what's his first name again?"

"Shvedric."

"Shvedric will not die anytime soon. He survived the worst stage of awakening. Many people didn't make it this far after decades of bio-sleep and such a harsh landing. But it is too early for me to tell whether his central nervous system avoided any problems. There is no mechanical damage, but he greatly overdosed on bio-sleep serum. Who administered it at the start? You?"

"No. We did all the prep by ourselves." The woman was lying. It was obvious.

"Fleur, you are on Noverca now. You will only fit in if you are honest. This is why I can't just promise you that your husband will be perfectly well."

The woman Zina called Fleur looked so miserable and guilty that Zina let go of her hands and sighed. "I know it will be hard, but not impossible. If you keep trying long enough, you will get used to it and even love it. It's a very different life."

"Doctor," a woman named Scarlett called out, a chubby young woman hypertrichosian only 1.4 metres tall.

Zina nodded to Fleur and went back to Shvedric.

The man's eyes focused on Zina's face and his hoarse voice said, "Avez-vous vu Fleur? She should be on the balcony."

"Il n'y a pas de balcon, but Fleur is here and worried about you," Zina replied.

"I am so sorry ... Every time I open my eyes, I see something different. *Pardonne-moi* ...

I was in my mother's house a moment ago, but it was demolished nineteen years back."

"A little more than that, I am afraid," said Zina.

"Shvedric! My love ... You are alive!"

Fleur got off her bed and tried to walk across the room, but her legs could not support her. She almost fell on the rubber floor, grabbing the corner of the desk for support. Scarlett was already there with a wheelchair, but Fleur screamed at the sight of Scarlett's hairy face. Zina had to leave Shvedric and deal with Fleur once again. When things calmed down, and Fleur finally approached her husband, a new problem appeared. Shvedric didn't recognise his wife. He called her an old woman and demanded to see his beautiful Mrs Beaumont. Nobody heard Vist coming to the ship's medical unit. The loader watched the man with interest, holding both hands in the sleeves of his or her wide robe. Zina stood over Fleur, who cried uncontrollably on the floor.

"A little help, Vist," Zina said angrily.

Vist stepped forwards and picked up the crying woman as if she had no weight. Fleur put her arms around Vist's neck, then hid her face on his chest. Zina didn't like this at all. Especially when Vist smiled handsomely and asked, "Where do you want her?"

Zina wanted to say, I don't, but instead, she grunted grumpily, "Over there ..."

The loader carefully put the sobbing woman on the patient's bed, and Zina approached her with a frown.

"Please don't try to get up again. It will take a few cycles of therapy before you can walk or run. Do you understand me, Fleur, or do I need to secure you with these belts? And prepare yourself for more strange-looking people. Do you think Scarlett has an unusual appearance? Wait until you see folks with plum-coloured faces and the local beauties shimmering like a silverfish."

When she looked back at Vist, he was standing next to Shvedric, who sat up, leaning on Scarlett's arm. She wanted to warn Vist that her patient was still very confused, but it seemed to her that the loader had no problems there. She heard them talking.

"The official information on your computer did not say much about Selest's assistant. I assume this person had control over the event."

Shvedric replied slowly, but Vist was patience itself. "Selest was not herself recently. After all, she was older than my grandpa. He used to be her pupil, you see. Oh, she stopped training staff almost twenty years before our flight. Now, what was the name of that youth? I am sorry, ma'am, but the name escapes me. He was her last and most trusted assistant. If it was not for him, she would not have gone at all ... Yes, mademoiselle. Old Selest would have died with that cursed planet. In fact, I don't believe anyone spoke to her or even saw her during the last six months. Is this a honey wax I can smell?"

"Forgive me, monsieur," interrupted Vist, "May I ask what happened to her pod signature? It is missing a certain code I was supposed to recognise. Also, we have a record of the passenger claiming that he had come out of the same transport. Were there two or three of them in the pod?"

"Passengers? No, there were no passengers. I am sure of it. One assistant, that's all she needed. She was old, my boy ... her mind wandered sometimes. The last thing she said to me ... umm ... it was a quote. But whose? My mind is clouded too. Darwin? Yes. She quoted the ancient wise man. I don't remember – something about not looking for the bogeymen under your bed anymore. Nope, it's gone. *Pardonne-moi.*"

"When we realised they were inside us," Vist said without addressing anyone. He thought for a moment and left the room without another word.

The old Shvedric didn't even notice the loader's departure. He squeezed Scarlett's hand and smiled kindly.

"Mademoiselle, are you a dwarf? You know what? Back on Earth, we had a fantastic beauty salon in the Object settlement in the Dead Forest. The young garçon Valentine could electrify every hair follicle on your cheeks so that you never had to shave. You could really use his service. He left Earth two hours ago. Look out for him, what was his first name? Nope, it's gone."

Zina was unable to leave the medical bay before lunchtime. Mr and Mrs Beaumont were finally well enough to be moved to the passenger room, where a vital signs detector monitored them. She found Vist in the dining room, slowly chewing on a smoked kipper and looking at the wall in front of him.

She sat with the loader on her right-hand side and finished her soup before Vist finally closed his eyes, sighed, and asked, "Zin, do you remember the old Earth story about the scientist who created a creature using parts of different dead bodies?"

"The Frankenstein monster?"

"Yes. The creature was too different. People did not accept it, but he didn't get the hump with them much ... he was angrier with his creator."

"That's right."

"Why? Any idea?"

"Well. That monster man was not very smart. He thought it was the doctor's fault for making him so ugly. Why did you bring that up?"

"Doctor Frankenstein created a very emotional but not very rational man, who was still smart enough to take revenge on an easy target."

Vist turned his head for the first time and looked at Zina. As always, she felt her pulse rise in response.

"I still don't understand."

"Zina, I suspect we have a Frankenstein monster on Noverca."

"Some people who came here in the last hundred years might think that the whole population of colonists consists of—"

"Oh, no. I am talking about a creature who is very different from earthlings and Novercians. He would not fit in with any of us. He is different from us all."

"You are different, but who are you talking about?"

"I'm not sure yet."

"But then, how do you know?"

"I don't know. I suspect."

A voice sounded behind them both. "I thought I would find you both here," said Captain Darkwood, who sat down on the loader's right with a plate full of deep-fried mini snacks in his hand. "What's on the subject menu today?" asked Tom before he started to eat.

"Vist thinks one of us is a Frankenstein monster."

"Really? Is she talking about herself?"

Vist turned away from Zina and looked at Tom, "Let's leave that for now. Tom, I need to share with you what I found in Beaumont's pod."

"It's about time. So far, you have been sending us to crazy places, hardly explaining anything before or after," said Tom, taking another bite.

Vist activated her amulet and doubled the screen size, so they could all see it.

"My assistants Cesario and Viola catalogued all the records for me chronologically. SD was pronounced hopeless from the start. Here's the initial signal I found in the temple. It shows the crash site for Selest's pod SD-211 at these coordinates, too far from where she was supposed to land. There is a small degree of inaccuracy, but insignificant. The pod ended up a couple of thousand kilometres north-east. What does this mean?"

"This means that her pod's computer accepted the instructions and initially navigated to the correct landing square," answered Tom, chewing.

"That's right. Something tampered with the coordinates, as if it was crashed on purpose. This has not happened so clearly and deliberately to any other pods. As you all know, we found nothing in that region, although we scanned deep into the ice and searched far around it. Now, because it went off course, three pods that belonged to Selest's friends tried to track it. The first two, GL-202 and DK-294, pointed at the same spot. The pod ZC-241 made the third signal register for Dr Cazacu's daughter Zhani. Her pod was practically still inside the wormhole at that time, just at the exit point. That is why there is a four-year difference between them. Zhani died twenty-six years later and did not leave any records about her interactions with Selest before evacuation. According to her computer, the SD coordinates gave a place few hundreds kilometres south, further away from the first readings."

"I remember that trip. It was way off the icy shores, and we found nothing on the seabed again. It wasn't very deep there."

"What about the owners of those first two pods? I know it was about forty years ago, but Selest's friends may still be alive or have some descendants who you can question. Surely," said Zina.

"Oh, I could, and I have, but let's discuss that later. Until today, we had two possible crash sites reasonably close to each other. This week we recovered Beaumont's pod, FB-569, and its records show something very interesting. We found it because their computer returned to life from time to time. On one of those occasions, it read the final impulse sent out by SD-211 pod before it became silent. Apart from us, no one on Noverca has tried to scan for the missing pods, which is why they ignored the impulse. Even if a geographical expedition had picked it up, they would have mistaken it for an error."

"Let me guess. You now have a third spot ..." said Tom, but Vist interrupted him excitedly, and hit the palm of her hand with her fist. The loader's voice, however, did not change.

"Exactly! And I guarantee that we will find nothing again if we go there."

"Why? And what are you so happy about?" Zina asked.

"Zina, I am a fool for not checking the geography of that area well enough! Let me show you the map of all three spots. They are on an almost-straight line, and what area lies north-east of Gera? The ocean ice crust is just above the cold current. What does it do all the time? It moves. Like a gigantic glacier ... it moves to the south. This is why the second coordinates were a little off, and the third – much later – pointed even further towards the equator. It came off the main crust. The pod is on the iceberg now, and it's drifting away. I have to check how fast the current is in those parts. If we don't apprehend it soon, it might melt, and we will not find anything in the warm depths. I hope it's not too late, and it hasn't crossed the belt yet."

Vist grabbed the amulet, got up, and rushed out of the room. Zina and Tom heard Vist conv-calling Rod, who was still on the cargo avion. They looked at each other through the space where Vist sat a few seconds ago. The vague smell of honey wax was still in the air.

"Do you want an early night tonight?" asked Zina.

"Sure," answered Tom, and they both walked their separate ways back to work.

Chapter 6. The Branch

From when I turned nine years old, she shaved my head and some other parts weekly. A fortnight ago, I refused to submit to this stupid ritual. My hair has grown almost fifteen centimetres since. Now, for the first time, I can feel every strand of my bodily hair standing on end. Some hairs are coarse and longer, kind of tactile. Am I nervous? Not anymore. In fact, I feel excellent. Right now, the computer is doing nothing but sustaining the bio-sleep tanks and an appropriate environment for itself. There are no lights, no sounds. Of course, no one would hear or see those indicators if I stayed in the tank. The air temperature drops to eight degrees centigrade to preserve all biological material on board. That includes the cell and tissue bank and some food stores – in case we land far from another food source. I am still hungry. So the first thing I must do is fix that.

There is not much space in the unit. I can just about stand tall and walk three steps between the egg-shaped tanks. There are no chairs, but I don't feel like I need one. I can sit on the floor quite comfortably. The unit's screen is quite bright, and its white light allows me to see my personal space's interior. The terminal is the size of a dinner plate, and at the moment, I can only access Bebia's personal journal – just her monthly log, as I was never allowed to have my own. It is not cyphered, though, because she needed me to use it sometimes during work. Never mind, this is all I need right now. I am going into the literature file.

The containers with our valuables are fixed under the floor and take up about one-third of the total volume. The essential storage is in the heaviest and strongest part – in the unit's nose. I pull off the hatch there and take out the box of ration packages. I am so hungry! I consume three portions in one go, but it is not very good. Most of it is synthetic proteins, fat and some dehydrated vegetables, preserved years ago when they still grew plants on Io-4. Some of this stuff is supposed to be sweet, but apparently I can't taste sweet. My birthday cakes were made of delicious, processed chicken meat and haslet. Nevertheless, I swallow all these compressed bars and capsules in a mere attempt to stop the hunger that is driving me mad. I drink some water and finally feel some satiety.

Time to take care of another necessity – the oxygen. The air is already heavier, and it will not improve. She took me through the transport operation dozens of times to ensure I knew what to do when we landed. I need the computer to adjust the life support for a fully functioning organism. The person who designed these transport units could survive in a much smaller emergency escape pod. According to the evacuation project's chronicles, this person created a system that integrated a vessel with the living body. I look at Bebia's tank. She is in a dormant state. She is using a minimal amount of oxygen, and all processes in her body have almost stopped. My source of oxygen is in my tank. I approach it and peel off the remains of the Kyros foam that now reminds me of the dry and porous tar they used last year to seal the waste and prevent its decay. Lying inside the tank feels surprisingly good. Its spoon-like shape is more comfortable than my bed on the station used to be, although it isn't soft at all. I didn't notice this before, but the tank's inner upholstery firmly accommodates my body's shape – every curve, every limb, and my broad shoulders. I have to close the lid to communicate with the computer.

The program doesn't respond immediately, but it recommends I return to the bio-sleep mode when it does. I turn down the predictable advice. Then it asks me for how long I intend to stay awake. I reply, "For the whole duration of the journey." The computer calculates my options and suggests I need a recycled oxygen supply for 172 hours of the pre-programmed flight. If I do not go into bio-sleep and use up the oxygen supply for one awake organism and one in stasis, I will only survive for forty-six hours. This option is unacceptable. After searching for alternatives, the computer comes back with a solution: if I recycle the oxygen, hibernate for at least eighteen hours at a time, and allow no more than two hours in between to exercise and to receive food, fluids, and mental stimulation, I will survive for 133 hours.

I ask how long I will stay alive if I take the stasis person out of the equation. The answer – for 165 hours. I see. The amount of oxygen was calculated to sustain two people in bio-sleep for 40 years. This same amount of oxygen would last about seven days for me alone. I can use a device on board to recycle oxygen from carbon dioxide by converting it into carbon monoxide and throwing it out, which means it would produce less and less of the precious gas each time. I am still a few hours short. What can I do? I can hibernate a little longer and stay awake a little less. I won't exercise – just stretch, so I respire less when awake.

For the same reason, I can eat less, but that may be harder. The computer also reminds me that I need to increase the room's temperature a little, check my calcium levels and suggest some games for mental challenges during my active periods. I agree to adjust the heat but refuse the games. I have other plans for engaging my brain.

Hibernation is a thing people did not do in the past. They borrowed an ability to use codons from a particular terrestrial mammal that went extinct long before *she* was born, but this was still a very different state, and it could only be short-term. It is not as harsh as a bio-sleep you may not even come out of, and it is not normal sleep, despite the heart still beating. It is a controlled function that people learned relatively recently, but they need technology to start and finish it. I have to argue with the computer, but after some haggling both ways, it accepts the terms. The computer will help to inject the sedative, which is much safer than bio-sleep serum, and then it will inject me with another drug 21.6 hours later to wake me up. My body temperature will decrease, my heart will slow down, and gas exchange in my lungs will be controlled by the computer, along with the uptake of cellular calcium ions and protein production. The chemicals added to my bloodstream will reduce the cells' response to the cold temperature and depress my metabolism. I will be closer to anaesthesia than sleep, but I will pass the time quicker and save oxygen. I don't need Kyros foam to equalise the condition of all body parts, but I will receive electrical impulses through my muscles to prevent sores, stiffness and tissue crushing. I digest food fast. Only one meal a day will be needed, at least two hours before each bedtime.

I look at her through the lid one more time. "Well," I say out loud, the first words since we left, "I actually may live through all this. But this time, Bebia, I will need *your* help."

Chapter 7. Mr Napovni

Andrea Hesley walked through the side gate to her mother's garden with a happy grin and hands full of packages of her favourite pastries. Today, the garden-watering program was set to epiphytes, so the garden was full of mist that hid the orchids like a veil but couldn't hide their smell. Andrea didn't even notice this, even though it threatened to loosen her make-up, leaving purple patches on her intentionally whitened cheeks. Nat was off for his very last expedition and would be back soon. She had so much to tell her mother; they needed to discuss many possibilities and make a million plans. She stopped on the steps to the gazebo, and her smile faded. Mother was not alone. There was a stranger in the chair next to her. The man was dressed as an official, and her mother's light-thistle-coloured face reflected the uneasiness Andrea felt inside.

"Andrea! At last! I am glad you came so soon. This is Mr Napovni. He represents the Gera-environmentalists group, and he has questions for you."

The little curls on her mother's head barely but perceptibly trembled with excitement or anxiety. The polite smile was forced but not insincere. Andrea carefully placed the boxes on the table and said "Hello?" in a tone that demanded an explanation. Mr Napovni did not hear it.

He got up and said, "At first, your mother thought you had done something wrong to receive a visit from me. Are you often a troublemaker?"

"Depends on your definition of trouble," replied Andrea. She still felt alert and defensive but could not say why. The man did not appear serious or threatening; he had a voice too high for a grown man, but something about him radiated danger.

"Andrea, don't be rude. This gentleman is interested in your friend. Mr Napovni, I hope our Nat is not in trouble."

"Not at all, but he is out of my reach now. I mean, he is away on one of his heroic missions. If I am not mistaken, madam, Andrea brought you something delicious for tea. I can smell fruits and sweet-bark icing. May I?" he asked, picking up one of the boxes and looking at Andrea with an almost childish innocence.

On his head was a fashionable Egyptian scarf, and between the strands of his shiny yellow beard, the red beads of a precious necklace flashed. His eyes were yellowish-brown. His skin was white but darkened by rays of Vitr. So, he was an earthling who travels out of town. He just studied nature, nothing to worry about.

Andrea relaxed and smiled, "Of course."

"I will make tea, and you two can talk," said mother and hurried inside the house. Andrea noticed her mother looked visibly relieved.

When Andrea and Mr Napovni were alone, he maintained that slightly infantile manner of speech. Andrea thought for a moment that it was not the same face she had seen a minute ago, but she soon forgot about her initial uneasiness. She asked him if he was a descendant of the new colonists.

"Oh, no! I take it as a compliment, but I am old enough to be one of the original and quite authentic evacuees from one of the first and earliest groups. Of course, I was a very young man when I travelled."

"So your parents built the pod-flier in the solar system?" asked Andrea with interest.

"No, I have no parents and was just a passenger. My friend lost a family member, and the family member's place was offered to me. I was too poor to evacuate myself and believed I would stay and die with the other unfortunate souls."

"But Nat told me that all people who worked for the project had a chance."

"As I am well aware, your friend, Nathaniel Alloyway, wasn't one of the regular evacuees. He had a very different arrangement. But that is not what I want to ask about him. Wow! This tea is delicious, Mrs Hesley. My thanks! Do you buy it in the White Capital?"

The mother's guest happened to be a very charming and funny man. He joked a lot and even flirted with Andrea's mother a little. But after tea, Mr Napovni became more serious and asked his first important question with passion in his high voice.

"Miss Hesley, would you be willing to take part in my research on the pod-recovery missions? I am working on my new offering to O'Teka. All my previous essays were just practice. I wrote a few articles on the environment and on Gera's ecological history. What Mr Alloyway and his colleagues are doing fascinates me. I already interviewed some people rescued by them, and I plan to talk to the whole team when it returns. So, I need to prepare."

"What do you want to learn from me? O'Teka knows everything," said Andrea. "Their leader, Vist, has made a few offerings already for each pod they found."

"Absolutely! Excellent work indeed! But the Architexter Vist is a rather modest person and gave minimal details about the project participants. Since you know one of them personally, I hoped you could ... introduce them to me one by one. I don't need to know their secrets. I have no intention of violating their privacy; I just wish to possess a few facts that summarise who they are as a potential subject of my admiration. Their names need to be remembered by the historical bibles of Noverca."

"But they are already there and have been for a long time. All of them, apart from Nat, came here before. The colony was only about three hundred years old – almost three generations before the first pod-fliers came from Earth."

"How is that possible?" Mr Napovni looked genuinely surprised. "But then again, my time on Noverca is limited by one generation. I have had no time to learn about everything that happened here hundreds of years ago."

"I am not the right person to talk about the architexter. I just know that Vist is an electronically enhanced genius. My brother Timofey can probably explain how they've done that. Tim said that the architexter's head contains all humanity's knowledge, achievements and history, and that he is closer to O'Teka than anybody else ever was."

"That is quite debatable," said Mr Napovni coldly, but he immediately laughed as if remembering a joke. "Andrea, is it true that the architexter is neither woman nor man? Or both?"

"No. Vist is a man. Tim told me so. He once saw the architexter in the temple. He overheard him talking to Priestess Bulgaria, and she loved it. It was ... the way earthmen talk to women. They make them feel ... good ... different somehow."

"Well, what else can you tell me about Mr Alloyway and his friends? I feel I must make that offering to the goddess. Help me to make it well. Please. I will pay handsomely. Here is the voucher for thirty outfits from the earthling market. For you and your mother. She told me how much you like their clothing. By the way, your mother is an incredibly charming woman, so delightful and exquisite ... I could eat her alive," Mr Napovni said with a wink and activated his amulet to record Andrea's contribution by touching his red necklace.

Since her father had died, Andrea had wanted more than anything for her mother to find happiness again. This man seemed to be of the right age, and he was possibly kind and decent beneath his strange appearance. The fact that he was not boring was already obvious.

Andrea told Mr Napovni what Nat had told her when they met. Soon, Mr Napovni learned that the main pod-recovery team consisted of ten people:

Their leader was a loader called Vist. The architexter himself. A creature born to be integrated with information technology on the molecular level. His usual abode was a house near the O'Teka temple in the White Capital. It was built specifically for the loader and reminiscent of those houses on the planet Mars from the first half of the third millennium, modelled not for an underground colony but for work on the surface. There was also something in it from the earthly mansions of the Platinum Age's wealthy elite.

Thomas Darkwood once headed a diplomatic flight to Noverca to organise the evacuation of the last people from the dying Earth. He was still the captain of the very same *Wasp*, which now did not fly in space and through wormholes. Darkwood assisted with geological and geographical research on Noverca. He sometimes rose into orbit and greatly accelerated such work. Flying transport on the Gera continent has been limited to low-flying avions and copters. Tom lived with his wife in New Tokyo – the same place as most earthlings – about two hundred kilometres east of the White Capital. Dr Zina Darkwood worked there at the science hospital, where medical personnel were more qualified to provide health care to the new colonists.

Mikael King and Steven McLeod lived in the same town as the Baker-Green couple, Tolyan and Rod, right here, in the southern city of Altyngrad. Rod had his farm, and Tolyan helped him with the business, but their two comrades, Mik and Steven, remained bachelors. The former space soldiers laid the foundation for several private schools to train the first proper army on Gera. They started a new type of scouting agency and training schools for security guards and ordermen in all four cities and their environs. This made them quite wealthy, so they sold the business to their apprentices, and now Steven built old cars for fun, while Mik made delicious wine out of local modified grapes.

Marta Larsson, formerly Brodsky, the owner of the most exotic kitchen in the colony, was a loyal *Wasp* pilot. She once agreed to return to Noverca to find a clone of her late husband, Chang Brodsky, but she gave up on this venture and married the local owner of the Old World Hotel, a man with lilac skin and a big lover of dinner parties. They had no children. The Larssons also resided in Altyngrad, at the opposite end of it, next to the airport. Marta and Nat were pilots on the only passenger flight between Gera and Carib City on Pettogreco Island. In that city, the only Nordian hypertrichosian on the whole island also lived. She was the tenth member of the search group – an indigenous resident of Noverca called Scarlett Da Costa. Andrea did not know her very well. Nat told her that Scarlett represented the science hospital of New Tokyo in Carib and happened to be an expert on earthling physiology. She helped Dr Darkwood as a nurse during expeditions if they found crash victims who needed medical attention.

Nat Alloyway was the youngest of the earthlings in that team. He was the only one who went through some quite-severe surgical alterations. His skin and hair colour did not change, but his sensory organs, muscular and excretory system made him more suitable for scientific fieldwork. He was always very busy, flying aircraft with Mrs Larsson (his senior friend and mentor), studying in the temple, helping the architexter with his research work, and sometimes just staying home alone. But he also found time for Andrea, which was always her life's best hours.

Andrea could not say much more, but Mr Napovni left looking quite satisfied. The inexplicable animal fear returned, and the garden dampness in the air became palpable and chilling.

Andrea's mother sighed with relief and said, "What an unusual man! I hope you told him enough for him to never come back for more. Never!"

"Mum, now I wish I had not told him anything at all. I am not sure why I did that. I am afraid we will regret having him here."

"Why, Andrea?"

"Not sure ... it's just a feeling, so it will go away like all emotions. Not to worry. Let me help you clean up."

Chapter 8. The Branch

The first thing I do every time is to check the timer on the terminal resting by my side. Indeed, it was just over twenty-one hours again. Naturally, I feel like I only closed my eyes a second ago. But no ... my body is numb, and my head hurts again. The computer advises me to take it slowly and not get up immediately. I am not listening. I am doing this, so I don't have to listen to her or to anyone else again. Why should I listen to this piece of technology?

Nevertheless, I remember what happened the first two times I got up too fast. I am careful and take almost four minutes to get myself into a prone position on the floor. I cough and regulate my breathing. I move my toes and fingers, wrists and ankles, knees and elbows, shoulders and hips.

I test every vertebra and finally stand up. I will jog on the spot before I return to the tank I call a bed. Right now, I need to eat.

I am satisfied. With my foot, I push the waste and pieces of uneatable fabric and plastic into the growing pile of rubbish in the corner. A smell is emerging from that corner, but I can do nothing about it, although I may be breeding some competitors for my oxygen. Two more days, and it will be over. Now it is time for extra mental activity. I open the next chapter in her journal and turn on the audio. Her voice was stronger just a few years ago. I listen to her thoughts and concerns, then I do my usual routine and check the work of the ZPE-converters, run the diagnostics on all electronic systems, and clean myself. Halfway through the week, I felt my clothes were constraining me. I remember how she punished me for running about naked when I was a kid. She explained that this was just as wrong as grabbing people by the legs in the corridors. But now I can do what I want. I tore my travelling suit off and loved the feeling of my skin in the cool air. The computer keeps telling me that I maintain the environment at too cold a temperature for a human organism, but I ignore it. I feel great.

I start my usual self-grooming, listening to Bebia's journal, when I hear her mention my name again. This is usually the best part.

I have no choice but to turn to Pilly again for some help. Two people who received implants (although not the same ones) complained again about the returning symptoms of rejection. I really hoped I would not have to do it again. He is getting older, and tricking him will soon be much harder. He is smart enough to understand the concept of donorship and is not getting much in return. I can ask our coach, Mr Soydan, again to meet him for a few sessions, but I am afraid he wouldn't want to risk another bite or scratch. Pilly needs to start reading something on psychology. He always perceives the information he has found in books better. Trying to tell him to do anything will make him do the opposite.

I pause to think for a moment. I had my suspicions, but these words have turned them into convictions. I will go back to find the recording that did not make sense when I first heard it. But now ... I carry on listening.

How could I argue with the chairman of Object himself? His reasoning is sound, but it wasn't the hybrid's mother who donated him for this research. Marta never knew I saved him, hoping I could have someone to love. It was Vist's idea to break the poor thing into useful genes and traits in the first place, not mine. But he is more than a group of cells now. Even in the past, when we bred hundreds of subjects, it was difficult for me to come to terms with what we did to them. Now I have only one. And he's mine. Taking from him is unbearably hard for me. Now, I find it highly unethical to grant life and then harvest it later and so soon. Something tells me that Mr Fletcher has no intention to wait for fifteen years and ask for his consent.

She doesn't mention my name here, but now I am sure she is talking about me. So I was not supposed to live at all. Someone needed something from me. Every now and then, she took blood samples, but I did not mind. It was a part of everything, and everyone who came to our medical facility had needles poked into them. But from me, they took something else too.

I instruct the terminal to isolate and move all the chapters that mention my name into a separate file, and I do the same for someone called Marta and any files with the slightest mention of the name Vist. I open one more record about myself, soon realising that I should no longer listen to any of those. This time I hear my own voice ... before it changed:

Two ... three ... Boom! (Laughter) – *Good*

boy, Piliali, now let's try this one. What colour is it? – Yellow! Boom! – Are you sure? – Greenange! Boom-Boom! (More laughter) *– Try again, and if you stop being silly, I will give you another piece of liver, – Orange! – Well done. Who is my best boy in the world? – Pilly! Boom and crash! (Sound of broken glass) Oh... Oh no... Bebia, I am so sorry! – It's okay, darling. It's only a silly old flask. Come here... Big hug! Aaah, this is so nice. Let me just clean this cut... No-no, don't lick it. Good boy. Bebia loves Pilly....*

I throw the terminal into the wall. The sound my throat makes is not a human scream.

Chapter 9. Let's Go

Epigraphica, offering to temple of O'Teka NT-544492

Call it a clan, call it a network, call it a tribe, and call it a family, whatever you call it, whoever you are, you need one.

Exhibit no. 15K58, English language quote collection by Texwell offerings, year AC501

Everyone gave up on arguing with Vist a long time ago, as it was hopeless. The loader did not insist stubbornly on anything, but he could voice a logical and irrefutable fact to any argument of dissent. On the loader's reasoning, there was not a word of demagogy, not a single fallacy, not the slightest crack into which doubt could creep in.

A few years ago, Vist gathered the entire old team in his or her living room, announced that everything was ready for the search, and invited them all to participate. Some of the earthlings' private pod-fliers very unsuccessfully fell to the planet. Almost three dozen crashed into various points, including polar ones – both in the northern permafrost and in the otherwise hot – indeed, extremely hot – south, where nothing remained of them, even if it had been possible to get there. For a long time, Vist tracked the identification signals received from these pod-fliers, from the moment they came out of the wormhole. He studied brief reports of the pod-fliers' contents, and their launch slot and time. Vist's assistants – Cesario and Viola – worked around the clock, bringing all the facts together and calculating the possibilities. Every detail was checked against the information from the pod-fliers that had safely landed. In due course, this information was uploaded and analysed in Vist's unique head, until the loader had generated a plan to find and possibly rescue the invaluable cargo these pod-fliers had brought with them.

"Not all of my instructions were followed during the implementation of the Object mission," Vist said, turning to face her friends. "But the most important thing wasn't completely ignored. Reducing the flight time through the Anev Wormhole made it possible to gamble on sending biological material in the pod-fliers and on extending its chances of survival. The maximum safe time for bio-sleep increased by almost a decade, and even if the pod lay unattended for a long time and the stasis tank was not damaged, there would be a chance that someone had survived. Those people must be found!"

"And I almost thought that by biomaterial, you meant the gene bank and tissue samples of the last living things from Earth," said Mik from the chair in the darkest corner. Over time, a frost had lightly touched his coarse hair. On his second arrival in Noverca, he flatly refused surgery to replace the retina and iris, and he now wore light intensifiying glasses all the time.

"Vist was not always a monster, and he has bursts of philanthropy," Steven said cheerfully, helping himself to a second piece of Marta's fruit pie. "Why not shake things up with antiquity? What do you say, Mik? I'll persuade Tolyan if needed. Let's get it back together like in the old days and ... what exactly are we needed for?" He looked at the loader with his mouth full.

Zina sat on the huge circular sofa next to her husband, and they both observed Vist with great wonder. She thought Vist looked even stranger than ever. She had never been able to be certain of his gender, but now she could not be certain of Vist's age. The loader rarely spoke so happily, despite his levelled metallic voice. The new robe of Vist's bio-suit was not black this time but the burgundy colour of the northern cliffs on the mainland. Long chestnut hair was thrown over one shoulder and fell on his chest in a wide wave. One temple of the loader's head was generously shaved, and the oval amulet clung comfortably to his ear. Vist's eyes shone like a sun reflected in a mountain stream. At this very moment, Vist looked no more than thirty-five years old. Zina had become a little stout recently, but she had not lost her beauty, including her rich braid, which she now wore like a crown.

"You won't have to persuade Tolyan. Where I am, there he is," Rod said.

He made a note on his amulet, which looked like a black sports medal, and deactivated it.

"You will stay at home with the children," Tolyan answered him.

This huge, muscular guy had become even larger over years of family life, but this intervention made him seem especially sweet and cuddly.

"Wait, but if I understand correctly, Vist, you need to look at dangerous areas of the planet?" Tom sat up straight. "Areas where only the *Wasp* can fly."

"Not quite? A medium-sized cargo avion can also do it, but it is slow and will take time," continued Vist. "You are right that the search itself needs to be carried out on the spaceship, but when we find the target, it will not work to ferry the find on the *Wasp*."

"No pod has brought more than four people in bio-sleep. I am sure the *Wasp* can manage them," Marta said and opened the box filled with homemade ice cream. She was no longer a blonde beauty but a mature, lean lady with very short-cropped silver hair who wore a large hat instead of a headwrap in Noverca's heat. Even before they left Earth, her co-pilot Nat, whose parents were executed by the religious fanatics called Cruisers, became like a son to her. She persuaded the young hunter to go to Noverca with Vist.

"Of course, in theory, we could only take people from the pods and download information from a computer," said Vist, "but we need the help of the colonists, and Grand, as one would expect, does nothing for free. The colony government offered us to disassemble the pod-fliers into metals and other materials for them. As you know, Gera is not very rich in non-ferrous metals, and every titanium fitting, every copper wire and so on will be useful for them. Moreover, the colony is growing, and northern mining is still difficult, dangerous, and expensive. More expensive than our expeditions. Grand will pay each of us well and provide a cargo craft, the necessary medical equipment, a moulting press, and storage containers. Provisions and medicine will be paid for by sponsors from the science hospital. Zina, you will have to invite an assistant. The best choice would be Da Costa – an adapted Novercian who is qualified to heal earthlings."

***

That was a few years ago. And here they were at the last mission together, sharing a drink in the *Wasp*'s common room and waiting for the next waking hours, when they would separate two vessels. With the pilots and Vist, the *Wasp* would depart to search for Selest and the missing SD pod location. Rod and Tom would take away the survivors of LU-569. Zina and Scarlett would look after them, and there would be three mighty troopers to load and unload the cargo vessel with scrap. Tom was not happy about it. Marta watched his face and tried to figure out what unsettled him more – the separation from Vist or the separation from his ship. Zina didn't look much happier. Her objection and remarks that Selest might need the help of a professional medic were politely dismissed by being overlooked once again. Vist, too, was more than qualified to provide such help. As soon as Vist left the room to prepare, she took her drunk husband by both hands and led him to his bed. She looked pretty miserable as she did so.

Marta looked at the rest of her friends. Scarlett was already sleeping in the depths of the soft chair in the common room. Two glasses were usually enough for her. Nat was staring at the chessboard, trying to understand how he had lost the game to Marta a few minutes ago. He was almost as big as his best friends now. No wonder they had stopped arm-wrestling with him last year. Marta smiled like all proud mothers do. Nat was now as strong as Tolyan. As smart as Rod. As brave as Steven. As handsome as Mik and with a voice just as deep. Marta thought that his father was probably a remarkable man.

Immediately after Rod slowly fished another beetle from the plastic bag, Mik opened one eye. His dark-brown iris went around the room and stopped on Rod. Mik stretched his hand and said in the demonic voice of the military commander, "Stuff!"

Rod made a face, hissed like a cat, shook a few sandy-beetles, or *sandies*, into Mik's hand and complained to no one in particular, "Stuff? Why is he always like this? Why does he call my product 'stuff'? So rude! Didn't he have enough of the delicious cherry vareniki Marta cooked for us?"

"He is Mik, my dear," said Tolyan.

"Oh yes, I forgot. Damn! I keep mistaking him for Charlie Chaplin. He really should work on his colour."

"Rod, shut up."

"Tolyan, are you trying to dominate?"

"You all should shut up," said Steven, "especially you, Mik. You talk too much."

With his mouth full of sandies, Mik opened his other eye.

"All four of you are the noisy bunch," said Nat, "Marta, please tell me this is not normal behaviour for the best friends in the universe."

"Nat, they are drunk, and this is normal behaviour for them when they share almost six bottles of Mik's wine between them. They banter and tell each other to shut up."

"I just told them to shut up."

"In case you forgot, you are drunk too."

"Oh, that's a relief. But this also means I belong. You made me so happy! I want to toast—"

"No. That was enough. See how sad Steven is growing? If you open another bottle, he will end up crying. Mik and Tolyan will start wrestling. Rod would be unable to work tomorrow, and you would be unable to fly. It's a good time to stop."

"Okay. But why might Steven cry? Is it because of Doctor Zina?"

Marta lowered her voice, "Yes."

"I heard from Tolyan that Darwoods aren't in love with each other. But why didn't she marry Steve instead of Captain Tom?" Nat whispered.

"You never heard of Novercian value-sharing marriage?"

"Andrea mentioned it, but she said it does not apply to us."

"Naturally. You see, there was a time when Earth people had to marry with no love. Family arrangements, religious traditions, relocation terms, genetic compatibility, etc. It was almost forgotten, but the first colonists on Gera had to resurrect that type of marriage because of a very poor choice of potential mates. Even polygamy was resurrected for a few generations. In those times, it was not for love but for a shared value – whatever that value was. I assume it was the survival of humanity, or a love of knowledge, or of a certain craft."

"Surely that is a recipe for disaster."

"Yes. Prearranged marriage rarely results in partners' happiness, but sometimes it does if they are not complete hypocrites," said Marta and got up, ready to retire.

"The mutual appreciation of something." For a moment, Nat appeared deep in thought, "I see the point. They both share ... what? Vist?"

Marta met his astonished eyes and nodded.

"Nobody could have Vist," she said, "but they can have each other, sharing their love for what Vist means, and this is better than nothing. Believe me, kid."

"But Vist ... Does Vist love anybody?"

Marta's eyes hardened for a second, "Good question. Nobody? Everybody? Herself? Himself? Everyone has their own ideas about love, but you always love the one who can complete you. Who can complete Vist? Does an ordinary person have anything to offer? Another loader could probably add something to a loader. Vist is the last of her kind. Maybe someday there will be new loaders. Why don't you ask her one day? Perhaps you will get an answer." Marta glanced towards the exit. "You know, I even envy Vist a little. Whoever he or she is, she's happy. Despite all the disadvantages and advantages, Vist is very complete. Very content, although I don't get it. If being myself is gone for me, I would like to become a loader. Who knows, maybe in a few years, when my time comes, they will make loaders on Noverca too. Then, in other words, if I die, I wouldn't mind donating my flesh and mind to test the new model. That's it. Time to sleep. Night guys! Don't stay up too late. Hey, Steven, help me with Scarlett, would you? It's her bedtime."

A minute later she was gone, and then Steven left with a plump Nordian girl in his arms. Nat watched Rod and Tolyan trying to sing in unison, accompanied by Mik's snoring, and he decided that sometimes something is better than nothing ... especially if it's truly great.

Chapter 10. The Branch

Epigraphica, offering to temple of O'Teka R-8893002

In the annals of the Niagara Monastery (33rd century), my attention was drawn to the young monk's confession. This is what he wrote, and if I were you, my friend, I would carefully hear his words, "The solitude, as proposed in the scripture, should have healed my immortal soul. But after four years of isolation, I feel my soul is now corrupted. Perhaps Satan himself takes possession of me, and I am not capable, in my weakness, of comprehending God's truth in a lonely cell. Being alone always, I can't compare myself with my fellow believers. My sinful vanity exalts me over those who are not even around. It seems that I am better than them, more worthy and knowledgeable. I am confident that I deserve more than them and am much closer to God. Why has no one ever warned me of such self-destruction? Am I the only one, or have all who have attempted this test experienced the same?"

"Cruisers. Their Start and End." Liam Nosoff, year AC403

I wanted to be awake for this and instructed the computer to ensure I was. I ran out of food a few hours ago, but apparently, I'm not feeling too bad so far because of the excitement. The screen projector is damaged, so the image of my destination is not clear. But I can see stars. One of them is enormous, and it's red and beautiful. Maybe the most beautiful thing I have ever seen. It's supposed to be much better than the one we left behind. The computer confirms that it is indeed Vitricus. I can't see other transport units, but they are here too. The computer receives and registers their signals, but I don't care about them.

Another hour and I will see the planet covered in clouds. Is it a gas giant? No, that can't be. We can't land. This is the wrong world! I am about to panic, but the computer confirms that we are out of the wormhole and now approaching Noverca. I stare at the fuzzy image and see gaps of something blue and grey between the clouds. I have made it! Soon I will walk on a proper surface with proper gravity.

Suddenly, the computer makes a new, unfamiliar sound. Up to now, it hadn't made even a single beep for the whole week. I am enquiring into what is happening. The computer explains that it is receiving commands from the surface. I felt a little worry growing in my mind. What commands? Apparently, people on the surface tell my unit where to land so that the rest will also land nearby. This way, we will be received by friends and taken to the settlement.

I turn around and look at her. This must not happen. No one should find us. The word I hated all my life is ringing in my head. *Consequences.* I tell the computer to ignore the command. But it is programmed to obey those who built it – not me. I demand the course alteration. It does not even answer me anymore. I grab the terminal. It is not connected to the main computer, but maybe I can do something with its camera outputs to interfere with this damn thing. The computer does not signal my success but advises me to return to the tank and prepare for a harsh landing. Stupid machine. I will obey you this one last time ... The transport unit is shaking violently. We are entering the atmosphere.

Why does it take so long? We have been shaking for a very lo—

The big red star explodes in my head, and everything goes dark and quiet.

Chapter 11. Iceberg

"It's here," reported Nat to all sections of the ship, "Captain Vist, I'm picking up metal confirmed on all scanners. This time it's definitely SD-211, not another incorrect iceberg or island. It's a large chunk moving slowly, but I don't think it will last. The water temperature is almost nineteen degrees centigrade, and I am surprised the iceberg has not gone yet. I also think the pod is dead, as we are not detecting any electrical activity there."

"I had no particular hopes," Vist's voice answered from the speaker.

"How far is it?" Marta asked from her room, where she was resting.

"A little less than forty kilometres. Captain, what do I do now?"

"Keep us on course, Nat. Marta, please replace our pilot on controls when you are ready. He and I need to work on the plan."

Soon, the *Wasp* circled over the iceberg like a huge vulture. They measured it and calculated its density and strength. While it was around a kilometre and a half in length, they concluded that its density would not withstand the ship's weight, and landing on its surface was impossible. The only way to bring a person from the *Wasp* to a block of ice was inside another pod. There was never a need for life pods on Noverca, and so there was only one on board the *WSP*. It was a museum exhibit behind glass in the common room, next to the models of the *Noah* and the *Ark-8*. It was a very old escape pod, much smaller than the ones that flew through the wormhole. This relic was the size of an Egyptian sarcophagus, and everyone called it just that. Vist had once escaped in it from the station on the Jupiter orbit where he or she was born. Many years later, when Cruisers tried to capture the loader, Vist ran from Mars on it. It had made the first known flight in history from the planet's surface to this ship, to this very *Wasp*, where Vist first met his or her new family. And finally, it had landed on Earth, carrying not only Vist but everything that helped humanity to evacuate. Bullet-shaped, covered with dents and scratches, and scorched upon entering the atmosphere, this cocoon had managed to preserve a vulnerable human life. It will have to do it one more time.

Nat stood and looked at the Sarcophagus with awe when he heard the metallic voice behind him, "I am afraid you will have to go in it this time, and you don't need to be a loader to use it. Not anymore."

Nat tried very hard not to show his disbelief at such luck. He never dreamed that he would even get inside the working prototype.

"I am honoured, but I have to ask why."

"Because only I can launch it."

"I was wondering about the launch. We haven't got a single launcher on board, and all the unnecessary equipment was removed long ago. Captain, how are you going to do it?"

"Well, you and I can get it to the cargo hatch and charge it there. And then one of us should push it out without following," said Vist and opened the glass case.

Vist tilted the pod and, with effort, dragged it into the middle of the common room. Nat watched the loader for a minute.

"And you call it a launch? Quite risky. Why are you so sure I can't do that?" asked Nat.

Vist took her hands off the Sarcophagus, "Be my guest. I might change my mind if you move it to the door."

Nat tried to push the pod with his hands, shoulders, and back but could only move it a centimetre.

"Bear in mind it is empty now. Besides a person, it will carry life support and control gear," said Vist in a metallic voice without a hint of mockery.

"Oh, I don't mind. I would rather go inside. I just don't want you to risk yourself. What if you fall out through the hatch too?"

"Moving heavy loads is not the only thing a loader can do. Do you know those half rings screwed to the floor in the cargo hold?"

"Eyebolts? Yes, I know. We secure cargo with them to stop the cargo from sliding about."

"We must weld a couple of these to these smooth sides of the Sarcophagus for my safety. Come on, give me a hand."

An hour later, they joined Marta in the control room to look closely at the target.

"I don't understand. On Earth, this iceberg would have melted long ago. Are you telling me it was drifting for almost forty years?" asked Marta.

"Not quite," answered Vist, "At first, SD-211 moved along with the glacier. Slowly, but still faster than the glaciers that crawled on Earth at one time. I believe this iceberg broke off only a few years ago, but it moved towards the equator only when the Galtstream touched it. Since then, it has been drifting south and melting, as it should."

"But with such an incredible amount of salt in the local waters, it wouldn't have withstood the warmth, despite its enormous size."

"With salt, it should indeed have melted faster, but the ice itself isn't pure ice on Noverca. Nat, remind us why you never drink iced drinks?"

Nat wrinkled his nose.

"Ha! No thanks," he laughed, "Except in Boa Trossy, all the bars add blobster drool to the ice so that it does not melt too fast."

"The blobsters are one of Noverca's most ancient inhabitants. They secrete plenty of smucilage – an organic compound that does not allow salt to dissolve for a long time, and so the ice does not melt. There is a theory that their ancestors did not make ritual spherical buoys out of salt but used pieces of ice, riding them from the northern shores. Perhaps, this species still exists in unexplored regions of the planet. The analysis of ice samples showed that this substance is present in all frozen seawater, but it was never found in snow or rain. Marta, can you enlarge the image on the screen? Look how porous it is. Nat, you must be extremely careful when walking on it."

"It looks like a peachy sponge," said Nat.

"Marta, do you have any suggestions? It is necessary to remain as high as possible for a drop and hover over a convenient area. I am afraid we will flip or split it if we come in too low."

"I am not sure I can do that. Is there any way to prevent it from moving so much, or better yet, to anchor it?"

Nat pointed his finger at the screen, "Further south-west. Can you see it? What is that thing? Another iceberg?"

Marta checked the mapping chart.

"An island. Not much land but a few cliffs."

"Well done, Nat," said Vist, "We will hook the iceberg to the island, and it will stand still for at least some time."

"How do we do it?"

"I need to think."

"I can create a wave," Marta said, "It will push our drift ice to the west, and hopefully, it will bump into the rock."

"Might work if you are excellent at billiards," said Nat.

"We can make sure we don't miss," said Vist, "We have a couple of power shields to build a bracket out of the island and create a bay-shaped trap. Marta, let's take a closer look at that rock."

Nat had been famous for being the best crossbow shot long before meeting Vist and the others. Being the son of a hunter, he did not fail this time too. Usually, the power shields were used to create a safe passage for the Novercian scouts when they made a drop to the hostile surface in Gera's south. Without these shields, the sudden blast of hot wind could toast a person, even in a protective suit.

The shield planter could shoot on the move, and so Marta flew twice over the small island. The first time, Nat planted the left shield, and the second – the right. When Vist activated them remotely, Marta reported that the water had changed its behaviour on the island's north side, as if the rocks were now spread several hundreds of yards on both sides. It was a good move. When the *Wasp* went into vertical landing mode next to the iceberg four times, it created a circular wave, one side of which changed the ice's course. Soon, the iceberg was hooked into the left wing of the bracket. Marta took a position above the iceberg, as she considered possible wind interference.

"Well done, everybody," said Vist, "and now for the difficult part. We have about forty minutes. Those shields are not meant to stay charged for longer. Nat, you will wear the space suit but without a helmet. It will not fit into the Sarcophagus. Take a scout hood instead – it has a cooler, a visor and communication means. Ready?"

Nat nodded. He got dressed in the cargo section for the trip, and then Vist opened the fully charged Sarcophagus.

"Be careful, boy. You are my only heir," Nat heard Marta say as she stood in front of the pod.

He sighed and got in. Vist lowered the cover, and a short hiss indicated that he was now sealed. In front of his eyes, Vist's face appeared on the holo-screen and asked, "Are you okay?"

"I think I can still smell honey wax in here ... But it felt as if I was getting into my own coffin."

"Yes. I felt that myself every time. Don't worry. You will not be knocked unconscious. The distance you travel is not far enough. Relax and think of the money you will get for this one. Marta, open up ... make it a metre and half."

"Yes, captain," said Nat.

The Sarcophagus lid cut him off from the world, locking him in a much smaller universe. But things on the outside happened fast.

With its usual loud clang, the hatch shook and slid to the left. Hot air filled the cargo hold when the gap was just big enough for the pod, making it incredibly difficult to breathe, even for the loader. Vist pulled on the mask, fastened the harness straps, and secured the measured cable with a carabiner on her chest. Vist lay on her stomach at the edge and peered out at the foamy surface beneath. It was not very far, and if the brake field was turned on just beyond the threshold, Nat would get off with only slight bruising upon landing. Vist got up and pushed a cable through the eyebolts that had just been welded to the Sarcophagus sides, passing this cable through the same bolt in the floor. Then the loader dragged their old pod to the hatch and pushed it over the edge. The Sarcophagus hung on the cable nose down. At the very moment when Vist commanded the inhibitory field of the Sarcophagus to activate, the *Wasp* suddenly tilted.

The brake force field slammed into the ship's hull and pushed a powerful blast of hot air into the cargo hold. At the same time, the Sarcophagus rushed down, and the cable tore the eyebolts off and whipped Vist across the legs. The loader was thrown against the back wall and then dragged out. Vist gripped the remaining bolts with all her might and heard Marta's voice ringing in her ears.

"Captain, we were hit by a hot storm. I don't know how the *Wasp* missed it, and the steam spout probably just formed right in front of our nose. This is because we are in static mode, I am sure. Are you all alive there? Captain? Vist? Nat?"

"Close the door," Vist said, wheezing.

Chapter 12. The Branch

The last thing I expected was a new planet made of something like solidified Kyros foam, but much harder to break, white and very cold. I can't stay here because no one will come and help ... I have made sure of it. I can't access the storage where my spare clothes are, but this does not bother me. I still have my shoes, although I can't find my travelling suit. I think I ripped it up in rage a couple of days ago. I have to find some shelter and food. My hands don't hurt anymore, but this stuff – I believe it's called ice – is really sharp. The snow looks much like the snow in the flicks I watched back at the station, but I never imagined so much of it.

My transport unit opened the main hatch and went dead. It is half-buried in ice. The terminal is also crushed, and so are the ZPE-converters. I have no time, desire, or skills to resurrect any of it. The only urge I feel is to move. So I begin my hike towards the bright horizon. I can't see the sun behind the clouds, but there is a light somewhere. This is obvious to me. Unlike the earthly sun, which I have never seen with my own eyes, I was told that the local sun does not move across the sky, and you must move towards it to find light and warmth.

I have no idea how long I walk for. My new beard is full of icicles. I am tired and starving, but I can't stop. It would have been better without this ghastly wind. Something makes me go, and I think that now my pace is actually faster than it was at the start. I took almost nothing with me. The water flask was the first thing I dropped. The snow cured my dehydration but not my hunger. Then I got rid of my shoes. It was always easier to hike without them, but strangely, even more so here. Now, all I have in my hands is something I have always wanted to possess but had never even touched. I found it three days ago in the emergency landing pack when searching the transport for food and supplies. The only weapon in the armoury of the transport unit is this sharp blade with a ZPE ray-gun built into the upper spine. The others used to call it a handzap, but Bebia called it a shoot-knife.

I stop. I must never think of Bebia again. It makes me more tired and sick.

I resume my journey. Another hour or two has probably passed, and the landscape has changed. There is solid and rocky ground under my feet instead of ice. The snow is not so deep anymore. I carry on between countless large boulders, weathered into similar shapes. They all seem to point in the same direction. There are hills now instead of dunes, and the crimson clouds look thinner and lighter.

I spot them from the top of the hill. Dark figures against this grey snow. Two people are walking towards the light ahead of me. They are slower than I am, and one of them looks smaller and weaker at a great distance. They appear to be dressed in identical dark coats with large, heavy hoods or animal hides over their head and shoulders. My first thought is that they may have food ... and I will have it, whether they give it up willingly or not. I am walking faster towards them. I am running.

They are still too far for me to call out. I am catching up, but before I get close enough, both turn around.

The snow in the wind is obscuring my vision. I struggle to make out their faces, but the tall one seems to smile at me. I see teeth, but I immediately remember the last dog at the station. An old sack of bones that always greeted me with teeth and a low growl before I killed and ate it in the abandoned waste chamber. I am sure I can hear a similar sound now.

Shall I slow down and greet them, or shall I just attack? I hesitate when the bigger person slaps the neck of the small one roughly. Then the small one settles comfortably on the snow as if to watch what happens next. It looks like he is not going to participate, so he is not a threat now. I focus on the big guy.

I keep running, but this person is running towards me. He comes closer and closer, and I realise he is not big. He is smaller than me. He runs on his legs, but occasionally he pushes his hands against the large boulders and chunks of ice to make magnificent jumps. He is like an acrobat, using his whole body to increase his velocity. I have never seen a person who could move so fast. He is definitely showing his teeth and demonstrating that he is far from being friendly with some battle roar. He will fight me, and I make my mind up not to risk the unknown. He is no more than three metres away when he launches into the air, raising both arms above his head.

Chapter 13. Nat

Nat lifted his hand slowly. So slowly. The heat was so intense that shutting his eyelids was not sufficient to gain relief from the onslaught. Besides that, seeing was essential, and keeping his eyes closed at this early stage was simply not an option. What would Vist do? Nat almost heard the metallic voice in his ears, "Slowly, you fool. Don't go now and lose it all just because of a moment of weakness or panic."

"Why so intense? Have I missed something? Was I distracted coming in so that some new or different factor wasn't taken into account?"

A wave of emotion seemed to come from inside his skull. It injected itself directly into the centre of his chest and then radiated outwards like a shockwave. It was intentional, of course. Anger was always at the top of Nat's mind, poised to present itself as a threat – and sometimes – as a resource. With a wave of fury, images came to mind that were the sum of all that Nat adored. In its wake – in front of it, and surrounding it with an air of mockery and malice – was a trail of all that Nat hated and despised. All that the young hunter lived to fight and subvert.

"We have found our scout! He is alive!" Marta's cheerful voice made the engine's noise disappear, and Vist's attention could not focus on anything else even if the loader wanted it to. "One heartbeat has been detected. Captain, what are your orders? Shall we try and land or perhaps ..."

"I will go after him," Vist's voice was still weak, but recovering muscles tested themselves in a series of contractions. Nothing was broken.

"Normally, I would not argue with you. I'd expect you to jump off the spaceship naked if necessary to save my boy! Despite all his physical alterations, he is only a human. But you ... you are injured, and he is moving. Things are not as bad as I feared they were."

"So he got out of the Sarcophagus. Where is he going?"

"Towards SD-211, believe it or not. Nat periodically gets hit by the hot wind and stops for a few seconds. Nevertheless, he is getting closer."

"Communication?"

"No. Too much interference from the storm. Can you walk? Come here and look at the ocean. It is quite a sight."

Soon, Vist lowered his beaten body to the second pilot chair, next to Marta.

"Have we caught him on camera yet?"

"Not yet. Vist, you look like shit. I never saw so much sweat on your face."

"I am fine, the bio-suit got the worst of it, but we are both good at self-repairing."

"Look, the storm is moving east. I will go higher and try to reach out again."

Marta started to navigate the cameras, searching for the Nat's silverfish shape against the dirty ice, while Vist looked out through the observation lens. There were no clouds above the ship, but yellowish towers of steam rose to the amethyst sky under it. Before even reaching the stratosphere, they became depleted and dispersed. Some curled up and swirled like a funnel, piercing the sea and sucking up the green water as if trying to pour the ocean into outer space. These columns of hot steam moved in one direction like a group of walking and swaying vagrants. Soon the disturbed waves and the edge of a rapidly ageing ice slab became visible below again.

"I can see him! Vist, look, he is almost there. Nat, Nat ... Can you hear me?"

Vist moved her eyes towards the screen. The pod was clearly visible. Next to it, the human figure slowly got up on his feet and stumbled closer to it.

Vist heard the voice from the speaker, "Hey ... Ladies ... Miss me? Sorry, Captain, I probably lost my lashes and eyebrows ... So no more frowning from me for a month."

"Well done, Nat. Apart from the eyebrows. Anything serious?" asked Vist.

"Not as far as I can tell. Bruised my knee trying to open the lid. I don't know if you can see me, but I am standing next to 211. It is sitting in an icy well with some water at the bottom, and I'm not sure, but it seems to me that the door is ajar. Any orders?"

"Try to get to the hatch. The ballast in one of the walls should leave the pod the right way up."

"How did you manage to find it in the steam?" asked Marta.

"Well, you dropped me north of it, and the wind was coming from the west. It was not that hard, really. Right ... I am climbing down."

"Be careful. It's a good thing you did not have to crawl more than 240 metres."

"Is that it? I thought it was 240 kilometres. By the way, the ice is not slippery. It's like climbing pumice ... Okay. I am here."

"Is there anything nearby?" Vist asked. "Your scout visor has a camera, right?"

"It does. This gear is from Mik's academy. Here, does it work?"

The second holo-screen at first showed a yellowish slash beneath Nat's feet and the curvy side of the pod. The numbers were barely visible but exact.

"Thank you, Nat. It does."

"Now, let's see. No, and I can't see anything. Hang on. What's this? A small box that looks like a supply case."

"Nat, can you hold it a bit higher and tilt your head forwards twenty degrees? Thank you. That is a handzap case. Somebody came out and armed themself. Can you get inside?"

"Sure I can. Oh gosh! The stench, shit! I wish it was still frozen! Vist, can you see this mess? The control is dead. Two bio-sleep tanks, the same as we have found in all the others. One is open. It has been used. The other is closed, but I can't see through the lid. It's too dirty. Captain, what should I do?"

"It is not active, so just open it up."

"Yes, sir!" Nat replied, pinching his nose, "Ugh! This is unbelievable, Captain. What kind of life support system did they build in this tank? It looks like excrement. Plenty of it. Possibly human. Parts of clothing, apparently it was a flight suit. I don't see any evacuees."

Vist looked intently at the screen and said, "Nat, leave it. Go to the right, deep at the narrowing front. Yes ... what is that on the floor?"

"Garbage, I guess ... and it also stinks. It is darker here, too."

"I am afraid you must pull out each item by item ... and describe them, please."

"Thanks, what a joy! Okay. An empty bag ... squashed. A shoe ... size six. A few empty water bottles. Food wraps, another shoe, another flight suit, more food wraps, a ... bone. A rib bone ... Hang on."

For about five minutes, he silently fished human bones out of a heap of rubbish and laid them on the floor. Finally, he took what seemed to be a head in his hands, on which there were still strips of skin and a few grey strands of hair. Without a word, he lowered it gently and reached for a book-like electronic device.

"Captain, I bet you'll want to see this thing for yourself," he said miserably.

Vist wiped both eyes on her sleeve and said, "This is Selest's personal terminal. Take it with you and—"

Marta interrupted with an urgency in her voice, "Vist, the power shield is down. The iceberg has broken free, it's drifting again. We have to get him back. That storm melted almost a third of the ice. Further south, it will get even hotter."

Vist spoke quickly, "Listen to me carefully, Nat. You won't have time to reach the Sarcophagus. It's not too far away, but you will break your legs running in those holes. The least damaged bio-sleep tank is your return ticket. It was carried in through the door when installed, so you can take it out. It is lighter than a sarcophagus, believe me. At the base, the clamps must be unfastened on both sides. No matter how, you must throw it into the sea with you and the terminal inside. And do it quickly. Marta, you have to go down to the surface."

"But we will raise the wave again, and he will be carried?"

"I might have time to catch him with a scooper-probe. It can take samples of water and soil up to two hundred kilograms, right?"

"Up to three hundred."

"Good."

"And what do you mean 'might'? You're not in your best shape. What if you ..."

"Ladies ..." They heard Nat's voice. "I got it out of the pod, but I can't get it out of the well."

Marta and Vist looked at each other.

"While he is in the ice well ..." started Vist.

"The wave will not push him off," finished Marta, placing her hands on the control panel. "Nat, get in and seal in, mama is coming!"

Vist was already running back to the cargo section, limping slightly on her left foot.

Nat curled up in the tank, closed the lid and looked up through the transparent cover. The iceberg started to shake, and it trembled more violently every second. Even through the walls, Nat heard a noise from the disturbed air above and the very unpleasant sound of cracking ice below him. The white cloud and ice flakes blocked the sky again, but the dark shade of the *Wasp* lowered vertically through it. Nat saw the scooper's mouth descend on him, and a strong jerk almost overwhelmed his consciousness.

The iceberg fell into three parts as soon as the bio-sleep tank was pulled into the ship. Two flew to the side, and one flipped over and threw the Sarcophagus and SD-211 into the ocean. Both filled immediately with water and sank. They slowly revolved and plunged into a dark-green haze, where no one had yet measured the depth and where the state of the sea floor was unknown to humankind.

Chapter 14. The Branch

I shoot him with the handzap. A short silent ray through his heart. He dies instantly, but his body keeps flying towards me, and I fall backwards under its weight. For a few seconds, I am shocked and frightened like never before in my life. But the body on top of me is limp and lifeless. I open my eyes and see his collarbone and his throat. I can smell him. This smell is familiar. This is how my clothes smell if I don't change for three or four days.

I push him off me and examine his body. There is enough light to see that he is not dressed in animal hides. He is naked. His body is covered in long dark hairs, thick and bushy. He wears no shoes and carries no bags. He is still squeezing a pair of dry bones with sharpened ends in both hands. I suddenly feel hot, imagining these bones stabbing into my flesh. My head feels dizzy, and I hear a female voice in the wind saying something like, "Waah! Mortah! Waah ... Waah ..." I remember the second person, get up and ready to attack again.

It becomes more evident that the second one is a woman as she approaches me. She moves slowly, hunching her shoulders and lifting her arms on both sides as if trying to keep her balance. I notice the broad bracelets on her wrists. She holds nothing in her hands and looks unthreatening enough for me to change my mind. I decide I can learn more from her if she is alive. At least for now. I just killed her mate, so who knows what that means to her.

The woman is hideously ugly. She has a broad nose and saggy cheeks. She is missing an eye, and her whole face is mainly scar tissue. She is also covered in hair, but not as much as her man. But unlike him, she is partially wrapped in a shaggy black blanket made of twigs and hay. I have seen dry grass in the books, but this looks black. It would have been better as camouflage in burned woods than insulation. A necklace of incomprehensible beads on her neck looks like red scales or husk flakes.

The woman stops to take a good look at me. I can't work out any expression on her face, but her only eye checks me up and down, paying no attention to the dead man. She speaks again. I don't believe that what she is saying is made of sentences. There are a few separate words, and I do not understand anything, of course. Two words she seems to repeat again and again. I start to think she is asking me something.

"Calcolo ... Mortah?"

I just guess when she points at the body with the first word and then closes her eye with the second.

"Yes," I say, "He is dead. Was Calcolo his name?"

The woman goes quiet for a whole minute, then slowly points at the corpse, saying "Calcolo," before pointing at the rock nearby and repeating "Calcolo."

"No," I said. "He didn't hit his head on the rock ... Hang on. Are you saying Calcolo and the rock? Calcolo is a rock. His name was Rock in your language?" I repeated her movements, then pointed at the rock and the man, closing my eyes on the third word, "Rock ... Calcolo ... Mort."

"Ahah! Ahah! Morta-ah ..."

I am sure she said it with a happy smile, followed by numerous nods. She has almost a perfect set of teeth, whiter than snow. Then she kneels by her man and turns him on his back. She takes one of the sharp bones from his dead hand and cuts him open, licking the blood off his skin with greed.

Chapter 15. Rod

Epigraphica, offering to temple of O'Teka P-432970

But how can anyone who has ever gulped down a luscious, live oyster at three-and-sixpence per dozen, turn up their nose and shudder at the clean-feeding and less repulsive-looking snail? The lobster, a creature consumed in incredible quantities at all the highest tables in the land, is such a foul feeder that, upon its sure capture, an experienced fisherman will bait his lobster-pot with putrid flesh or fish too far gone even to attract a crab. And yet, if at one of those tables there appeared a well-cooked dish of clean-feeding slugs, the hardiest of guests would shrink away from tasting it (...)

It is hard, very hard, to overcome feelings that have been instilled in us from our youth onwards; but still I foresee the day when the slug will be as popular in England as its luscious namesake the Trepang, or sea-slug, is in China, and a dish of grasshoppers fried in butter will be as much relished by the English peasant as a similarly treated dish of locusts is by the Arab or Hottentot. There are many reasons why this is to be hoped for."

Vincent M. Holt "Why not eat insects." Earth. Year 1885

"Tolyan, is it me, or is the tea on Noverca not the same."

"Of course it's not the same. The

environment is also not the same, in case you forgot. Try adding blackcurrants or bergamot."

"I just want a nice cup of good old Rosie Lee with milk and sugar. Maybe, there is something wrong with the local milk, or the sugar." Rod peered into the large ceramic mug, sighed, and sat on the sofa.

Tolyan took his mug and sat down next to Rod, stretched out his legs, and exhaled with satisfaction. "Finally!"

"Yes, it has been a tiresome journey."

"I missed this place."

"Me too. Now I want to go and see how the business is doing without me, but I'm too tired."

"Come on, Rod. Jaxon is still there. We haven't even unpacked yet."

"How about this – you unpack the case, and I'll pop out quickly and see if the goods are still alive."

Tolyan frowned. "No, Rod. Tomorrow, we will do it together. Tonight, you should rest. You haven't slept in twenty-six hours."

Rod was about to agree, but suddenly a small voice came from the nursery door.

"Daddy, Papa, I can't sleep."

Tolyan got up and put his cup of tea on the table. At the door stood four-year-old Phoebe in yellow pyjamas, rubbing her eyes.

"Hello again, princess, what's up?" His voice changed in a flash, from a deep bass to a soft cooing. "Your big sister is sleeping, but why aren't you? Didn't you like your presents?"

Tolyan crouched in front of the little girl and hugged her.

"I want Nanna Winnie!" The girl was on the verge of whimpering.

"But now your fathers are back. Nanna Winnie has gone home. She needs a little holiday."

"Nanna Winnie sang me lullabies. I want Nanna Winnie."

Tolyan looked back at Rod.

"There!" Rod said, "This is what happens if you leave children with babysitters for half a month. Hang on, sunshine, I can also lullaby."

He tried to get up and immediately sat back down.

Tolyan waved him away, "Relax, Rod. Papa Tolya sings better anyway."

He stood up, lifting the girl with one hand. He gently pressed her to his broad chest and carried her into the darkness of the nursery. Soon, a quiet growling was heard from there, which should have been the promised lullaby about little grey wolves.

That should work. They used to crash out to it before, Rod thought. He sipped his tea again, thought for a minute, and then got up without effort. He silently put on his shoes and left the house. The house was purposely built close to the farm because only Rod and Tolyan worked there for the first three years, substituting for each other without any outside help. Now the children have got bigger, there were more than enough apprentices, and Vist offered to participate in a new search almost every month. Finally, Vist found all the pods. After all, it was impossible to refuse his call, but time at home was becoming more precious every year. Maybe they are all getting too old for adventures.

Rod approached the large facility, which looked on the outside like a large solid building with no windows, but inside it had almost a real Earth seaside landscape. From the concrete platform, you could see dunes of authentic quartz sand, metres deep, a few saltwater features, some slow-growing *Ammophila* and artificial sunlight, bright like an afternoon on Earth. Even a gentle beach breeze had been recreated with silent fans.

Rod's apprentice Jaxon was on his post. He wore very dark visors, as his eyes could not bear so much light. He was also dressed in warm clothing. Jaxon was a typical fifteen-year-old Uzhan. His nose, forehead and cheeks were covered in reflective star-like scales and his thin lips were usually curled inwards.

Rod greeted him, jumped down to the sand, made a few steps onto the dune, and crouched. He dug a small hole in the sand until he felt the moisture with his fingers. A minute later, the tiny pit was filled with water. A small patch of dry sand stirred almost immediately, and a shiny brown beetle appeared on the surface. It was about the size of a walnut, and it shone in the light like molten chocolate. The segmented abdomen looked fat, almost spherical. The insect approached the pool, turned around and attempted, with its hind legs, to push some sand into the hole to close it. Rod held it between the thumb and index finger of his right hand. The beetle pretended to be dead. Rod kicked the sand with his toe cap to close the hole so other bugs would not crawl out.

"Didn't lay any eggs yet," Rod muttered under his breath and added louder, "Jaxon, is everything up to date?"

"Yes, sir. I did not expect you back so early, sir. How are you?" replied the boy.

When he spoke, his lips unfolded and looked almost like a normal human mouth.

"Fine, but is this why you are late with the fall?"

"No, sir. I followed the instructions. I shortened the cycle, so it darkens gradually for fourteen hours. I projected the Moon at the angle described. The phase change lasts twenty-nine cycles. I also lowered the temperature to sixteen degrees centigrade."

"Days, Jaxon! Twenty-nine days! At this farm, we say *days*, not *cycles*. This is still an October setting. We need to be in November now. Lower the temperature to twelve and add more minutes to the night. When did you rain last time? Yesterday?"

Rod got up and walked back to the concrete floor.

"Two cycles ... days ago, sir," answered Jaxon, checking his amulet.

"Good. Wait for another *day* and rain again. Not too much, just a morning drizzle with a bit of fog. Last feeding?"

"Stopped any feeding last week. Their guts should be empty. That is why I thought they had already started to lay ..."

"It's okay, don't worry. I'm sure we can start harvesting adults any day now. Prepare the traps, and I will buy the ingredients for marinades."

Jaxon breathed into his hands, trying to warm them with his breath. His scaly face turned dull, and the purple skin between the scales darkened.

Rod gave him a long look and said, "I should have taken another tiny Nordian for an apprentice. I don't understand how you can freeze at sixteen?"

"I am fine, sir. I just forgot my gloves. When I start my own farm, I will have Nordians helping me with winter seasons."

"You will not have much to do in the winter season. Just ensure the cold climate does not malfunction, and eggs don't get cooked accidentally in the hot sand. They will hatch when you warm them up by the end of April. I don't want to waste time cloning a whole new population."

"Yes, sir. End of April. I thought they hatch in the first month of the spring season."

"April is the first month. March was in the ancient calendar! Bloody lizard!"

Rod spoke without any malice but looked the boy straight in the eye. He brought the beetle to his mouth, bit through the abdomen, and squeezed and sucked in a truly dead beetle's soft insides as if it were a grape.

Jaxon winced.

"You need to memorise all the seasons, my young friend, if you want to successfully grow sandies. But I'll tell you more. Even if you grow them, you have to sell them for someone else to cook. This will be less profitable, though. You won't get rich this way."

"I want to cook them too. I've learned all your recipes, sir."

"Jaxon, how can you cook them well if you don't even like them?"

"I do ... just not raw. I prefer them grilled. What's a lizard, sir?"

Rod flicked the remains of the unfortunate beetle into the slit of the decomposer and clapped Jaxon on the shoulder.

"Lizards used to be very handsome beasts on Earth ... a very long time ago. They also didn't like cold weather, were covered in scales, and ... I actually don't know if they hated bugs. Ask Tolyan. He used to hate them too."

"Thank you, sir."

"You are welcome, mate. Who is replacing you?"

"Harlow. She should be here in two hours."

"Go home and have something hot to drink. I will wait for her," said Rod, walking towards the control panel and taking off his amulet.

He left it on the flat surface of the contact port to synchronise and started reading the most recent logs. He did not hear Jaxon leaving. The numbers were mostly satisfying, and Rod decided to transfer a bonus to all four of his apprentices for a job well done. Rod started to process the information they had collected, which was useful for the new idea of a bug-harvesting device, which he had come up with during the last expedition.

Rod was so carried away by the observation diaries that he didn't hear the door slam again. He almost jumped when an unfamiliar high-pitched voice spoke behind him.

"Mr Rodion Baker-Green? I knew I would find you here."

Rod unwillingly pulled himself away from the holo-screen and turned around.

Instead of the apprentice Harlow, there was a stranger in front of him in an expensive suit. The stranger's head was covered with a striped pharaoh's headscarf, which had recently come into fashion and now completely concealed the intruder's hair and shoulders. Rod noticed red jewellery on the stranger's neck, mostly covered by a yellow beard. Above the elbow, a ribbon had been sewn on his sleeves, the same red-brown colour as his headscarf. So this was a Gera-environmentalist. Rod gave him a mocking look and suddenly felt a cold sweat behind his ears. The former military engineer didn't like the stranger's face at all.

"Who are you? How did you enter without a code?"

"Well, let's say your code was easy to guess. My name is Ramus. Ramus Napovni. You've probably heard of me."

"But of course. You ran for mayor of the White Capital, didn't you? Unsuccessfully, if I remember."

The intruder humbly bowed his head and threw up his hands, which were folded on his stomach.

"There are defeats, but you can always try again. There is a year left before the new elections, and my supporters have multiplied in number recently."

"I will not join them. That's what you came for, wasn't it?"

Rod stared hard into the face of the mayoral candidate Ramus Napovni. This man, it seemed, did not belong to any of the pre-evacuation ethnic groups of Noverca, but he was not an earthling either. The man was probably a result of the new crossbreeding. He lacked phioletine in his skin pigment. Neither small glitter nor large scales were exposed on his skin. He had high cheekbones, and sharp teeth. His irises did not look like pearls or mirrors but were bright brown, almost yellow, with two tiny dots for pupils. His eyes were not protected by goggles but remained wide open. He did not exhibit any signs of shaving or of subdued hair follicles on his broad forehead, but he had a real and rather thick beard found only in true earthlings and local Nordian hypertrichosians.

But it wasn't even the beard size that struck Rod. It was a yellow golden colour, which had almost disappeared among earthly blondes. Even Steven's mop of wheat and Tolyan's light-brown curls would seem dark next to these shiny strands. Perhaps only Marta's colour was similar before she turned grey during that year of her first visit here. She was silver now and always had a very short cut.

All this time Ramus spoke. His voice was confident and stern, but similar to the breaking voice of a teenager, although he appeared to be a mature middle-aged man, "I am very sorry to hear such negative sentiments. But I must become the Grand of the Capital next year by any means – and at any cost. This means that if something can help me win the election, I must get it. Anything, any resources, any person. Many of my followers made voluntary decisions to support me, and some had to be persuaded. Especially useful people like yourself."

"I only have two questions before you leave," said Rod, infuriated by now, walking to the door and throwing it wide open. "First, where did you get the idea that I am useful to you? I am an outdated Earth engineer whose knowledge and skills became antique several generations ago. Now I am a humble farmer. I breed edible beetles. Second, since when did elections on Noverca get won by such primitive means? As far as I know, not a single Grand has ever gathered followers. All the previous leaders were always elected by colonists only because they were proven loyal to O'Teka and to the colony's survival."

Rod crossed his arms over his chest and stared expectantly at the strange man. Inside, he was very afraid. He could not yet say why he was fearful of Ramus. Still, everything about the stranger was so unpleasantly familiar that his thoughts took him back to the past. All the way back to the times of the Resistance and to the struggle against the Cruisers. Back when even the leaders of the rebels betrayed their own people. This gold-bearded man looked like, talked, and even gazed in the same way as those people from the ancient past. His voice had the same self-confident and mocking intonation, which reduced the interlocutor to a powerless and already defeated beggar.

"I will answer with pleasure," Ramus replied seriously. "Times are changing. Our survival on the planet is already guaranteed, but we greatly overdid it, and now it's time to swing the pendulum back, restore balance, and reverse our steps. Gera is increasingly losing its original appearance, as is humanity itself. A little more, and we will cease to be humans, and Noverca will be set on a path to self-destruction. Do we want our planet to repeat the Earth's fate? Certainly not! But to turn back, we need power. That power can be obtained only through a certain means. And you, as a representative of a real human race, coming from Earth, simply must take our side."

"Bollocks!" exclaimed Rod, "Some nonsense!"

He could not believe his ears. It seemed impossible that this mental disease, this infection, would start again on Noverca. Where did Ramus come from? How had he not been figured out and rehabilitated on time?

"Why nonsense?"

"Because … I refuse."

"I knew you would refuse."

"Then why did you come? Leave immediately!"

"We'll leave together. I don't care if you accept my offer or not. You and your companions are my only way to get what I need to be successfully elected."

"I'm not going anywhere."

"If you want to see your husband and children again, you are. And I'll show you the way, by touch."

Two people entered the open door, put a sack on Rod's head, twisted his arms and dragged him out. He did not resist or shout. He realised that there would be no point in it. An incomprehensible fear paralysed him and was replaced by a completely understandable and sickening fear for his daughters and for Tolyan's safety. His beloved would not go quietly. Phoebe and Groonya would be scared to death.

Ramus calmly closed the door, which clicked with the automatic lock. Rod's amulet beeped desperately on the control panel.

Chapter 16. The Branch

I remember yesterday with astonishment. We spent a few hours by Calcolo's body, which was like a birthday party. Even greater! He was young. His meat was much better than anything I had had in the last few weeks, so I felt almost intoxicated by the taste of his warm blood. And the woman. I don't know their relationship issue, but she appeared grateful for her freedom. She touched my body in a way nobody has ever done, and I liked it. She did things I thought existed only in the books about human physiology I have studied. It felt good, but afterwards, I fell asleep and woke up in fear that she would stab me with my own weapon.

But no. We are wrapped together in her strange, grassy blanket, and I can feel the heat from her skinny body next to mine.

I wake her up, and this time I know what to do to feel so good again.

She likes touching my beard and tries to speak to me from time to time, but I still don't get anything, apart from the few words that seem vaguely familiar. How did these people manage to take over my transport computer? I thought we were going to join a civilised colony. But then again, I have only met two people so far, and they are humans. I am sure of it. They are just like me. Okay, they have dark hair on their heads, backs and shoulders. Some people on the station also had dark hair, although not so much and none of this tactile hair. The patients on Bebia's operation table were naked, and I never saw so much body hair as I saw on Calcolo and his woman. Maybe someone shaved them regularly, just as happened to me. I run my hand through the long hair I never knew I had on my chest. I wonder what it will be like when fully grown.

My knife works better than a piece of dry bone. After breakfast, the woman, with signs more than words, suggests that I remove as much flesh off the corpse as possible. She covers the remains – bones, skin, and blood – with snow and stones until all of it completely disappears from view. After that, she takes off her bracelets. They are just metre-long pieces of wire about 3 mm thick, coiled up into wrist bands. With one end, she strings the pieces of meat and liver on the wire, like on a skewer, until there is no room left on it. Then she links the ends, thus making two wreaths of human flesh. She puts one around my neck and the other on her left shoulder. It looks like she expects me to follow her towards the sun. Why not? I have enough food now to last much longer, and this woman can be useful to me in more than one way.

We walk for some time and stop to catch a breath on the top of another hill. We can see many more hills ahead of us, but some versicoloured clouds are thinning on the horizon. Suddenly there is an opening in the cloud, and their lower sides turn bright orange. A blazing narrow beam of sunlight pushes through the gap like a shot from a handzap. The woman excitedly touches my arm and points at the light beam.

"Ray!" she says loud and clear. I can't believe my ears. She makes me look at her and places her hand on her chest, "Ray," she repeats and smiles. I know that the word "ray" could come from many Earth languages, and I should not be surprised, really.

"Okay," I say, "your name is Ray. RAY!" I poke her in the chest and point at the light beam, but it has already gone.

So it looks like their names are the words of the things they see. Calcolo was probably as firm as a rock. And she was perhaps as beautiful as a ray of light ... some time ago. My name means "branch" in one of the Earth languages, but I see no trees around here. Then I look at the blanket on her back again, made of grass and twigs, and I pull the longest twig to show her, pointing at my chest. She looks at me for a moment.

"Ramus?" she says before I have time to open my mouth.

I look at her with new interest. She is not as ugly as I thought yesterday. She is probably the same age as that Kaila woman on the station. I suddenly like my new name. I have left everything behind. My past, my Bebia and my sun. I lost everything. Now I have lost the name Piliali and become Ramus. Ramus the foundling! In Bebia's language, Napovni, which sounds better. I am Ramus Napovni.

Chapter 17. Tolyan

Epigraphica, offering to temple of O'Teka J-81149

Why do we always want someone else to tell us what to do? Didn't we learn that if we let someone lead us, all they need to do is to frighten us? After that, they can lead us anywhere ... And I mean anywhere. They can tell us what is good and – much worse – what is bad for us. They can petrify us into submission as easily as a child gets his mother to pick him up if he wants her to.

It's nothing to do with being a coward. Even the bravest man in the world falls on his knees, fearing for his family. But then again, why does the most courageous man give power over himself to others? Why is he so afraid to make mistakes and to be wrong, that he makes the biggest mistake of all? He gives up on his own mind and starts to think someone else's thoughts, appreciate someone else's taste, adapt someone else's ethics, and agree with someone else's judgement, all his life.

Fadzia Herman, *Letters to Parents*, Sea Shimmer publications, year AC422

Harlow, a beautiful squat girl in a white headwrap and stylish beard, found Rod's amulet a few minutes after his abduction. She wondered for a minute and decided to take it back to Rod, thinking that he simply went home without it.

When Harlow approached Rod Baker's house, she heard a child crying inside, then a rumble as if someone had turned over some furniture. From the glass window (new colonists usually preferred screens), a dark-purple man in the bronze uniform of a Gera-naturalist flew out and remained motionless at the girl's boots. She barely had time to jump back. Otherwise, he would have knocked her off her feet. Again, there was a roar with which a strong man usually lifts a heavy load. This time something banged on the door from the inside. The door opened, and a second man wearing the same environment-guard uniform fell out of it on the threshold, and a third ran out and started down the street. Then Rod's husband, Anatoly Baker-Green, known as Tolyan, appeared on the doorstep. His left hand held on to his bloody side as he dragged the fourth guard by the collar with his right hand. Harlow stood frozen in shock, but the fierce earthling's red eyes found her, and Harlow began to breathe a little slower.

"Harlow!" growled Tolyan, "Where is Rod?"

The girl could not answer right away, "I don't know. I thought he went home and forgot his amulet at the farm?"

She held out the black disc.

"What? Tvoyu mat'!" Tolyan swore in a language Harlow did not know. Tolyan shook the man who hung in his hand like a doll, and he lifted him off the ground so that his face was at eye level. "Where is he? And don't try to lie. Otherwise, I'll shake off all your scales like dust."

But the man was unconscious. The intruder, who lay on the doorstep, was too. The girl leaned towards the man by her feet and realised that the dark-purple one was not breathing.

Tolyan abandoned his captive and went into the house. Harlow remembered the child crying and hurried after him. In the destroyed room, two more lay on the floor. One was alive and groaning, holding his head. She found Tolyan in the children's bedroom, where two tear-stained girls of eight and four years old quietly held each other in his mighty arms. Tolyan whispered something in their ears until they calmed down and agreed to do what he asked them to. The oldest, Groonya, led her sister by the hand and began to dress her as if for a walk. Then she dressed herself up. They were no longer sobbing but got themselves ready to go quickly and quietly. Phoebe put on her shoes herself, pulled out a school bag from under the bed and emptied its contents on the blanket.

At the same time, Tolyan pressed some towels to the wound on his side, tied it with a belt, and turned to Harlow again, taking his husband's amulet from her hands and pushing it deep into his trouser pocket.

"Do you know where Paisley Kornoki lives? You know, a former cadet of Master King?"

"A land-scout trainer? A carogering agency?"

"That's it."

"I know it. If you take the main road, you can walk there in fifteen minutes."

"Take the girls there for me, please. I will contact Paisley right away. The Altyn's ordermen will come soon, and most likely, I will not return home today. I need to find Rod and check on the others. Groonya, Phoebe, are you ready?"

Both girls stood dressed and ready for a short hike. It was evident that they had some training. They had always taken Papa Tolya's favourite game seriously, but no one had thought before that it would become useful.

"Papa, where is Dad?" Phoebe asked.

"I'll go and bring him, don't worry," Tolyan answered. "Groonya, Phoebe, listen to me carefully. Go with Harlow to Aunt Paisley's and skip school for a couple of cycles. Do what she says and wait. Do not go for walks. Study at home only. You must learn two of Queen Regi's songs by heart and write a letter to O'Teka about what happened today, but not right away. Wait until tomorrow. Do you understand your mission?"

"Yes, sir," Groonya answered, putting her hands on her sister's shoulders as she stood right behind Phoebe.

"Yes, sir," Phoebe repeated after her and bit her lip to keep her from crying.

Tolyan saw Harlow and the girls in the main street, which was busy but calm. Some passers-by stopped, attracted by the obvious disorder near the house, and called the ordermen on their amulets. Tolyan's time was running out. He grabbed his amulet and called his friend Kornoki. He quickly explained the situation and received a promise to hide the girls from any possible harm.

"But that all sounds too unlikely," Paisley added, "you are not on Earth anymore. Such things did not happen here even after the division into races."

"I've got a fresh hole in my side, Pais!" Tolyan said calmly to the face on the screen. "Only a flesh wound, though. These guys are not well trained but know how to use zappers. I miscalculated a bit since you are terribly vulnerable people, but I'll interrogate the survivors if I have time. I'm not very concerned for Steve and Mik, but I need to find Rod. He is not a combatant. Does Rimma Herschel still work for you?"

"She does."

"That's good. She knows how to deal with earthly children. Do not call our regular babysitter. I am not yet sure she is not involved."

Tolyan didn't get much from the captives of his house. Two of them could speak, but only one said he was on a mission from the True One of O'Teka to save the planet. The other one was silent – either from the horror, or because he was stubborn. Tolyan was not going to be merciful at the cost of his loved ones' lives. He was about to start breaking fingers, but then two ordermen and a medical operative entered the house. As befits representatives of the law in any world and at any time, they presented amulets with a code order and explained the reason for their visit. Tolyan invited them into the kitchen for a conversation, leaving the intruders to the medics.

"Mr Baker-Green, an order violation has been reported at this address. It is already obvious to us that you have indeed injured citizens. The severity of the violation will be determined by an examination, but you will have to come with us to the temple right now."

"I will go, but you must take these guys with you. They broke into my house without permission, wounded me, and threatened my—
"

"They will be dealt with accordingly. We know what to do." One of the ordermen held out his hand. "Your amulet, please."

Tolyan deactivated and handed over his amulet – a large turquoise finger ring – and then allowed the medical officer to dress his wound. Rod's amulet was still in his pocket.

Leaving the house, Tolyan saw two body bags with corpses and stretchers with the wounded being loaded into a medical conmot. The escaped Gera-naturalist was nowhere to be seen.

Tolyan was taken to the O'Teka temple in the conmot, a special vehicle that, unlike an ambulance, headed slowly to the city centre. It seems that on Noverca, nobody ever ran down the route to the temple, so Tolyan managed to effortlessly disappear from the conmot in a noisy area when they drove past the city waterfall. His hands were free, and he silently fell out of the vehicles back, flew over the broad rails, and sank like an eel into the huge city pond built by earthlings. The bridge was only three metres above the surface, and the pond was shallow. Closer to the shore, the water reached the huge hero's chest.

He emerged under the bridge. Only a forehead, eyes and nose appeared above the water. Tolyan listened for a long time and looked for signs of alarm among the pedestrians in their colourful headwraps and among the transport traffic. If his disappearance was noticed, it would not be immediately, and the conmot would be a couple of blocks away. Everyone here walked about with their noses in their amulets and their eyes on the numerous holo-screens. No one was looking around anymore. What was the point of all these beautiful flowerbeds and the magnificent waterfall?

Tolyan wished he could wait until dark, but the artificial twilight and nights projected by a dome only existed in one city on Gera called New Tokyo. These newly arrived earthlings made up most of the population. There was no such luxury in Altyn yet. Tolyan had to think of something else.

The pond was filled with running and very salty water. It was pumped directly from the sea, which could only be heard outside the city wall. Gallons of the material used by the waterfall were returned there so that the pond did not overflow. The pumps were powerful, and the pipes used were wide enough to give the falls an earthly grandeur. Once, along with the water, a blobster the size of a sheep was sucked into the pipe and fell into the pond. It was not hurt, but it did cause a big splash. The environmental guards wanted to catch and return it to sea, but the animal swam out through the broad outlet pipe. Since then, the filter gauze in the pump had been repaired. But was the outlet pipe open? Tolyan had not thought much about this as there had been no reports of blobster corpses stuck in the outflow.

Rod would never have allowed Tolyan to test this method on his own skin, but Rod was not around, and Tolyan didn't think twice. He was much larger than a sheep and, in theory, should be smarter than one. He dived again and let the current carry him to the outflow. He found a drain hole that seemed wide enough for his torso. There was a lattice there, which meant there was unlikely to be one at the other end. Tolyan put his hands on the decorative rock and, with two kicks of each heel, loosened the lattice hatch's bolts. This made his wound bleed again. He tore the lattice out with his hands, left it on the bottom, and then rose to the surface. Here, he took several deep breaths, sucked in as much air as possible, and returned to the outflow.

He only half entered it, but going back was impossible. The pipe, faced with such resistance, indignantly sucked him in as befits a good sewer. Tolyan had no idea of whether there were sharp bends or forks in the pipe. He flew with the stream of salt water without feeling squeezed, gathered himself in a ball, and closed his eyes. Now he was most concerned about the pipe's length. Blobsters are deep sea residents. They have gills. And Tolyan decided that if he didn't get stuck, he would simply drown. This path seemed endlessly long to him. He began to feel the suffocation creeping in, but he knew that in no case should he give in to the urge to inhale. He hit the pipe wall several times, slowly releasing the used air from his lungs. In that moment, he felt like he had shot out of the pipe like a cannonball. The surface of the water was not far away, and he managed to take a breath before falling into the sea waves.

He was pushed to the rocky bottom and had just enough time to think that he was free. Just when he thought he could plan the next step, a blow to his head deprived him of the ability to think or plan anything.

Chapter 18. The Branch

"Ramus! Ramus! Mbroj ..."

Ray's pushing and pulling awakens me. She is pointing in the direction we came from. After four intervals (I don't have a timer with me, so I can't call them days. They are gaps between camping for sleep) of the journey, I am so used to sleeping on the ground or the snow dents I start dreaming again. But this is not a dream. Ray looks frightened and frantic. She is holding my handzap, pointing away, and shaking me again, "Mbroj!"

I have no idea what it means, but I take the knife and get up. A man is running towards us, just a few hundred paces away. Today the wind is not so strong. The sky is getting lighter with each interval of the journey. When the running man crosses the snowy patches, he becomes visible against the white background. He runs with purpose. Just like I did a few intervals ago. Just like Calcolo ... and he looks just like him. My sleepy head thinks for a moment that Calcolo has come back from the dead to chase us. This time I do not let him come too close. I shoot him, but my aim is not good. He rolls to the ground and screams from pain. I am still bewildered when he jumps up and disappears into the cliff's dark shadow. My clear mind returns to me with Ray's voice saying, "Perseguir, perseguir, fin-tak ..."

I think she wants me to chase and finish the guy. I have no desire to walk into his ambush, but there is not much left of Calcolo. I don't know how long our journey will be. Ray tried to tell me once, but I am not sure she can count.

I can't find the uninvited guest. I see blood on the snow and some footprints, but he is not wounded badly enough and escapes this time, running on the frozen soil alone. I cannot tell which way he went, but I will be more observant now. It looks like this is a common event ... a stronger male kills and eats the weaker male, taking his flesh and his woman ... This has happened before on Planet Earth. Only those men did not build space stations and transport for wormholes. What is going on here?

Ray looks disappointed. She turns away when I reach out to touch her. Does she think of me as unworthy because I failed to kill and bring more food? Does she think I am weak? I will show her who is weak. I slap her on the back and force her down. She resists me. This has never happened before. I hit her face, and her skin splits under her good eye. She screams. Now I know where her scars came from. She easily becomes disrespectful and disobedient. When I grab her by her ankles and go inside, she screams again instead of sighing with delight. This makes me laugh. She looks horrified and ... surprised. Well, well! If being hit on the face is not new to her, rape is most certainly. For me ... this is even more satisfying. I laugh again. I feel much better. The unpleasant taste of failure has almost gone.

"Nay ... Ramus ... Zogs!" Ray shouts again, but I am already done. I roar with pleasure and toss her aside. Her torn red necklace is blown away by the wind.

It has probably been an hour since I left her whimpering on the snow. I am sitting on a blanket eating a chunk of meat. We have only one wreath of Calcolo left. The wind and cold air make it less enjoyable, but eating is still good. I throw a scrap of meat at Ray, but she does not move. I know she is hungry, but she does not touch the piece. Sometimes she turns away, digging her fingers in the snow. It looks like she is eating snow. Stubborn fool. I am angry again, but an alarming thought stops me from hitting her again. How long is my road? By waking me up, she saved my life today. What if another runner is welcomed by her, and she will smile in gratitude when she licks my blood? I can kill her, but I want to feel good every interval. Surely this can wait.

I had better mend things between us.

"Ray, I am sorry." These are my first words since the attack. "I shouldn't have hurt you, but you made me so angry ..."

I get up and cover her curled-up shape with a grassy blanket. She stops sobbing and looks at me carefully. She does not understand my words, but surely she understands the tone of my voice. "We need to go soon. Eat, don't be silly."

I pick up a piece of meat and hold it by her lips. She pushes the meat away and covers her face with both hands.

"Fine," I say, grabbing her by the arm and forcing her on her feet. "Be like that!"

One of her bracelet wires is meat-free now. I use it to bind her wrists together and hang the remaining wreath around her neck. She stands still.

"Jet!" I use the word I learned from her recently, "Go!"

Only when I show her my knife does she turn and start walking towards the light.

Chapter 19. Steven

Epigraphica, offering to temple of O'Teka W-964966

Cruisers burned her at the stake. The same mystics burned witches in the same way in the old times. They burned scientists a little later. Father Darron made a short speech, which all boiled down to one thing: we did not tolerate the abomination of your attempts to make a man out of an animal. Why would we accept your attempts to turn a man into a beast? The first is the privilege of God, and the second is the impudent intention to trample on his work.

Dr Emilia Hofer has saved many lives by increasing the ability of humans to hold their breath for eight to eleven minutes by activating some of the dormant genes we share with amphibians. Yes, that means different internal organs and a slight change in appearance, but the Earth's conditions are getting harsher. The air now is thinner; extraction of every molecule of oxygen from it will allow us to continue a little longer. She laughed when I quoted from the ancient book: "The trouble is not that man descended from an animal, but that he has not ceased to be an animal." She said this means that there should be no problems then. What's wrong with the fact that we take back what is already ours?

Peter Roy Javen, *Diary 51*, Earth, 18 October, year 3397

Mik always thought his friend spent too much time in front of the mirror. Steven examined his own reflection with satisfaction. His big arms stretched the sleeve's fabric a little, but this time his chest fitted his shirt perfectly.

"I am glad you made an effort too," he said to Mik, "Tilda said tonight she will introduce you to a very special lady."

"I disapprove of double dates," Mik replied, unbuttoning his shirt collar.

"I've known you for years, which tells me that this may be the only way. You will be complete only if you have someone with whom to share your glory and your success ... and your money. Ask Tolyan."

"I can share my money with a woman if she can share hers with me. Although, I am more interested in her lifestyle and her purpose."

Steven picked up a shoebox-sized package from the chair and dimmed the lounge lights. "Every woman on Noverca has a purpose ... and money, if she has chosen the first well. Tilda said that you will surely fall in love this time. We have a bet."

"What will you give her if she wins?" Mik replied.

"A trip to Pettogreco," Steven said, pushing the box into Mik's hands and doing Mik's collar button up again.

"And if she loses?"

"She will find a new date for you every month," Steven said.

"Damn you!"

"Sorry, mate, but we will never rest until you are happy and broody. Let's go. I will introduce you to my new interest, Victoria. We need to be on our way."

"I thought your date tonight was with Tilda," said Mik, following his friend to his workroom.

"That's right, but it's going to be even sweeter this time. Victoria will take us to Boa Trossy," Steven replied. He opened the door and made an inviting gesture. His smile was full of pride and excitement.

Mik stared at the vehicle inside the workroom with surprise, "This one has four wheels. Are you sure this is Benz and not Ford? Where did you get the schematics?"

"Only the very first Benz model had three wheels. This one I pulled from the records of O'Teka, dated by the very first offering on the subject. Rod helped me order the parts. I put it together all by myself ... well, almost. Madam Ursula does not ask too many questions but does what she is told ... most of the time. Victoria is ready to go. And here is your part of the plan. Open it."

Mik opened the box and pulled out an object that looked like a rubber ball with a brass horn.

Steven beamed. "It arrived today, the last thing I needed. The real brass cost me a fortune, plus an argument with Ursula about the percentage of copper. Go on, give it a squeeze."

Mik pressed on the rubber ball, and the horn made a horrible high pitch screech. Mik made a face, and Steven laughed and got in the driver's seat. "You know the way. Your job is to walk in front of us and signal to the pedestrians."

"Go to hell."

"Already been there! Ha ha ha! Okay, okay. *Ich mache Witze.* Give it back, here it goes. Now we can clear the way if needed. Get in, mate. When was the last time you ate in Boa Trossy? There are earthling chefs too, and the music is from the best collection of twenty-third century Earth."

They left Victoria outside the main entrance and went in. There was no parking space, as people walked a lot in this small city. They used the electric train if they needed to hurry, but inside the city walls any moto-vehicles, such as electro-mobiles or conmots, were used only by official services. Steven and his comrades got away with a lot, being local heroes and the main city attraction.

The place was busy and noisy, but the table reserved for VIP guests received exquisite service. When Mik and Steven approached it, one of the girls sitting there got up and threw her arms around the blond former soldier. Tilda was an earthling, one of the second generation of newcomers. Her skin was already much darker, with a violet hue on her neck, ears, and eyelids. Her lips had red lipstick over her natural purple colour, and her silver eyes were decorated with lenses, imitating the brown eyes she probably would have had anyway if she had been born on Earth. Her black hair was braided. Her dress was plain red velvet, tailored by the earthling craftspeople. Mik wondered if Steve explained what he preferred to see on her to Tilda.

Steven laughed happily and said, "Mik, you remember Matilda Crossich. Tilda, I miss you too, baby. Will you introduce us to your friend?"

Mik took off his lightglasses and stuffed them into his breast pocket. Tilda pointed her finger at the young woman sitting next to her.

"This is Nikolaya Gil, an apprentice of someone very important, but she is too shy to talk about it," said Tilda and went back to her seat, beaming. "She is not my friend yet. We only met last week at the bible club. But I hope we will become closer soon. We have so much in common."

The girl Tilda called Nikolaya was about the same age as her, around twenty-seven. She was also dark-haired, but she did not wear any lenses, make-up or jewels. Her only accessory was the ribbon of her amulet – bright red-and-brown stripes, which looked nice against her yellow dress. Her skin was darker than Tilda's, almost plum-coloured, and her eyes were well adapted to twilight. They were black with an occasional deep-green retina reflection, which flashed like lightning every time she turned her head.

"You must be Mik King?" she asked in a deep but pleasant voice.

"I am," answered Mik, "You don't look shy to me. Where is your apprenticeship?"

Steven was already sitting next to Tilda and whispered something into her ear. Mik also took his seat next to Nikolaya. She immediately placed an empty crystal glass in front of him and said, "I asked if they serve the wine you make. They do, but it's too expensive for me. Do you have a discount at this restaurant? I really want to taste some."

"As a matter of fact, I do. I can let Steve choose the wine, but what is there for me?"

"Just say what you fancy."

"I already did, Miss Gil," Mik replied. "The answer to my question, you ignored."

"Is that all you want to know about me?"

"Maybe not, but it's a start, and I prefer to do things in the order I choose."

Steven's voice interrupted them through the music. This time they played some songs from The Martians' album *Take Me with You.*

"Hey Mik, today's special includes fresh tocks. I will also order sandie soup and rabbit roast for the girls. What do you want? The usual?"

"Sure," said Mik, turning back to Nikolaya with a certain interest.

"Tock Platter to share as a starter, one sandie shchi, one rabbit with pea mash, one goat de volante with lemon and one flame beef burger with potato and extra chilli for the mains. No seaweed on the peas, please. Oh yes, and two bottles of Mik and Ann Jello, from the year 1005 or 1006. We will decide on the desserts later," said Steven into his amulet.

Tilda leaned over the table and said loudly, "Nikolaya trained in one of your scout academies. Show him your brows, Nikkie!"

Black eyes flashed a green reflection at Mik once again. Nikolaya turned her slow smile directly at him and frowned. Her extra muscles under the skin of her forehead contracted, and her eyebrows, which a moment ago looked like ordinary broad and smooth arcs, unfolded. Every hair was erect and almost five centimetres long. Now they looked just like the bushy whiskers of the *Felidae*. Tilda squealed with exaltation and clapped her hands.

"I love it when she does that! I wish I had the same implants, but I am not entitled to them, as I chose a different purpose. I am so glad they let her keep them."

"I have seen this before," said Mik. "Vibrissae come with nocturnal eyes for most scouts. But if you didn't graduate above pride grade, then you will not receive maintenance treatments, and the superfluous neurons around your eyes will atrophy. Your antennae will become useless in a year or two," said Mik.

"I have a plan to take care of that – and some help," answered Nikolaya, returning her eyebrows to a flat position and smoothing them with her thumbs.

"Then my second question would be – what help? I am still waiting for the answer to the first question."

Nikolaya stopped smiling and frowned again, but her face didn't bristle this time.

"Your friend is no fun at all," she said to Steven, watching all of this with interest.

"Oh, he is," Steven replied. "Just play along and answer his questions. Avoiding direct requests is the first sign of dishonesty. Very unusual for the colony. I would even say – here it is frowned upon."

Tilda laughed loudly.

"Okay, you win," said Nikolaya. "How long do we have until the food is served?"

"About five minutes until the starter arrives and forty minutes till the mains. People need a chance to talk before they eat," answered Steven.

The waiter brought wine and confirmed the order.

Nikolaya flashed her eyes at Mik, "Then why don't we let the lovebirds smooch alone for a bit? Tilda mentioned that they have some private simulation rooms here, where the Earth's most famous restaurants can be projected on all four walls. She and Steven had a date last month in a French bistro. We can visit Mugaritz. My ancestors were from a place on Earth called Spain, and they mentioned that restaurant in the family chronicles."

Mik poured the wine into four glasses.

"It will double our bill. Are you paying?"

"Oh, we won't eat there. We will just ask to take a look, for future plans, perhaps?"

Mik stared for a moment, then picked up two glasses with both hands, "Why not?"

Master Mik King was a special guest, so five minutes later, he walked with Nikolaya into the screen unit. It was not big – three by three metres with a simple round table under a long white cloth, and two chairs. But the illusion created by the screen walls took them to a sunny day with green grass outside huge windows between wooden walls. Mik tasted the wine and nodded with satisfaction and pride. Nikolaya lifted her hand to her glass, but Mik moved it out of her reach.

"Lady, I am a very stubborn goon. You can't dodge forever. Flirting rules are not for me. The number of my questions grows every time you ignore them."

"Oh, I am sorry. It is so nice here, although my eyes don't like all that light. What were those questions again?"

Mik took another sip, "Mmm, that was a good year indeed. Okay, Nikolaya. Let's pretend I believe that you are just not a very serious person. In this case, it's very unlikely that there will be a second date, but the questions were simple. I tried to get to know you. Curiosity is a part of my personality." Mik put both glasses on the table, pulled out the chair, and sat down. "Tilda mentioned your apprenticeship with someone important. So I was curious as to who that might be. Then she said you dropped the academy. That happens very rarely, so I was curious why?"

"Tilda needs to keep her mouth shut," said Nikolaya without her charming smile.

She turned to face the window. Her deep eyes reacted by narrowing the pupil into a slit, revealing her irises, which were the colour of rust. She was incredibly attractive, and at the same time, there was something unpleasant about her. Like an unfamiliar multi-coloured insect, about which nothing is known. What if it bites?

Mik carried on, "I am a professional, and there is no such thing as a passing comment for me. I still have access to the personal data of cadets – past and even future ones. But I would like to hear it all from you, Miss Gil. You also mentioned that you have the means to maintain your implants. That is also uncommon, so ..."

Nikolaya turned around and, in one fast movement, she jumped on Mik's lap, squeezing his thighs together with both her knees. Her hands grabbed his head, and her mouth dug into his lips. Mik's reaction was as if he expected that, but it was automatic. He would not let her insert a small solid object between his teeth; something that could not be her tongue. He pushed her abdomen away with both hands and, at the same time, fell back, throwing her over his head. Nikolaya yelped, rolled over, and jumped back to her feet. She was a well-trained land-scout, but not a fighter. It was too late. The element of surprise was lost. Mik lifted her into the air, threw her on the tabletop, and swaddled her in the tablecloth, together with spilled wine and shards of glass. Nikolaya could not move – only her shoulders and head stuck from the cocoon of the fabric.

"Would you now answer my questions? This time I have the right to ask them with some encouragement."

"No. I failed. The True One will kill me anyway, and not only kill. Please, don't let him have my body!"

"Who? What else? Come on, girl! The True One? Whoever your patron is, don't you want to get him back? You could have been a great scout."

"Get him back? Ha! He is the true priest of O'Teka. Not a corrupt one." Almost immediately, her body went limp, and she lowered her head to the table surface, "I deserve this. My task was conditioned – it was you or I."

Nikolaya moved something in her mouth and swallowed it. Her head rolled on one side, and Mik thought it could be another trick. He waited for a minute, but as soon as he saw yellow froth filling the girl's mouth, he grabbed his lightglasses with an amulet built into them, and called the emergency services to these coordinates. They should arrive in less than five minutes. Mik rushed back to Steven and Matilda but found that Steven's date was sitting at the table alone.

"Where is Steve?" shouted Mik at the girl's face.

She recoiled. "Hey! What are you doing? Stevie tried his starter and went to the toilet. I don't think the tock was very fresh. What's the matter? What's wrong?"

Tilda looked at him with bewilderment, which transformed into real concern as she spoke. Mik was already on his way to the lavatory. It was empty. Mik ran to the kitchen and checked the back door and the warehouse, not letting anyone stop him. He searched the entire restaurant and returned to the toilet. He took a small airtight case with a tracker's eye lenses from his pocket. He didn't even need to use the mirror on the wall, as he had put them on thousands of times. He closed his eyes, trying to slow down his breathing and pulse. Two minutes had passed. He heard a commotion in the restaurant as paramedics and an ordermen arrived. Someone's powerful and professional voice urged customers and employees to remain calm and stay at their tables until the officer on duty had spoken with them, and he gave them all an address to which they could send their statements from the amulets.

Mik opened his eyes. Through the lenses, the bathroom looked very different. All the colours had disappeared, but the bluish light showed the traces of various body fluids on the clean-looking surfaces. There was no sign of blood plasma, which usually lingers for a few hours after blood is wiped off. Mik ignored indications of spit, urine and even tears in that room, but the compound of goon-fly venom shone nice and bright, like a sparkle. Mik removed the lenses and crouched over two tiny drops of orange liquid. They were still wet, smeared slightly, as if with a shoe sole. He found another drop by the back door.

Back at the table, Tilda said Steven had only been gone for a short time, so she hadn't worried immediately. She did not see anybody going after him, as the furniture and decor concealed the entrance well. She did not see anyone coming out for the same reason.

Mik left her to repeat all that to the approaching officer and checked on Nikolaya. But the emergency medics had already taken her away in a body bag. Mik looked around the empty room with the simulation still on and picked up the girl's amulet. Nobody had noticed it because of the room's bright light, which was so disliked by Novercians.

Soon the ordermen were questioning everyone in the building, Mik included.

"An assassination attempt? I don't think so," said the professional, who pronounced Nikolaya dead. "Mr King, I have removed the remains of the 4 ml capsule from her craw implant. The enzymes there are slow-acting and dissolve only the seal. For a slim female, this much pure goon-fly venom was lethal, no doubt, but you are probably more than three times her body mass. You would have slept most of the cycle and would not end up like the poor girl. The dose was calculated with great precision. May I ask, that friend you are missing...? Is he just as big? What is his name? Oh, I see. If the same amount of venom was injected into the fruit he sucked up, he will not die."

Mik put his lenses back on and looked for traces of the froth on the street. He did not find any. Outside the restaurant, between a few emergency conmots, stood the Victoria Benz, looking abandoned and incredibly wasted as a means of escape from a crime scene.

Chapter 20. The Branch

I will miss entering the warmth of her body, but at least I don't have to butcher her up. She is not heavy, and I can carry her in the blanket over my back. I left her head and one of her arms on the spot where I enjoyed her last time. A few hours later, she was not the same. She was cold and unresponsive, so I even wished for a moment that she was still alive. With every interval she becomes lighter, and soon there will be no meat left on her, but I am not worried about hunger anymore.

I have learned that this race does not feed only on each other and their women. The less snow there is around, the more I come across the small animals that live in it. They are yellowish and like large caterpillars, but they are warm-blooded and probably feed on microorganisms. Since the sun is already much higher above the horizon, I have enough light to see that the snow is not as white as I thought. The brownish hues near the ground can be evidence of a snowy plankton. Three times bigger than a finger, these caterpillars dig tunnels in the snow closer to the ground, but Ray did not need to show them to me. I caught one and saw that the red husk from which Ray's beads were made were dry caterpillar heads strung on coarse long hair. They taste too oily but not unpleasant. Apparently, this is what the locals eat until they get lucky.

I wonder where they are coming from and where they all heading. I often notice dark spots at a great distance, slowly creeping in one direction. They are all walking towards light and warmth. Where is their home? Up ahead, or where they make their long and dangerous journey from? Alone, in pairs, or in small groups. I don't see large groups yet.

I have reached a sort of canyon or a mountain ridge. My knowledge of them is limited to a few pictures in geography books. The snow and its caterpillars are very rare now. When Ray has nothing useful left on her, I throw her bones into the smoky hole in the ground. It's very smelly, but warm vapour is rising from it. I want to rest here but am not the only one attracted to its comfort. Two figures step from behind the cliff, and I can tell they are both females. This does not mean I don't have to fight them, but the first thing they said sounded like a question. "Oon?"

"Whatever."

"Oon? Ma?" one of them kept asking. She looks old, but I can't be sure since they are covered in scars and dirt. This one has three rows of caterpillar heads around her neck. She carefully approaches me and touches the blanket I am sitting on. The inquiry on her face changes to deep sadness.

"Ma, Morta-ah!" she moans with unmistakable grief.

Does she know Ray? "Ray," I say, testing my theory. No reaction, "Calcolo?"

I note that both women have similar blankets on their backs. Do all women here carry them? To dress or to wrap up their children? Probably. They can see I am a man, but they also know that the woman to whom this blanket belonged has gone.

The younger one is staring at my hair and my beard. I don't believe the locals have seen hair of this colour before. Ray also used to be impressed and kept touching my head. She also seems fascinated by my height, so I get up on my feet. Both women step back, and their eyes open wide. At least these two have both eyes intact.

I want to be part of their group. Resting will be safer, and they can make me feel good again. I wish to show them that I can offer them protection. I hold my handzap out, but ... it does not work. The deadly beam of energy does not appear. I don't know what the problem is, but its ZPE-converter must be malfunctioning. It could be that I need to be done closer to the sun to recharge it. Damn! I have no means of fixing it. Another fight could mean certain death for me. But the shiny knife is still making an impression. Both women nod at me and at each other. The older woman shakes the blanket off her shoulders and produces a wire wreath of cold and dried caterpillars.

"Vorms. Gust," she says.

So far, so good. This halt promises to be enjoyable.

Chapter 21. Losses

Tom looked at his amulet with surprise. His wife had never called him from work before. He was glad to take a little holiday after their return from the last rescue mission, but Zina insisted on going straight to the hospital. Her bags were still unpacked, and her messages were still unheard. Tom activated the amulet response.

"Tom ..."

Zina's voice was far from calm.

"I need you to come to the hospital ... quick."

"What's the matter?"

"I don't have time to explain. I need you here, and I need you to check on our team! Are they all okay?"

"Why? Any bad news from Vist and the pilots? Last I heard, they are on the way back and will reach the continent tonight."

"Not them ... the rest. I am worried about Rod more than the others, I don't know where he is, but his amulet is in front of me. Also ... Tolyan is in trouble ... Please hurry."

"On my way."

Tom knew that asking for anything else would have meant slowing things down. Zina was not a drama queen, and if she sounded so urgent, there was a reason for that.

The former captain of the *Wasp* washed the garden dirt off his hands but did not bother to change his clothing. He rushed to the rail line and stopped, waiting for the next tram. Tom tried to contact Steven, but he did not respond. He tried Tolyan and Mik with no result.

He was already on the tram when Mik returned his conv-call, "Captain?"

"Mik, are you okay? Are any of the guys there with you?"

"No. I'm giving a statement to the orderman here, at the Earthling Affairs Department. Steven has been kidnapped."

"What? Here? Who could overpower Steven here?"

"The poisoner has overpowered Steve. I hope he's alive."

"You have to tell me everything in detail ... Earthling Affairs Department? You are here, in New Tokyo?"

"Yes, I was *summoned* this morning."

"When will you be free? Zina called me urgently."

"I'm already free. Where shall I go?"

"To the science hospital."

Mik disconnected. It sounded like somebody next to him had protested before that, but Mik could not be stopped. He and Tom arrived at the hospital almost at the same time.

"What's this?" asked Tom at the gate, looking at the strange vehicle that Mik had parked clumsily, nearly crashing into a linden-like tree.

"Another project of Steve's. He finished it just before the expedition, and we took it out last night, and I was able to take it with me on the train this morning."

"Mik, you are taking advantage of your reputation."

"The owner of the line offered this idea. I wanted to leave it by the Altyn station, but he insisted that I make good use of it in New Tokyo."

They entered the spacious hospital room and hurried to the broad escalator.

"When and where did the kidnapping take place?"

"Last night in Boa Trossy. I spent the night there, trying to investigate."

"And they let you?"

"Who? The ordermen? Only on condition that I go to the Earthling Affairs Department and report everything I knew and learned."

Both men approached Zina's office, although she spent little time there. The young nurse waited for them.

"This way," he said after the greeting, "Doctor Zina wanted to stay by your friend's side until she was sure ..."

"Whose?" asked Tom.

"Steven's?" asked Mik.

"No, It's Mr Baker-Green."

"Which one?" asked Tom and Mik at the same time.

"The big one!" answered the nurse.

In the ward, they found Zina sitting by the hospital bed that looked small under Tolyan's huge size. He was covered with sheets up to his chin, and the neuro-helmet had hidden his head from view. His eyes were closed, but his face was badly bruised on the right-hand side. Next to the bed was another person, who wore the uniform of an orderman.

As soon as they came in, Zina got up. She looked seriously worried but gave a deep sigh of relief.

"He is alive. He has a zapper burn on his side, but it's not lethal. He suffered a serious head injury, drowned, and his body was covered with bruises all over."

"Why isn't he on the temporary system preserver?" asked Mik.

"He was – all night and on the way here from Altyngrad. Tolyan was brought in yesterday evening, and no one thought to tell me. Dr Plamidi was on duty, and he saved his life."

"So what happened?" Tom asked.

"The villagers from the shore camp found him. They always search for possible waste from the city that might get washed out. So, they saw Tolyan floating, and dragged him ashore to rob him, taking him for dead. The border patrol investigated the signal when they found the amulet on him and activated it."

"It is their duty," said the orderman suddenly. "They are keeping a watchful eye on technology that might make its way outside the walls. Your friend was lucky that one of the city spies in the camp immediately rushed back to the beach and contacted the emergency medical service."

"I am sorry, but why are you here, officer? It does not look like Mr Baker-Green will give evidence any time soon," said Mik, turning to him.

"I do not expect that, sir. I am here to secure his presence because he was arrested. He attacked civilians, and two lost their lives. He will give evidence during his rehabilitation."

"What? Two dead? When did that happen?" asked Tom.

"Yesterday. The amulet was taken off the suspect at ..." the orderman checked his own amulet, "21.02."

"But the amulet villages found—"

Zina interrupted her husband and said, "That was Rod's amulet. We don't know where he is and why Tolyan had it, but another orderman took it back to the office as a piece of evidence."

"What was the location of that attack?" asked Mik.

"At his address, and sir, this is the only information I can reveal. Please do not ask any further questions."

"At his home address? So he was defending his home ... his children!"

Tom turned to Zina, and she answered the question on his face, "Scarlett left for Altyngrad as soon as she heard. The smart girl thought of them before I even did. I am sure she will let us know soon enough."

Mik stepped closer to the orderman. "Tolyan is not a murderer, and if someone died, it must have been an accident. Some Altyn civilians would die if he sneezed at them ..."

"Sir, I believe you. This is why he will not be exiled. But people died, Master King. He will have to serve his ..."

"Who is in charge of the investigation?" asked Mik.

"I am afraid the case is already with the magistrates," said the orderman. He looked at Tolyan with sympathy and turned back to Mik. "Try talking to Senator Petrich, sir. He used to be a great fan of the famous Three Giants."

"I will talk to Grand if I have to," said Mik, putting his sunglasses on and activating his amulet on the way out of the room.

Zina sat back down, and Tom put his hand on her shoulder.

"Officer, as far as I am aware, you can do your job on the other side of the door."

"Yes, sir," answered the guard.

"Please do that and ask the nurse to come in and replace Doctor Darkwood. Thank you."

"Tom, Tolyan is being monitored by the centre."

"I know, but I have reason to double secure him if I can help it."

When they were alone by Tolyan's bed, Tom listened to the breathing pump for a minute and asked, "Is his head fried? What is the chance that he will not end up a vegetable?"

"After a couple of days of intensive restoration therapy, the brain tissue will grow back, but he might not remember his life," Zina answered without lifting her eyes.

"Did he have a will for such a case?"

"I don't know. Both Bakers could afford one, but ... I suppose we can check in the temple. Don't rush to tell the others. Please. Have you found them all?"

"No. Zina, I think you must let your colleagues look after Tolyan for a while. You also need to take time off and disappear from the scene. Yes, I am afraid so, and I will go and see what can be done about Rod and Steven."

Zina looked up.

"Steven?"

"He is also missing."

"Oh ... Tom, what is happening? Rod and now ... Steven."

The door opened, and the duty nurse entered. Zina's expression immediately changed from concern to authority.

"Thank you for coming, Nurse Matthew. This patient is a victim of an assassination attempt, and I know you enough to trust that you can protect him."

The nurse nodded calmly, "Yes, ma'am."

"Do not leave him with any strangers. That goes for the guard too. Is that clear?"

"Yes, ma'am. He is due for a review in two hours."

"Be present all the time. Contact me with any changes without delay. Thank you."

They found Mik frowning at the already blank holo-screen outside the room. His attempt to contact the magistrates ran into typical bureaucratic obstacles. All three went to Zina's office, and Mik told them everything that had happened in Boa Trossy. The doctor's office was also a meeting room. The walls were a faceted series of screens. There was also a round table with chairs. Zina sat in one of the chairs, Tom sat on the table, and Mik walked around it.

After listening to him, Tom shared his thoughts. "Rod and Tolyan were attacked on the same day as you and Steven. The kidnappers tried to sedate you two because they knew you would fight back, but I am not sure why they thought Tolyan wouldn't."

"They thought he wouldn't if they had his girls and Rod as hostages," said Zina. "Mik, why do you think they need you guys?"

"Captain, I think we are all the target, the entire rescue team. They started with us in Altyn. Vist, Nat and Marta are not on Gera yet, and you two and Scarlett are here and could be next."

Zina grabbed the amulet, "Scarlett? Oh no ... She is in Altyngrad right now!"

Chapter 22. The Branch

Epigraphica, offering to temple of O'Teka R-8893002

This man with violet scales on his thick cheeks and the top of his head insisted on defining all the concepts I used to try to prove my point of view to him. Why does he need it? He explained that we belong to different worlds, both geographically and psychologically. Our languages have evolved separately. If we want to come to an agreement, we must make sure we are talking about the same things. We have to access the temple and refer to "Oxford." I asked him what Oxford was, and it turned out that he meant a dictionary. "Do you see already," he sneered, "how definitions are useful for communication?"

I couldn't help but argue that even if we both had our dictionaries, who would decide whose definition is correct? He turned to me from the screen and said, "What do you mean, 'if'? Don't you have it? When you have your own Oxford, you can argue which is correct. Otherwise, your definitions will change depending on your mood, time of day, and situation. It's ridiculous to hear this from a debater who doesn't even have his own Oxford."

Brother Dan, My first contact with the colony. Year AC1001

Eating vorms with brown mucus scraped off stones is not as pleasant as meat but it is satisfying. Very satisfying. One handful is enough for most of the interval. Although how long intervals last, I cannot say. The sun does not rise and does not set like in the old flicks. There is no common timer device like there was at the station. I go to rest when I want or when my strength runs out. During each stop, two women with me begin to collect vorms in the rare but still available pieces of ice and snowy shadows under the rocks. Both give me little pleasure. They do not rejoice from my attention, and if I treat them harshly, they close their eyes and silently endure, hanging in my hands like their grass rags. At least now I get enough sleep and learn their language. It may be useful to me. I know that there were once many languages on Earth. When the remnants of the people lived only in cramped stations, they used two or three at most. Bebia told me that many words appeared in different languages and passed from one to another so much that you can work out what is being said if you listen carefully and look out for something familiar.

For now, I call these creatures – *pilgrims*, and I already know that they are not speaking here in sentences but in single, essential words. But these words come from many languages I have not even heard of before. I bend fingers in front of the old hag's nose and learn that she could only count to twenty. She shows me her name and her relative's name – I still don't know who they are to each other. The older woman's name is Shadow, which sounds like Tma in her language. And the young woman's name is either a voice or a scream, I am not certain, but she wants me to call her Anthem. I told them my name was Ramus. That was easy enough.

"Mortah" means death or dead. "Zogs" means stop. "Chov and Ma" means man and woman. "Mbroj" means fight, and so on. By the time we come to the crater, I know at least two dozen words. Oh yeah ... I believe these women ate their man some time ago because he was "hvor," whatever that means.

The crater was a surprise, and I did not expect that the next climb to the ridge of rocks would open a fantastic sight of a huge hole in the black stone cover of the planet. I know of volcanoes, but I thought they were supposed to be tall mountains. This one is about two sleeping camps of walking, not active, although something is heating the air and water under the crust. The small cracks with steam and smoke are now more frequent, but there is no more snow or ice. And of course, no more vorms. But now we eat something else.

Not all but some of the steaming cracks hold water. We encounter small puddles of warm clear water with a slightly acidic taste and larger pools in which all three of us could fit and wash. It is a very good environmental change. Most of the small pools have creatures called *ee* living in them. I wouldn't have known they were there if it weren't for the women. They are the size of my palm and practically transparent, flat and slippery. These creatures are less fat than caterpillars but much tastier. Catching them is hard and frustrating because you have to slowly move your hand in the water and grab it as soon as you touch the slimy body. The women laugh at me every time I try and fail, but only until I push them to the ground and kick a few times. After that, they do not laugh anymore. They catch some ee for me and try to apologise by offering me pleasure. I decline the last offer, as I prefer to do that when I choose to, whether they are willing or not. It's more fun when they are not.

As we approach the crater's edge, I see more pilgrims coming from the same direction. They do not attack each other anymore. Some even make resting camps as close as a few paces from us and exchange a few words with Tma. Sometimes they point at me and ask something about the "Chov" I can't guess. Most of them are couples, but once I saw a group of three men and two women. What don't I see? Children. Do they have young ones at all? They must.

The wind is still strong, if not stronger. The sun now is high enough to look less like the dawn, and more like a very early morning in some flicks I watched about mountain climbers. It is much lighter and warmer now. I can see more details about my alien companions, but this does not help. I prefer them in the dark. But dark has been left behind, and it will only get lighter. I point at the crater and ask old Tma what that is. There was never any use asking the girl questions, as she never answered but just stared at me in fear. I use the same word that Tma and Ray used, enquiring about my weapon, "Shta-evo?"

She throws her arms as wide as she can, and then touches her forehead.

"Dostup," was her answer.

"Shta?"

"Dostup ... Casa-Tvo."

I did not need to guess that casa means home, but the rest is still a blur. I express confusion, and she repeats those words. Then she points back in the direction we came from, "Casa-Oon!" She points at the crater once more, "Casa-Tvo."

Suddenly I begin to understand. This crater is their Home-2. And they have been walking from something they call Home-1. How far is that? Do they often wander from one home to another and back?

Chapter 23. What Now?

Zina breathed a sigh of relief when she saw Scarlett's beardy face on the screen. "Why haven't you said a word for so many hours?"

"Because there was nothing yet to report. I'm talking to pretty Harlow here. She witnessed the incident in Baker's house, and Tolyan himself forbade her from telling anyone where the children are. But she assures that they are with reliable friends."

"That's nice. That's right. Well done, Harlow! What can she tell us about the incident?"

"Nothing. She is afraid. Why do you want to know? The order takes care of it."

"It is very important to me. After all, Rodion has not yet been found."

Scarlett thought for a moment. "If it helps, I'll talk to her again. Nordians trust Nordians the most."

"Will you let me know right away?"

"I promise, Doctor Zina."

As soon as Zina put the amulet away, Mik, who had been walking clockwise around the table all this time, changed direction.

"Okay," he said, "so far, we have got no help from official Novercians ... quite the opposite. I did not get far with the senator either. All he could tell me without breaking his integrity is this: Rod's amulet was not damaged, but it has nothing on it that could help us. I am pretty mad now! I am missing two of my mates, and I can't just sit and wait now for two hypertrichosian girls to become useful."

"We might all have to sit back and wait anyway. Vist will be back soon, and we have to make sure one of us is still around to tell the story," said Tom.

"While we are waiting for Scarlett, why don't we talk about Steven?" said Zina. "Mik, you spoke to the others in the restaurant. How many people saw a 'very drunk man' taken to the back room? From the toilet?"

"Just one, a customer. The ordermen took the statement. The description fits Steven." Mik grabbed the chair and sat next to Zina and Tom.

"And how did that customer describe the waiter who took him?"

"There were two. Earthlings, most likely, with purple make-up. Novercians would not be able to move Steve. The witness described the uniform and those stupid hats they have to wear ... and said that both waiters were medium-sized and ... This is all crap, guys! I should be looking for him and Rod!" he said, getting up again.

Tom put both hands on the table and calmly said, "I know, Mik, but we're trying to see if there is a way to recognise those two men when they come for you again – or for either of us. If they could dress up as waiters and then as medical officers and take Steven away in an ambulance without any problem, then they can come to you as cadets or as ..."

"As far as I know, they may actually be ex-cadets, like that girl with the implants. Maybe I taught them to merge with the environment myself."

"But why do they want to capture our rescue team?" asked Zina.

Mik stopped pacing. "I just remembered. The girl said something before swallowing the venom ... something like, 'he is a true priest of O'Teka.'"

"Who?"

"The person who sent her on the quest to seduce and sedate me."

Mik put his hand into his trouser-leg pocket and pulled out the intricate amulet with the red-and-brown ribbon.

"That is a lady's trinket. The new fashion returned most amulets to a necklace format," Zina commented.

"How could I forget about this? I was so focused on Steven's kidnappers that I had completely forgotten about the attempt to drug me. Am I getting old? I need to investigate that girl."

Tom's wrist watch – his amulet – demanded attention. He checked who was trying to contact him and looked at his friends.

"This is the Grand's conv-call. Let's talk to her." He activated the response. "Afternoon,

Grand, Tom Darkwood here. How can I help you?"

The heather-purple face of the colony leader smiled a friendly smile.

"Citizen Darkwood, my greetings to you. I hope things are as good as they can be. I wanted to congratulate you on your successful return from the final mission. I was made to believe it was final. Am I right?"

"I hope so. Thank you, but we are not all back yet. Both pilots and Vist will be here in a few hours."

"I was going to wait for the architexter, but now we both have a problem, don't we? I just finished listening to the account of the recent events involving members of your team. Are you aware of this?"

"Yes. I am missing two people, and a third is seriously injured."

"I am sorry, Mr Darkwood. Such atrocities and conspiratorial events have not occurred within the walls of our cities for many generations. According to the professional report of the doctor who saved Anatoly Baker-

Green, your friend will not be able to serve rehab. I withdraw from him the charges of beating up the intruders who broke into his house. My people are working on those who survived his self-defence methods, and the information we hope to receive could potentially aid the investigation. Finding Rodion Baker-Green and Steven McLeod should be a priority."

"I can't agree more. Who is investigating the disappearances?"

"This is why I decided to put you in touch with our order-supreme, Officer Werner. I recommend you liaise with him and share your experience. After all, you still have an advantage in dealing with extreme situations. He suggested I send our conmot after you. Here in the capital, you can use our resources well."

"Coming to the White Capital is a good idea, but all we really need there is Vist."

"Werner counts on the architexter's return too. He will be with you in about three-quarters of an hour. Please get ready. I am sure together, and with the help of Architexter Vist, we will find our citizens sooner."

When the holo-screen disappeared, Tom looked at Mik as if to say, "See? They are not as useless as you thought."

"We will see about that," answered Mik. "You can go to the capital tonight if you want, but I am going home to Altyn. I need to see Tilda and ask her more questions about that girl ... Nikolaya Gil and the True One she mentioned."

This time it was Zina's amulet that interrupted him.

"Scarlett, what do you have for us?" asked Zina.

"I told you – Nordians trust each other more than they trust O'Teka herself," said Scarlett happily. Then she became very serious, "Harlow was too afraid to tell the ordermen that she found Rod's amulet on the farm and brought it to the house when Mr Baker-Green was fighting. She recently received a threatening note and refused to cooperate with the investigation. I am the first person she described the whole thing to. I am sending it to you in the file, and Doctor Zina, do you mind if

I take her away to my place in Carib? I want to hide her until things are clear."

"Good idea, Scarlett, but please do not stay in your place. Go to a friend or some other place nobody knows of."

"You think? Never mind. I understand, Doctor Zina. I will think of something. A disguise perhaps. We will shave faces and apply more purple make-up and glitter cream. Oh, and another thing. Harlow said that the older daughter of Mr Baker-Green heard uninvited guests say the words, "Otherwise your daddy will be eaten by the god of the svoloch.""

"God of the svoloch?"

"Yes. Groonya asked Harlow what it was, but she couldn't answer. What is the god of the svoloch, Doctor Zina?"

Chapter 24. The Branch

At first, I thought they preferred living in the crater because it provides effective shelter from the strong surface wind. But I see now that this is not the only reason. The spiral path, just about 1.8 metres wide, takes us into the crater's depths. It looks darker from the edge. Inside, everybody descends slowly one by one, and I see at least a hundred men and women of similar age, all hairy and dark, approaching the centre. Now I can make out the crater's flat bottom, and right in the middle is their home's dark shape, rising at a slight angle like a tower. Curiosity pushes me to walk faster, but I can't do that without knocking down a few of these people. Since I am unaware of the possible consequences, I must be patient. I will have a good look at it when we are there.

I suspect ... Yes. Just as I thought. It's a spaceship, and it's huge. I saw the pictures of the *Ark* and *Noah* ships. This is *Noah* ... or what is left of it. The Object chronicles described it as a military ship that could transform into a defence fort or a boat. This one hasn't even unfolded itself to come to a temporary stop. I wonder what happened to it.

Here I am, at last, standing at the foot of one of the greatest structures of the Platinum Age. I walk slowly around it and can just work out its name on the side and then ... the number. This is not the *Noah-8* as I thought, but the *Noah-4*. The one that didn't even send a byte of communication and was pronounced lost in space before entering the system.

Anthem carefully touches my arm. This is the first time I hear her voice. "Ramus ... Dentro."

I take my eyes off the magnificent, old, dark human creation with effort and follow her.

The doorway looks more like a cargo gate forced open. Our transport units were made of a similar metal alloy that does not corrode easily, but this ship looks severely beaten by ... what? Heat and pressure? Space and time? I try to remember the year this ship was sent on its way. A few hundred years ago? But it looks like it has been sitting here for millennia.

On the inside, I suddenly see the light. What is this? Are these walls painted with luminescent paint? No, but human hands and fingers have smeared the walls with lines, waves, and circles, using a substance that gives out fairly bright light. I guess this is some microorganism that is carefully replaced as it fades away. Maybe something grows somewhere nearby and gets harvested by these dwellers. At the same time, I can feel the hair standing on end on my shoulders, neck and arms. Not all hairs, but only these new shiny, hard tactile ones. They are almost twice the length of my undercoat and grew a couple of centimetres apart just a week ago. I suspect they have something to do with these new feelings of knowing my surroundings without looking or listening.

There are hundreds of people inside the ship. I don't know what they do here or what they eat, but this is their home. I finally see children of all ages who seem to be looked after and fed by anyone whom they approach and ask for food. And they have plenty of food. I am yet to find out where it comes from, but I see strange fruits and small fish-like creatures in pots and bowls made of dry dirt. The toddlers are chewing on some dark vegetation, but I can't work out any of its colours in this strange, dull light. I would expect such a crowded place to be noisy, but everyone, even the children, moves slowly about their business and speaks in whispers. I hear no laughter and no battle roars, as if this were a place of worship.

I didn't notice where Tma disappeared to, but Anthem seems determined to show me something. She speaks quietly and pulls me down the corridors and up and down the ladders, prompting a memory of my orbital station. Only instead of electrical light, everything is hardly visible in the dull light of the luminescent smears. The girl brings me to the room that was probably the ship's bridge. It is decorated in glowing lines and circles with great care and attention. The device in the middle is covered in a thick layer of the glowing substance. I can see the lines running out of the centre mingling with images of ... hmm, this also looks familiar. A solar system! Of course! The middle hemispheric computer structure must represent the sun and those circles ... they are planets and moons. These lines must be their orbits, and these waves ... a wormhole? The rest is a space full of stars. Small figures of men fill in one of the circles. Is it Earth? It must have been because the Vitricus system does not have so many planets. Is this the room from which my unit received instructions? There is only one way to find out.

I approach the hemisphere, clear my throat, and pronounce the standard command, "Access!"

Something inside the glass dome flashes a yellow spark of light, barely visible through this glowing mess, and it immediately fades away. This computer is dead, but the main ZPE-converter somewhere else on this ship is not. I need to find it and see if I can bring it back to life. Unlike my transport, this ship is not stuck halfway in the ice.

Anthem looks at me with shock and exaltation. Hmm! I wonder if they have a leader here.

Chapter 25. Vist

In the capital, Officer Werner brought Tom and Zina to the Temple of O'Teka first. It was the biggest branch, although it was not the original spire they had come across during their first visit to Noverca. The incredibly tall tip of the tower disappeared into the yellow clouds. It almost reached the thermosphere and protected the city with a much larger diameter power shield. The shield was responsible for protecting the town from the radiation of Vitricus. The spire was anchored to the geostationary satellite launched into orbit by Tom in his *Wasp* a few years ago. Otherwise, it would have collapsed under its own weight.

"The architexter's secretary just told me that Vist is waiting for us on the eighty-fourth level," said Werner, who was the first to walk towards the elevator doors.

Werner was a native of the White City, and apart from his colour, he did not differ much from the recently evacuated earthlings. His narrow eyes looked like emeralds because of the micro-cameras built into his irises. His face was scaleless, hairless, and dark, almost like an aubergine, and it shone like polished purple metal. His short hair was completely white. His voice was so low that it sounded like he was speaking into a trumpet.

The ascent had to be slow, but as soon as the lift doors opened, Tom and Zina saw the person they both adored greet them with a most beautiful smile, "Welcome back to the White City! Hello again, officer."

"Vist, did you get our warnings?" asked Tom instead of greeting him.

"We got it. Two hours ago, we all secured *Wasp* in the hangar and went home. We were vigilant and took great precautions. We did not see anyone suspicious and did not talk to strangers."

"Are you taking our caution seriously?"

"Of course. It all happened the cycle before last, and there is every reason to take this seriously. One of our comrades is fighting for his life, and two are missing. Was anyone else hurt?"

"No. Mik is eager to investigate someone in Altyn. So far, he hasn't been successful.

Steve's girlfriend left the city to stay at the remote farm with her parents. And the deceased cadet at the academy apparently had no friends left who could tell Mik about her. I was unable to persuade him to wait for you. Now he is waiting for our conv-call. How are Marta and Nat?"

"Mr Larsson assured me his wife would be safe at his hotel, and Nat didn't go home but arranged to meet Miss Hesley at ... I don't even know where."

"Why are you here? It's not safe," said Zina. She missed Vist but would not dare hug him unless Tom did so first.

"Nobody's going to get to me here since nobody knows the temple as well as I do. I had to start working on the new material we brought with us. I suspect I know who is behind the kidnappings," said Vist.

"Who?" Tom asked. He finally shook Vist's hand but held it for a second longer than appropriate.

Vist continued, "This is why I wanted you to come with me to the capital's temple. Both of you. We'll talk about what we have learned over the last few years and just a few hours ago. I have booked a study room for the evening, and we will contact Nat and Mik and ask them to join us remotely."

"Scarlett has already returned to her place in Pettogreco," said Zina, "Do I need to contact her too?"

"I don't think Scarlett is in any danger. The target is us – the first delegation to Noverca before Operation Object. But I am not sure about the reason yet."

Officer Werner interrupted. "Forgive me, Architexter Vist, but are you aware that I must be at your meeting too? Also, I need a reference to every bible or prayer you used in your research."

"Of course, officer. I will also need your help and your opinion on a few issues."

All four walked into the cylindrical room with a disc-shaped refreshment table in the middle and a few rotating chairs. The dark wall surrounding them was one huge holo-screen, already shining with a series of images and texts. Vist had stopped smiling, but the reflection of the cold light in his green eyes merged with a sense of excitement.

Tom sat down. Vist turned to the screen and blinked without raising her hands. A few seconds later, besides the other images, two ovals with the faces of Mik and Nat appeared on the screen.

"My regards," said Mik.

"Sorry. I couldn't find my amulet immediately," Nat said and coughed in embarrassment.

"Well, now we are all assembled, let us start with a bit of the history. After all, I have found some of what I was looking for. We have retrieved the missing pods, and it was a great commercial project that paid off well. But as you know, I was looking for answers regarding one particular pod. Selest Dvali was a very old woman who played an unusual but crucial role in certain events. Her pod was on the drifting piece of ice, just as I thought. Nat found human remains in unit SD-211. It was impossible to conduct a genetic analysis, but I don't doubt it was her. Thanks to our brave Nat here, I have got my hands on her personal terminal."

"But how did you track this pod, or any other missing ones?" asked Officer Werner.

"All KOSI units were launched successfully from the Jupiter station because they followed my instructions. One of those instructions was to carry at least some brief information about all the others. That is why we know how many arrived and how many were lost along the way. After all, not all units were built properly. Remember the records of the pod explosions on the way here and the damaged pods in every party? In the year that Selest arrived, only sixty-one units arrived safely. They all carried the same list of pods, which included SD-211. The list briefly mentioned two people – Selest and an assistant. After all, she was too old to travel alone."

"We did not see any assistant in the pod, and there was only one set of bones and lots of shit," said Nat.

"The bio-sleep tank you used to escape the iceberg had the DNA of that assistant on it. I am sure that person has survived, and we are still to find him among us," said Vist with a slight frown. "Selest also carried a message from the late General Alan Lillypond, already uploaded for you to view. And a small five-volume record of her latest work in her personal terminal. I have read all her previous dissertations and diaries, but I didn't know what she did in the last twenty-odd years before the flight. She and her research group worked on the svoloch's adaptation features. You could observe the result in the new colonists who arrived here aged ten or less. Nordians and Uzhans can only envy their ability to withstand frost and heat. And their digestive system! Not to mention their acute senses and muscle strength."

"Samantha never dreamed of it," Zina said quietly.

"Who is Samantha?" asked Nat.

"Doctor Nguyen. I am sure you know this name, Officer Werner."

Officer Werner nodded and said, "Doctor Nguyen died at the hands of the same beast you caught at her request."

"That's right," confirmed Vist, "Abraham still managed to prove that he and his kin were descended from the men of Earth. How this happened remains to be seen."

"What happened to Abraham?" asked Zina.

"He was killed during his attack on the scientists, and the research stopped. What Selest has achieved on Earth may be dearer to Noverca than all the pods – those landed and found by us – put together."

"Are you still working on the svoloch puzzle? Is it true that they either died out or moved further north-east?" asked Tom.

"I have a few theories. Their number has greatly decreased, and their ability to make themselves invisible in the shadows has improved. In addition, they could find a place to migrate further away from the colony."

"But what does that have to do with the svoloch? These are wild people, no more. Worse than those mystics in the villages of believers and even less capable. What do they have to do with Steve and Rod?" Mik asked.

"Our kidnapper is one of them," Vist replied. "He is not that wild or incapable if he managed to persuade some people to assist him."

Zina gasped, and the faces of the others expressed sheer disbelief.

Vist raised her hands like a conductor. The images on the screen moved and flickered with varying intensity.

"Before you argue with me, I want to show you my findings, which I dug up in these archives almost immediately after our second arrival. Here. See this bible. The number of offerings made by the medical professional who examined the new colonists. I studied them long ago carefully, in the hope that one would describe Selest. Most of them are very similar to each other, but then I found this."

The image on the screen was of a very slim and tall man on a hospital bed. His face and bald head were covered in first-degree burns.

"This person was discovered by a city spy who lived in the village by the Laguna. Yes, the same salt village where we met May and Massimo. That spy reported to the capital that his search party had found a stranger wearing the fishermen's tunic instead of the missing fisherman. He was stretched out on the sand by the river Thanile. The stranger was covered in fresh burns and claimed that he was the passenger earthling from the crashed pod. He said that his clothing was also burned. And that he found the torn tunic in the resting camp of the savages from the North. Everyone believed that a svoloch had killed the fisherman, and the injured stranger told the truth because he had proof of his origin. This proof was enough to take him in because he produced the same ZPE ray-gun some other earthling brought with them. I think Nat found its case on the iceberg. The man also spoke the language of Earth. He was very confused and mentally traumatised. My assistant Cesario noticed and brought to my attention that this man's anatomical data had more in common with Abraham than with the evacuees."

"You mean, some wild svoloch found Selest's pod first and ... but how would he learn the language?" asked Zina.

"No," replied Vist, "the truth is a little more complicated. I believe the creature did come in that pod with Selest from KOSI, and he found his way to the warm parts of Gera."

"Select used the cells you brought to Earth to clone the svoloch she brought with her. Right?" Tom said.

Vist tilted his or her head a little, "For now, I would only say that she indeed brought a very educated svoloch with her. I don't know how he survived the landing, but he was covered in burns, not frostbite. This person could not explain his burns, even when he regained full consciousness in the city hospital. A few earthlings came to see the man but could not identify him due to his scars. His memory also failed him, and he asked everyone to call him a name not mentioned in any of the evacuees' manifests. Ramus Napovni."

"A politician?" said Nat. "He spoke to Andrea in her mother's house some time ago."

Chapter 26. The Branch

How long have I been living in *Noah-4* with this simple race of colonists? It must have been a few months because I have noticed women's stomachs grow. I have never seen it happen before, but I know this is where children come from. Anthem didn't get pregnant, nor did the other two women – Suave and Zhel – who became attracted to my status. I assume this is because we are not quite the same species after all. Not anymore. This makes them unhappy, but they do not dare show it. I could tell them to go and find other mates, but why should I? They still bring me food from the caves, take turns to warm me in bed, and follow me to the surface to bathe in the steaming pools. I never liked washing on the Jupiter station, but here I need it. *Noah-4* is also occupied by insects that bite. The very small ones live now in my hair, and the bigger ones fill my bed when I try to sleep. If it weren't for them, I would have been quite comfortable.

I have taken some time to observe and study this society, and I discovered that they do not have a leader but, instead, a few exceptionally popular individuals. They follow some very strict traditions and behaviour patterns and do so with precision, almost religiously.

While at the Jupiter station, I read about the animals on Earth that lived in groups. They also had alpha males who produced healthier offspring. I, too, had to kill a few in their sleep to take their women and rooms. I don't care about producing offspring, but I think these women do, so I don't yet know how it will work out for me if they all end up with empty wombs. I will cross that bridge when I get to it.

As for the bridge, I spend many hours there. I am unfamiliar with the ship structure, but I used to service equipment in the medical department, including ZPE-converters. A ship of this size will have to carry more than one such power generator. I found maintenance sections in four parts of the spaceship, and I had to evict a family of six from one of them by killing the eldest male, and finally found one converter that seemed to be damaged less than the other three.

I don't know how to fix the broken ones, but I can clean them and run tests. The converter struggles to absorb energy from its environment, so it can't produce much.

I am unable to restore the electrical light. Shame. That would have raised my status enough to let me get away with my infertility. If I had I been able to talk to the dome and provoke a series of light flashes and beeping and buzzing, everyone who witnessed such an event would have been filled with sacred awe and fear of my abilities. I still don't know exactly what I have become in their eyes. All I got from those women is that I am worth the attention of "Dostup" itself.

They don't know that the light on the fuzzy display now shows me the ship's map. It looks like one small section of Noah is still powered, somehow. It takes me many hours to find it, but I am very excited to discover this compartment the pilgrims never go to. I am not surprised. The entrance is covered. There has to be an unused space behind this strange decoration on one of the walls of the largest room. I had seen it before when passing through and decided it was a trophy display of a particular man or clan – a thick curtain of human skulls, hanging like beads from the ceiling to the floor. To get behind the several layers, you must move the garlands aside with your arms, which are quite heavy. As I start moving in, my women, including Anthem, who always follow me around, express deep concern. They make noises and repeat "sefaar" and "mortah." I ignore them.

I enter the corridor with no glowing paint on the wall, and it appears to be a completely dark hallway. I take a few steps and notice that one of the women is following me in. It is Anthem, of course. She is terrified. I can hear her fast breathing, and she trembles as she grabs my arm with her wet hands. She has less body hair than me, but her sensitive hairs are much thicker. She bristles like a mop and, apparently, can feel the environment better. I pull her towards me and make her go ahead, so she would fall first if there was a gap in the floor.

It is so dark that I have to rely completely on my hearing and touch and on the sensations from my new hairs. I keep one hand on the back of Anthem's neck and another on the wall. Sometimes my fingers touch something that reminds me of the pocket doors on our space station. But they are all closed and won't budge when I try to force them open.

Soon I can hear a faint noise. Now Anthem refuses to go first, and I release her neck. The noise comes from the opposite side of the corridor we are following. I leave the wall I am touching and take four steps to the right. I feel another wall and listen out for the noise for another minute. It is a very familiar beeping. In our medical department, the monitor of the temporary system preserver used to make this same noise when the patient was disconnected or dead. Here is another door, but this time it opens when I push it aside. I see the light inside the room, which also makes me feel almost at home. It is a reanimation room. The dim light comes from four matt round hemispheres on the walls – enough to see a body inside the cylindrical bed with an open lid. A dead man or a woman is lying inside something much more primitive than our station system preservers. The emergency ZPE-converter is inside the simple computer and is almost passive. No wonder. There is not much energy here to convert. The air is too cold, with no sunlight and no vibrations.

Anthem is still afraid to enter the room. I look around. The equipment is covered in dust, and the system does not respond to my call. I wonder if I can redirect the little power the converter produces to this huge and clumsy terminal. I walk towards the dead man and pull off all the wires and tubes attached to the bed. It works. The programme gives up on the hopeless attempt to keep the man alive and powers the control. The lights are now brighter, and I can see a thick layer of dust flakes on the floor. Anthem screams and, for a minute, disappears into the darkness of the corridor. But her curiosity is impressive. She slowly returns and looks at me with admiration and fear. It seems like she is afraid to touch anything here, but she keeps repeating quietly, "Oh minii gud ... Oh minii gud ..."

Chapter 27. Marta

Martin Larsson loved his wife very much. He knew her life was full of crazy and tragic events but preferred not to know too many details. All he wanted was to make her forget it all and feel like her life had started when she met him, and he thought the same about that cycle. But Marta looked completely happy only in two places: her pilot seat and her kitchen. In Martin's luxurious and expensive hotel, Old World, she lacked both.

After Marta arrived back from the last expedition, she spent the first morning with him in their bed in Martin's private suite at the hotel. This made him late for work, and she laughed like a child when he spilled coffee on the carpet. But Martin could tell that, although she was glad to see him, she would rather go home to their cottage by the woods. In that cottage was a kitchen with a huge chopping board with "Marta and Martin" written on it and nailed to the wall, with a real fire stove and iron frying pans. It was a walkthrough kitchen. You could access it from the greenhouse, which was full of herbs, garlic containers and garlands of dried fruits. Then, you could follow it into the dining room with a table made of real wood. It was big enough to feed a party of twelve and was covered with a natural cotton cloth. In her absence, two cats oversaw the kitchen and probably grew fat on the dirteaters and local lake fish.

"I had promised Vist I would keep you safe," Martin said again when Marta expressed her desire to go home. "Here at the hotel we have guards, a security system, and plenty of people and regulations to facilitate your safety."

Marta leaned her head back on his chest as if on the back of a lilac sofa. She interlaced her fingers with his and pouted her lips. With him, Marta behaved like a young girl, spoiled and capricious. Martin liked that she was unafraid to show her weakness in his presence when her friends weren't around.

Marta replied, "But I don't understand why Vist is doing this to me. Let me speak to her. I am sure she is wrong, and those attacks have something to do with the academy or with politics. Why would anyone kidnap me? There are so many skilful pilots that are much better than me."

"But there is no better cook on the whole planet. Someone went to all this trouble to get your recipes. Just kidding. Look, darling, this hotel is not a prison. You can contact Vist whenever you like, although only her secretaries have answered the call when I've tried lately. And if you don't want to wait for me and go home before the weekend, then go. But I can come up with dozen wild ideas why you shouldn't. You missed me, for starters."

"Yes. Yes, I missed you."

"Second, you can use some warm pampering after your journey to the north."

"Oh, yes please." Marta smiled.

"And if you want a more serious theory – you and Nat are the true *Wasp* pilots. You told me somebody always wanted to take over that ship. What if our country mystics—"

Marta sat up, turned around, and looked him in the eyes. "What exactly did she say to you? Doesn't that mean that Nat is also ...?"

"Vist said it would be good if people did not know you had returned just yet. And as far as I know, Nat can look after himself and fight off the kidnappers just like Mik and Tolyan did. He is a strong boy."

"But look what happened to Tolyan. I have to talk to Vist." Marta got up and started getting dressed. "She must have known more details now about what is happening."

"Wait, finish your breakfast at least."

But Marta had already switched her amulet on and clipped it over her ear. The holo-screen bowed like a broad ribbon and hung in the air in front of her face.

"No, Viola, I want to talk to your boss," Marta said in a couple of minutes to a female face on the screen, "I will try Tom. Hang on, what's this? A message from Zina."

"Let's hear it," said Martin, then stood up.

Zina's voice was calm, but she spoke faster than usual.

"Hello, old girl. Zina here. Listen, Vist is hunting whoever is behind this mess, but he asked me to insist, yes, to insist that you do not try to contact anybody from our team. Do not go out, do not show your face at work, and do not go home. Vist is sure that your house is being watched. He also thinks that the hotel could be under observation too, but it is a busy place, and identifying you will be difficult if you are wearing a hotel uniform and powdering your nose with purple sparks. I am not joking – this is serious. If someone called Ramus Napovni comes to talk to you, do not see him under any circumstances. For some reason, Vist is sure he is after you more than the others. Say hello to Mr Larsson, and tell him that I will personally hold him responsible if anything happens to you. See you in a couple of cycles. Zina."

Martin said, "Did Zina say Ramus Napovni? The political figure in the White Capital?" His lilac face went pale, and Marta stared at him.

"I am sure that is the name. I have heard it before."

"He is here. He has stayed in one of the best rooms in the Black Sea Wing for the last two cycles and is supposed to leave tonight."

Marta paused for a moment and said, "I know I should be hiding from this person, but I actually want to see him ... to challenge him. He hurt my friend. He has kidnapped two of them."

"You are a crazy woman! He is deliberately here ... for you! And I didn't know ... stay here. I need to talk to my staff. I must warn my people and place a couple of men at the door."

Still dressed in his spa robe, Martin went to the door. When he opened it, he looked into the yellowish eyes of his guest of honour.

"I was told I would find you in your private suite, Mr Larsson. I have a complaint to make," he said and pulled a small spray bottle from his pocket.

About an hour later, Martin opened his eyes to find himself on his bed, but this time he was alone. Marta was gone. Only her earring, her amulet, remained on the pillow. His staff members did not see her. They reported that Mr Napovni had signed out about an hour earlier and left in his private transport. He was alone with his luggage. What was his luggage? The same huge suitcase he had a cycle ago on his arrival. No, it did not look heavy. He carried it himself quite effortlessly.

With trembling hands, Martin Larsson found his amulet on the bedside table and searched for Tom Darkwood's location. He was terrified to talk to Zina about what had happened, but he was even more scared of speaking to Vist.

When the holo-screen showed Tom's face, Mr Larsson almost shouted about his wife being taken. Tom begged him to slow down and explain the details of Marta's disappearance. Martin told him about being assaulted by the Gera-environmentalist's party leader with great reluctance.

"Mr Larsson, do not blame yourself. You could not predict Napovni's involvement. We only learned about him less than a couple of hours ago. If you want to help, contact your local ordermen office and gather all the evidence you have to support your word against him. You have to make an official accusation."

Martin interrupted Tom, "But I have nothing ... he drugged me, that is true, but nobody has seen him doing anything. Captain Darkwood! This Napovni, he is a powerful man. He will destroy me and my business! My hotel will become a place to avoid. If he wants a ransom, I would rather ..."

"Mr Larsson. Do you care about your wife or your hotel? That man wants something you can't give him. But I think Vist knows what to do. Let her worry about that, but you can help her bring Napovni to order. Will you do that?"

"Yes, yes I will. I just got scared and didn't think clearly. Of course."

***

Tom disconnected from the link. The couple sat next to Officer Werner in his conmot. Vist had already gone home, and Mik and Nat had gone to the head of the academy looking for information. Werner was taking the Darkwoods to a safe place of their choice.

Werner heard an angry voice, "I can't believe he hesitated ... even for a second."

Zina was frowning and shaking her head.

"Don't be too harsh, Zina," Tom pulled the sleeve over the amulet on his wrist. "Martin is overwhelmed with things he is not used to. Many Novercians, who will watch tomorrow's news about this politician's strange behaviour, are destined to feel something very similar. This happens in a rational and comfortable society, where the worst thing that can happen is the occasional economic fraud or crime of passion followed by rehabilitation or exile. This world is not ready for organised crime."

Zina turned to Werner. "Officer, these Gera-environmentalists, what do you know about them?"

"They are a political party formed about five years ago as a social group of interests, but then they started to grow. If I am not mistaken, Mr Napovni was their founder and leader. Nobody had heard about him before the last election, and now he is famous enough to make a second attempt at becoming the Grand in the next term."

Tom said grimly, "People like Mr Larsson will vote for him out of fear, and Gera will never be the same. The changes in society will be most catastrophic."

"But there will be a new Grand then?" said Werner.

"There will be no new Grand," said Zina. "The rules will change. The whole new and reformed system will not allow that. You've studied the history of Earth. It's full of such cases."

Werner went silent for the whole minute and then said, "Captain, Doctor, my duty is to turn my attention to that group."

"Are you going to the Gera-environmentalists? Let us come with you," asked Zina.

"Yes, I want to talk to their members and try to understand how some Novercians could betray Noverca's most approved traditions. Everything they did recently goes against the order and against reason."

"According to what Martin said, Napovni will not be back in the capital for another hour or so. Where are they based?" asked Zina.

"They have an office in the north district, by the training grounds," answered Werner, "but the architexter wanted me to—"

"Vist will understand," Tom interrupted, "We might find out if this is a genuine organisation with a mad leader or if those kidnappers have nothing to do with the environment and just used the label."

Werner paused for a moment and then said decisively, "We will go there now. I am an official. I will go in and check a few things, talk to the members, and ask questions. But you will agree to wait for me in the transport. I am responsible for your safety."

All attempts to change his mind were in vain. The ordermen's transport had turned around and soon arrived at the city's northern gate. Werner parked his vehicle next to the old industrial conmot, went into the building, and emerged less than thirty minutes later. He was unhappy that the only person he met was a clerk of some sort who politely stated that he was not authorised to answer questions without the chairman. That clerk asked Werner to wait for a minute and disappeared behind the office door for half an hour. When the clerk returned, he said that the chairman would be back in the office tomorrow afternoon and that the officer should come back.

Werner found his vehicle wide open and thoroughly searched. Both the Darkwoods were gone, and so was the old conmot nearby.

Werner, mad with anger, almost hit himself in the ear, activating his amulet. Werner played in his head the words of those who did not really belong to Noverca but who seemed to know a lot about how things might go. He had to trust his knowledge and those records in the temple of O'Teka and accept that what was about to happen must not be allowed. His ancestors were humans with different skin colours and internal systems, but their history on their alien planet had taught him enough to know better.

Whether the star above your head is red or yellow does not matter. If you let one man decide for thousands of others, then peace and harmony will be gone, and to get it back, you will have to start from scratch again. This world is too young and unprepared for totalitarianism. He will not allow that. And nor will his comrades, the ordermen. Werner called for the whole operative group to attend and arrest this nest of deceivers. That cycle, the Gera-environmentalists' organisation ceased to exist. But Mr Napovni was not seen there when expected or ever again. When Werner activated his amulet once more that cycle, he saw the face of Mik King.

"Officer," Mik said after hearing him out, "We can get them all if we work together. Meet us tomorrow at the northern City Gate at about 16.30."

Chapter 28. The Branch

I don't understand what these people are saying, but they are saying many words. Maybe they are surprised that Anthem and I have returned safe and sound. Perhaps they are mad at us. Maybe they are showing some appreciation. I don't care. I spent a long time trying to get Tma to show me where they get the glowing stuff until she stopped hauling and beckoned me to follow her. She went the same direction as all the women go to get food – to the cave in the wall of the crater, east of the ship. I suspected it was somewhere over there but did not rush to explore because no men ever went there. Also, to get to the cave, you must walk for ages along a narrow and low corridor, perhaps a former underground river. But it was worth it.

The cave is large and full of dull-white and turquoise light. It is not enough to see the ceiling, but I feel it is rather high. What I did not expect was a cave so full of life. I see the leafless plant branches and billions of tiny bugs covering them. These are even smaller than the itchy *buve* that now live in my hair, and I had to look closer. Every part of their body is luminescent, even their tiny antennae. They must be living in a symbiotic relationship with plants.

In the dark areas free of plants and bugs, there is water. I explore the cave, while the women keep busy, taking what is needed. Some go knee-deep into the water and catch some animals living there – animals much bigger than *ee*. Some dig something out of the ground, while others remove large growths from plants – perhaps fruits.

Tma, Anthem, Suave and Zhel do what I tell them: they get my glowing dirt. They scoop water with the clay bowl and pour it onto the ground; they shake the slow bags off the branches into the wet soil and rub them into the dirt. Then they scrape the mud mixed with crushed bugs into the bowl. We make our way back home after they have got us as much as we can carry. Now glowing smears also mark my dark corridor behind the skulls. After a few trips into the cave, my women have made enough glowing dirt to light up my secret place for a while. I call the discovered room "my lab" – it's short enough for them to pronounce it.

Today it is Suave's turn to warm me at night. I don't like it when they all sleep in the same room. I make them sleep where they can guard me. Anthem and Suave are the only ones brave enough to follow me to the lab. After Suave pleases me, I decide to see what else is working in the room. I go from item to item, surprised at how little is left. If anything, this room reminds me of our station and its state a few days before the evacuation. It was stripped of every recyclable item, every useful molecule. I wonder why these people did the same here. They did not have to evacuate. They are still on the ship, so where has everything gone?

My thoughts are interrupted by Suave, who also looks around. Now she stands up straight by the dead body on the surgical bed.

"Mortah ... Chov ..." she says quietly, and then she adds a few more words, which, I think, express her surprise. Why this chov was left here uneaten, and why weren't his remains concealed?

Of course, she can see that the body is nothing but a dry and uneatable mummy, but curiosity forces her to lift her hand and gently touch the skull's forehead.

The next second, she screeches and jumps back. The dead man begins to crumble like ashes, starting from where her fingers were. I move closer and watch him turn into a pile of dust. A conjecture springs to mind and amazes me. These are not just dust or ashes. This is all that remains of the corpse after the ZPE transformed it into energy. Okay, this converter is not a regular part of the ship's ZPE network. The regular ones can take power from the outside, mainly from space radiation. This one is a spare emergency installation that we had in every medical unit. The stupid machine didn't know what it was doing. When other sources became unavailable to it, it turned to this man. He was probably already dead by then. No. It can't be. Even this old generator has to have been set up for such things. ZPE-converters are programmed not to consume living things, but they could use any energy if meddled with them, including that of their owners. The reprogrammed computer could use any source inside the system preserver, dead or alive. Or anyone who puts a hand inside. I wonder if this was done deliberately. And why? This converter is dormant now and does not have enough power to reboot back into safe mode.

The sudden idea enthrals me so much that I don't want to wait. I grab the preserver's cords and plug the cylinder back into the system. Then I spend a few minutes trying to catch the frightened and screaming woman. She resists, but I punch her face, put her on the open cylindrical bed and lower the lid. I take my hands off the preserver, turn it on and stand back. At first, nothing happens. She regains consciousness and looks at me in horror through the transparent cover. It reminds me of Bebia in her bio-sleep tank, and I feel sick for a moment. Somehow, I'm glad it's not Anthem. I find her much more fun than Suave or any of the others. Suddenly, Suave opens her mouth wide to scream, but I assume that the ZPE-converter was now hungrily focusing on everything beneath the lid, including the sound.

I can't hear her, but I watch her go limp first and die within a few minutes. The lamps on the wall burst into a familiar bright light, and the computer comes back to life. It has an old-fashioned hemispherical holo-screen, and it beeps and clicks as it carries out its self-diagnostic procedures. It finally has enough power to recognise that there is no living patient on the bed and disconnects from the energy source with its typical long beep. Now, if I reboot the converter, it is charged enough to restore the original program and become safe for me to use. With one hand, I open the lid and slowly mix the dusty flakes of the ancient man and the woman whose body I was enjoying only an hour ago. I brush it off. Only now can I see colourless ash of all kinds covering the floor. So that is what I could feel with my feet in the dark corridor. But I believe that not all this ash is human remains.

Now I understand that to keep this emergency converter alive, the arrivals brought and maybe used everything that could be used. Every piece of chemically stored energy, carbon-based substances, paper, fabric, wood, plastic ... dead comrades, and who knows what else. They allowed the ZPE-converter to absorb energy from everything inside the ship to generate badly needed power. But what for?

Chapter 29. Gera-environmentalists

Zina opened her eyes and saw the back of Tom's head trembling as the floor moved. It immediately became clear that both were lying in the industrial conmot, driving pretty fast on the uneven, bumpy road. There were no such roads in the city. This means that they were somewhere in the wildlands of Gera. On the way to where?

Tom had a dark bruise on his head from a blow, but the wound looked superficial. Most likely, he was unconscious, nevertheless. Zina listened to her own body. Her wrists were bound together behind her back. Her left shoulder appeared to be dislocated, judging by the pain. Although she had lost consciousness when pulled up by the arms, this pain woke her up here. Fighting it, Zina wiggled herself into a sitting position.

She bent over Tom's face, trying to hear his breath, but the rumbling of the wheels made it impossible to hear anything else. Light came in through a single round skylight. Load-securing belts and nets dangled on dark walls. They were in a truck for heavy loads and for transporting materials. There were no seats or benches. Instead of a door, there was a square double hatch at the rear.

"Tom," Zina called, "Tom, wake up."

She called and nudged him with her forehead until he groaned and opened his eyes.

He soon grasped their position and asked his wife, "How did they bind us? Turn around. They tied your hands with my own belt."

"It seems that they used whatever came to hand. What's this you have? Oh, it's a plastic tube from my first aid vitals monitor. Yes, I can easily gnaw through it with my teeth. Get up a little. Yes, like this. Don't move."

Zina overcame the pain and freed her husband's hands in a couple of minutes. Tom retrieved his belt, released her wrists, and examined her arm as far as the poor light allowed. Zina took off the white headwrap with her good hand and let her long braid fall on her back. Then she laid down on the floor and said, "This is an anterior dislocation. Bend my arm up at forty-five—"

"I know what to do, Zina, don't worry. We will pull on three. Bend your elbow a little more. Relax. Are you ready?"

Zina gritted her teeth and nodded; her face was beaded with drops of sweat. Tom took her upper arm with both hands.

"One ... two ... three," he said, then pulled.

The pain was too much, and Zina fainted again. But she managed not to scream. When she opened her eyes, Tom had already made a sling out of her wide headwrap. Zina sat down, moved her arm back and forth, and put her hand on her opposite shoulder.

"Everything seems to be in order," she said and smiled at her husband. "You are a jack of all trades too now. Hah!"

Tom helped her put on the sling and thread her arm through it.

"And you are a master of self-control, my dear. Take it easy now. I don't see our amulets. Probably taken," he said, touching his wrist.

"Mine was in my back pocket. Check it for me, will you?"

But Tom found only a handkerchief in her pocket. He wiped the sweat off Zina's face with it and said, "How are you feeling?"

"Better. How is your head? Let me see. You have a lump."

"Doesn't hurt that much. Ouch! Until you touch it."

"Do you feel sick? No? Then it will heal soon."

"Why do they always go for my head?"

"It's your most precious part," Zina said with a smile. "What do you think they did to Werner?"

"He is not one of us. I am sure he is fine. Otherwise, he would have been here with us too. I wonder how long we have been on the road."

"I wonder how long we have been knocked out. How did we allow these people to catch us?"

"That was stupid of us."

"They had nothing to tie us with, and we walked right into their claws." Zina winced from the conmot shaking.

"We did not know that those Gera-environmentalists were the real deal. We all thought the kidnappers simply dressed up as other people. Waiters, cadets, medics." Tom clenched his fists.

"But the masquerade was to blend the environmentalists with their *environment*. They came to the Baker-Greens as themselves," said Zina. She flinched again as the conmot made a sharp turn. Tom reached out to support her.

"Yes, I didn't even think about it. How can someone even turn people in the city to break the order? I could understand if this Napovni guy had successfully preached to the villagers."

"Vist said that Tolyan's identified attackers have certain things in common. They are first-generation earthlings or colonists who failed in their first- or second-found purpose."

Tom got up and walked around the section on unsteady legs, examining the walls. He jumped up but could not reach the ceiling window. He tried the hatch, but it was locked from the outside. Zina hugged herself, trying to stop the shake of the vehicle from hurting her injured arm.

"So, the outsiders and losers. How typical! I thought that the first generation of earthlings would be humanity's best, who left on the day of the evacuation."

"Most were the best. Did you know that some of them were Cruisers?"

"What? How is it possible?"

Tom sat next to Zina and put his arms around her, trying to create some comfort for his wife. She leaned on him and her back relaxed. Tom decided that some destruction would help.

"It looks like we can't get out of here. We'll just have to wait and see where we'll end up and then deal with it. Do you follow Rod's work on his *Summary of the Earth Evacuation*?"

"I always meant to but never had time." Zina hissed with pain when the conmot once again shook upon hitting a road bump. "Tell me about it."

"Well, when Rod was working on his book, he found some interesting stories in Vist's collection of pod logs. Most of them were the personal accounts of family members and messages for other travellers, friends, colleagues, and whoever might find them if things didn't work out."

"It was part of Vist's recommendations to them."

"Yes, and most saw sense in following it. The best way to learn about people is to hear them out and see what they have brought with them. The more information you have, the more likely it is that your conclusion will be close to the truth. Some people thought it was important to describe the final days at the KOSI station. Rod found a recyclist's diary and very detailed planning by the provisional team leader. These reports were very interesting. For example, when the survivors relocated to one last station, the caretakers had to invent a new way of dealing with human waste. Some of the ideas were incredible. When Rod finishes his book and offers it to O'Teka, we will have something to read on our way to Pettogreco and in Carib. Hold on ... I think we are stopping."

The back hatch of the conmot opened soon after, and four men rushed in, forcing Tom and Zina on their feet, dragging them out. The rough treatment made Zina cry with a pain, but managed to glance around to notice the cave's stony walls and ceiling. It was some form of underground vehicle storage, large enough to serve as a garage for two or three industrial conmots.

One of the walls was concrete, and this strange facility had a brightly lit entrance. This is where they were taken. After a brisk walk, they were brought into a dark cell with locks on the door and piles of dry and rotten leaves on the floor. This cell was definitely a cave with a long, narrow crack in the ceiling, which allowed in leaves, warm air, dim light and – occasionally – some rain. But the first thing that got their attention was the cave's other two occupants. They saw Steven first, although he was hard to recognise. His large shape was lit by the ray of light from the hole. One hand was chained to a granite pillar in the corner. His face was one big mess of bruises and lacerations. Rod wasn't chained, but he lay flat on the dry leaves and raised his hand to the air to greet his friends.

In a weaker voice infused with his usual mockery, he said, "I was wondering who he will bring next ... Welcome to alien hell!"

But the reunion had to wait. The door opened again, and their captor came in. He was tall and dressed in an expensive suit of wide trousers and a long jacket. Both ends of the red-and-brown scarf hung loosely on his chest, which was decorated with a red necklace. His head was not covered, and the shiny masses of his golden mane reminded Zina of an Earth-beast called a *lion*. Light-brown, almost orange eyes added to this image, making this man look more like an animal than a human.

Zina had never felt more frightened in her life. When this man with long blond hair walked into the cell, she thought the air around him was thick with hate and madness. He did not speak for a whole minute, and he looked at the new prisoners with cold and expressionless eyes.

When he finally said his first words, Zina was surprised to hear a high-pitched voice, like the voice of an adolescent.

"When I first decided to invite you into my party of honourable deeds, I imagined a civilised and much more dignified way of socialising with your group. But my first guests were so uncooperative that I thought not to waste my time on pleasantries anymore. We will do business right away. I already know your names, roles and relationship with your leader. He is the one I am really interested in. Not you. Not any longer. I hope to learn as much as possible about him." He turned to Zina and almost smiled, but he was talking at Tom all this time – that much was clear. "I hope you love your wife enough to preserve her beauty and physical integrity. We will talk tomorrow morning. Think long and hard, Captain, and ... sleep well tonight, if you can. It may be your last chance to rest. I know how hard it is to sleep when you are in constant pain from multiple wounds."

He turned around, walked out, and locked the door.

"That was ... Napovni?" asked Tom, still looking at the door.

"Yes. Don't underestimate him. You never met a more unpredictable man in your life," said Rob. "He is strong like a svoloch ... and a professional torturer. He broke my back just enough to demobilise me but kept his promise to reduce my pain if I told him where Marta might be."

"And you told him?" asked Zina.

"Don't judge Rod," said Steven, "trust me, you would have too. This Ramus knows how to hurt people. He brought Marta here just before your arrival. We did not see her, but we heard her scream once. We don't know what he did to her."

"Oh, no ... Marta! Rod! And what did he do to you, Steven? Why is your leg bandaged? Let me see."

"I am his punch bag. He does not ask me for anything anymore. He just enjoys delivering blows. I don't think my kidneys will last much longer. Most of my teeth are gone. Zina, don't bother to look under the bandage. You will find stitches. He performed the surgery by cutting out a muscle – he called it my *rectus femoris* – and then ate it in front of me. That was on the second cycle. He was well pissed off with something going wrong with his plans. But all he got from me was what it means to be a loader. As you can imagine, I am not the best person to talk about that."

"That is just ... horrific. Tom, what is he going to do to us?" Zina could not say anything else. Her breathing quickened, and tears ran down her cheeks like rainwater on a window.

She lifted her trembling fingers to her eyes, but Tom grabbed her by her good shoulder and squeezed a little, "Calm down. I don't know. We were pulled out of civilisation into some wild barbaric world. But we will do our best to get them all out of here to the hospital, and you will replace what he took. If he wants information, whatever that might be, I will feed him as much bullshit as possible. I am not a native Novercian. I have no moral issue with deception here."

Chapter 30. The Branch

Epigraphica, offering to temple of O'Teka B-693288

There is grandeur in this view of life, with its several powers, having been originally breathed by the Creator into a few forms or into one; and that, while this planet has gone cycling on according to the fixed law of gravity, from so simple a beginning endless forms most beautiful and most wonderful have been, and are being evolved.

On The Origin of Species, Charles Darwin. No date. (Record lost on Mars during the explosion.)

Most pregnant women on the ship look like they have less than a month left to carry. So, where are they all going? Wouldn't it be safer to give birth here rather than in the cold wilderness? But I am wrong to think they are going on another pilgrimage to the place they call Home-1. They grab their blankets and some provisions and head in the opposite direction, towards the sun in the company of their men, their siblings (if they have them) and other close relatives. I am curious. I want to follow them, but the women – more so than the men – with unusual aggression have made it clear that I am not welcome on this journey. I am significantly outnumbered, so I stay. My women would have stayed with me, but as none of them managed to conceive, I have only one left now to guard me and bring me food. A few weeks after they stopped looking for Suave, Zhel decided to take her chances with a different man. Tma wasn't pregnant either, but she also went south. I didn't mind. She is a bit older and uglier than the others. She seems to be welcomed by any clan as she is knowledgeable and helpful. Maybe she is a midwife of sorts. They will be back. I assume the children on the ship were born further south and then brought back here. I guess the southlands must be warmer and richer. It's all a part of the ritual, fulfilling the purpose – to breed. I don't see any other. They do nothing else.

From my primitive conversations with them and my observations, what I have learned is pretty simple. Men do nothing but eat and mate mostly with women. Sometimes they make simple knives from sharp fragments of human bones. Women bring food and glowing paint from the caves. Children, more often male and less often female, frequently and loudly fight outside the ship, at the bottom of the crater. Those who reach maturity will silently and quietly kill the weak and old ones inside the ship in competition for the best place, food and company. I do not see any really old adults on the ship. I reckon the lifespan here does not exceed thirty or forty years since the slightest signs of weakness or illness become a reason for consuming those unfit for reproduction or self-defence. To survive, I have to kill too, but I don't have to limit myself to the weak and old. I can outwit the strongest male if needed. The thing is, I am not going to wait to grow weak and old here. I must find a better habitat for myself. A place where my age and physical state will not cause so much concern for my life.

Adolescent boys often fight to the death as soon as their bodily hair is a couple of centimetres long. Young girls make grassy blankets. All religiously follow the path of their life. The children are well fed, and their growth is carefully monitored. As soon as they stop growing, they must make a trip to the extremely cold and dark place they call Home-1, most likely for some rite of passage, test of strength, loss of virginity or something. Most do not return from that trip. Occasionally, an older family member will volunteer to accompany lucky individuals and even offer themselves as food if necessary. Not quite natural selection, if you ask me. More like population control.

Those who return are ready to mate, sometimes forming couples on the way back or later. The rest of the women on the ship also choose a man to father their children. In that same moment, they stop using what I suspect are herbal contraceptives. They try very hard to synchronise their breeding for reasons unknown to me, with a few weeks' difference allowed. If a woman fails to get pregnant, she will stay on the ship and help the teenagers look after the younger children. Also, I don't understand why all the men leave with their women. Is it to protect newborns? I doubt it. I bet it is a leisure trip. Apparently, there is a danger further south too. Beings called unbeharts. But to find out more, I'll have to go there myself.

Everyone, even the kids, have been looking at me with silent contempt recently. It's possible that thanks to my strength and knife, I have not yet been rejected, but I am not sure how long this will last. Next year, I have to think of some way to survive and get my ticket to the southlands.

Soon after they all left, I solved the fuel problem for my ZPE-converter, as the fish-like creatures in the cave lakes turned out to be quite fat. This unlocked a few adjacent rooms, and I now live in a brightly lit section of my own, and I no longer need the glowing paint. It is also warmer here because the heating, albeit weak, has come online somehow. All this keeps the remaining women and children away from my corridor. It is not dark anymore. On the contrary, it gives the impression of a fiery vent against the background of the dim spaces.

I am the only man on the ship, apart from the adolescents with pathetic body hair. With fewer adults to discipline them, the children are becoming unruly and playful. Now they behave more like youngsters should behave, as far as I can tell from the old histories of humankind. However, they are still afraid to go behind the skull garlands into the corridor. They crowd with childish curiosity at the entrance, nudging each other. Several scary sounds and bright lights drive them away. After Suave disappeared, even Anthem stopped coming to my lab. Good. Because the next thing to do is to examine the relics in this secret place.

Humans tend to constantly write reports and diaries for someone else to read or listen to afterwards. The man whose corpse we found was no exception if he truly was one of the pioneers on this planet. I turned out to be right, but viewing his log wasn't easy since the emergency converter had eaten everything that could have been transferred. But it seems he knew this and kept his last notes on the walls of one room. All the insulation has been torn from these walls, and scratching letters on bare metal is difficult. Therefore, the notes are short and just present the most important things. This record of events is written in one of the languages of Earth, but I still recognised some of it. On the Jupiter orbital station, people hardly read any books. All information was brought to one's awareness technologically. The messages and diaries were audio recordings, and writing became more of a hobby than a necessity. Bebia insisted that I read books. Thanks to her, I can make out what is written on the walls of *Noah-4*.

The notes were kept by someone named Alexander Irrean. He was the ship's doctor, and one of the first to wake up when the ship had already sat in the crater for several years. It seems that the walls of the crater, or something in its geological structure, did not allow contact with the another ship or send messages to Earth. Besides Irrean, two more rose from bio-sleep. Of those who were still sleeping, almost half died in stasis. The energy resources available to the ship gradually depleted. The equipment became unusable, and it was clear that the colonisation programme could not be carried out according to plan. Survivors faced inevitable death in a few years.

One of the awakened people suggested a good, in my opinion, course of action – to disconnect the sleeping people from the ZPE-converter and thus extend their own lives. But Irrean convinced his two comrades not to kill and not to awaken the rest of the crew yet, but to give humanity its only chance to survive on this planet here. He claimed that he could make some genetic changes, adapting not the crew but their future children to the local environment. The environment could also be altered and populated with organisms to build a suitable habitat and form food chains. There was enough biological material on the ship. And yes, something was found on the planet too.

I did not understand the mechanisms of their strange experiment, but they created glowing insects by modifying something called a *louse*. And they cloned other organisms, improving their genome. Only six women and men woke up out of two dozen sleeping people. They probably never realised that their bodies had also become biomaterial for creating human embryos with new inheritable traits. They used the ship's resources, and a few kilometres away, they found the second ship of a pair, the *Ark-4*, with no survivors and with completely frozen corpses. Those corpses and everything else they found on the *Ark-4* allowed the experiment to last more than sixty years. The result was a small population of new men who were stronger and hairier, and able to survive on the surface, but with the cognitive ability of an uneducated nine-year-old child. The scientist Alexander Irrean was so busy working on their physiology that he had no time for teaching. The people he created generated knowledge from nothing but their own experiences, mental states and beliefs – such a limited and unreliable way to interpret the world. At the end of Irrean's life, just over eighty individuals lived a very similar life to that of the people I see now. The only skills they passed on to each other were how to make a few simple things ... like those blankets and bowls. They have a long way to go before they build a spaceship. Both of Irrean's companions perished, tragically died or were eaten halfway down the road. Irrean was forced to barricade himself in the medical department and scare off his creations by ensuring that those who entered the room never came out.

I am particularly interested in the lines explaining the garlands of skulls. After reading the end, I leave the room very excitedly and approach the peculiar curtains. I turn one of the skulls towards me and peer at the letters on its forehead. It reads *Charlie Delhi, day of awakening.* I pick up another, a third, a fourth ... *John Santiago, day of awakening. Venpeculiarus Vlaho, day 102. Nicholas Antonio Omer, day 1341. Isla Vortko, day of awakening.* The first few garlands near the wall are made from the skulls of Irren's crew. Many others are from the next generations of colonists. I imagine Alexander Irrean lying in the preserver's cylindrical bed after turning the ZPE-converter into a weapon that absorbs the energy of anyone approaching him until the source dries up. If they didn't die in the hallway, then they would certainly die soon after leaving it. Later, the tribe of new people made garlands themselves, from the heads of those who dared to explore this cursed section.

Finally, they settled, forever deciding that this part of the premises is forbidden under the threat of death. Since then, they have lived and multiplied independently, remembering and passing on to their children the pitiful remnants of the knowledge and rituals they had acquired several hundred years ago. I don't know how, but this scientific genius had successfully carried out his crazy plan. His last words were, "Is it any wonder? After all, I turned them into cannibals through my own example. I used everyone and everything to get things done one way or another. Now it is up to them. I gave them everything I could, but not myself ... I will not let them eat me."

Chapter 31. Viola

Two men in uniforms with a red-and-brown insignia approached the tall gates. One was a young native, and the other was an older man who had come from Earth just over a generation ago. They sat on a bench beneath ever-flowering lindens and waited.

"Unusual gates," said the young one, "what do they protect? A vault?"

"Possibly."

"But besides the wealth in the temple, what else would someone hide like this?"

"In the last sermon, the True One said that a great blasphemer lives in this house. That he is hiding a treasure from O'Teka herself. This means that the knowledge of this atheist exceeds the temple's knowledge. He is a false architexter."

"So, this is the famous loader. I did not know he lived here. Wait, he's a hero. He rescues evacuees like yourself. I prayed about it last year in volume 2.3 of the Offering V-450. So, he built a second temple here. What's wrong with that? I thought that more O'Teka temples means more bibles."

"Well, yes, but only for a handful of his closest friends. All knowledge belongs to O'Teka. No one should keep it locked away," said the older man, clicking his fingers on both hands.

"You wasn't born here, were you?" asked the young man with a sniff.

"So what?"

"You can't keep knowledge from the great goddess O'Teka. If you do not offer her something you learned, it will become forgotten and therefore worthless."

"Are you saying the True One is wrong? Why are you working for the god of svoloch then? Do you know what we are doing here?"

"You need to decide who he is to you. The True One or the god of svoloch. I took this apprenticeship because I am looking for my purpose," the younger one said with a sniff.

"We only call him that because he's so hairy and loves raw meat, according to the rumours. But he is truly great and authentic.

And you are not young enough to start looking so late."

"This is my second search. There used to be another plan. I wanted to build inter-island bridges so the synthetic rails would run further east along the island chain. But the next closest continent is too far away, and Gera is not overpopulated yet. The financiers abandoned my project in favour of a new city north-west of Gera. I was told that my idea was great but very premature. The colony has to triple in size to contemplate such an expansion."

"Then you were accepted into the Gera-environmentalists." Now it was the older man's turn to sniff.

"I feel this organisation is doing right thing. What purpose have you lost?"

"And why are you so sure that I have lost anything? Maybe I have always fought for the rights of nature. People here are well taken care of, but what about Noverca? Very few of us still truly know what can happen to the planet if you keep changing it. Trust me, son. I was about your age when I saw the death of Planet Earth and the whole system with my own eyes."

"According to O'Teka, the Earth died as part of a natural process. Give it up. We are all second-chancers here, and you can confess to a friend in misfortune. Our movement is fairly recent, no older than ten years. What crazy project did you fail? Did you want to genetically modify a chimaera and create a gryphon or a mermaid? Like that idiot who was accidentally killed in Altyn last week by one of the three giants?"

"Watch your mouth, boy. If I tell the True One what you are saying, then maybe the god of svoloch will chew on your liver next. Ha ha!" The older man's laugh was malevolent. The young man did not react to this laughter.

"But it is true. Can we say anything else? O'Teka does not lie."

"She does not, but those who listen to her may hear what they prefer to hear. The True One teaches us that knowledge can survive for a long time without entering the temple. People pass knowledge on to each other, from one generation to the next. Every time they do that, it changes from truth into a lie."

"I know that. That is why you need the bible if you have doubts. No one makes important decisions based on what your grandmother told you."

"Yes, but what if you write a lie in the bible?"

"O'Teka will not accept it as a true fact and would place it in a more appropriate category. After all, the computers check your information against everything else in the temple. If there is the slightest contradiction in my offering, it will be challenged and treated as a subject of further study. O'Teka does not claim absolute knowledge. It treats any information as knowledge, but you decide whether to trust it or not. This is why the loader is not a threat to O'Teka. He is more of a danger to our boss. I think the True One is just trying to eliminate his opposition. This loader could become a serious candidate for the Grand next term."

"Okey, I almost forgot. You people are too naive. But you are wrong. This loader has never run for office before and is not going to now. But our victory is assured if he speaks in support of the True One."

"I see. Many will listen to the opinion of the hero and the famous loader. Clever. When the True One is a Grand, we can do something about the planet. That is a good purpose, right? Today, my task is to accompany you and assist you in recruiting a potential follower. Our decoy facility was visited by the ordermen last cycle. This must be the reason why we are doing this sooner than when it was planned before."

"That is, if I need an extra pair of hands."

"Have we come for this man? The instructions clearly state that two people alone can't take him. He is too strong."

"No. We need to learn more about the loader and make him more accommodating. Wait a minute, look, someone is coming out."

The gate opened, and a figure in a long dress with a flirty motley headwrap emerged. She immediately slammed the door shut with a reliable click and buzz. A woman in a headwrap walked down the street, slightly swaying her hips and talking with someone over her amulet pinned to the wide lapel on her collar.

When she passed the two men on the bench, they heard the words, "If you want to make an appointment, then Architexter Vist will be in the capital until Thursday. Huh? Then let's make it at three next Wednesday. Okay, I'll tell the architexter that you'll need an hour and three-quarters. Great, don't be late. All the best."

The older man lowered his voice. "I know her. This is the loader's second secretary. They say he taught her himself when she chose her purpose and became his assistant. But in my opinion, she is his concubine."

"What shall we do?"

"Come with me, and ... smile."

The older man got up and rushed after the woman, "Excuse me, miss. We have been waiting here for a long time. Tell us when we can see Architexter Vist?"

His voice became soft and rang ingratiatingly. The woman turned and staggered away from the Gera-environmentalist looming too close over her.

"Get away from me. What do you want? If you are after the architexter, then contact him or myself through the channel in the temple." Her voice shifted from sweet to frightened.

"But we would not want to waste his time. We just want to see him face to face and give him these leaflets with an appeal to urgently save Noverca."

"Leave me alone! You don't know who I am."

The older man's voice quickly became harsh and threatening. "You are Vist's personal secretary. Your name is Viola Crystal. I can't leave you alone. Moreover, I invite you to come with me to that conmot. Let your architexter come to pick you up. Otherwise, you will never see him again. He'll postpone urgent matters for your sake, won't he?"

The woman turned and looked at the two vehicles parked side by side at the end of the alley, "A conmot? Which of the two?"

The older man was surprised to see a second conmot. It was exactly the same as his vehicle, and so it was impossible to say at first glance which one he had arrived in. He told the young comrade to grab Viola's arm and not to let her go. Then he quickly walked to the conmots. Because of the mirrored dome's reflective glow on top of the vehicle, it was hard to tell if someone was inside. As soon as he was nearby, two ordermen got out of the first conmot, introduced themselves, took the amulet from the Gera-environmentalist, pushed him inside, and drove off towards the capital's business centre.

Viola and the young man followed them with their eyes.

Then Viola said, "Why are there only two of you? I hoped the True One himself would come for me too."

"He is afraid to do it himself after one of the Baker-Greens resisted. He does not want the risk. He is especially wary of the architexter, and he doesn't know what to expect from either of his secretaries," the young man answered, then let go of the woman's elbow.

"I understand, but even so, how will you explain to him that you alone managed to get me? What happened to your partner?"

"Surely I can handle a woman. That old earthling is in poor health. He said he was born and grew up in the lunar catacombs before the evacuation."

"Are you going to lie?"

The young man smiled. "I'm a spy for O'Teka. We do not lie – we play a role. Let's go, miss. I am still trying to find the cave by the map since I never went there alone. Just don't forget to put this bag over your head when we drive up to the place. You are not supposed to know the way."

"And don't forget to enable a tracking device for Master King. He will be able to follow us from the city."

Chapter 32. The Branch

Almost all the tribe has returned with their newborns wrapped in blankets. Not only the babies but also the adults look well-nourished and healthy. I need to check out this place they visit once a year to fatten themselves up in just a few weeks. But that is not the only reason I want to go there. My puzzle of who might have given the order to my transport unit to land is still unsolved. I am sure that the command has come not from these genetically modified people who I have decided to call the Irreans. The command came from the southlands. Would you believe it, the clue has come from good old Tma. I have seen her outside the bathing pool, wearing a new necklace around her neck. She was easy enough to rob, and I examined the necklace in the surface light. Unlike everything I have found on the thousand-year-old ship, this object is not an ancient relic. I am holding a real piece of polymer between my fingers, which used to be a teapot lid not so long ago. It is bright green, a colour I have not seen since the last lime plant died in Bebia's room.

So, there *is* another colony on this planet. The mysterious unbeharts are not dangerous beasts but people. Those who make tea in the pot usually eat at the table, have kitchens and bathrooms, sleep in beds, and build computers. They are quite capable of sending a signal to the space unit. I have to find these unbeharts. I suddenly feel the weariness of my current life, being gnawed by insects, constantly worrying that another man might kill me in my sleep, and eating without knowing what I am eating. I feel different about personal space now. Being alone and free is good only if you can choose it. These moments are priceless, but still, I need useful cohabitants for the rest of my time. And if I have to manipulate the unbeharts to serve me, I'd prefer it if they were like the Earth people I hate, rather than the Irreans I despise. Maybe the people of the southlands are exactly what I need, and I am determined to find them.

The plan that has formed in my head makes me feel so good that I return the necklace to Tma and walk away, looking for Anthem. I need her to trust me and feel safe in my lab again. It will take only a few intervals to darken the corridor again, smear it with the glowing paint, and treat Anthem nicely when she is with me. I can be very patient when I want to be. It will take only a few weeks to get her to sleep by my side again.

The new initiates are coming back from the north, which means that I have been here for about a year or more. It is hard to tell. Now all the women should stop taking their contraceptive herbs. My priority is to make a woman pregnant. After a few more months, I will go south too – hopefully for good. It is time to remember that I was a medical assistant in the past. I can use my knowledge and wits to make it happen. The best place for me to find what I need is in the dwelling hall. A few families occupy this large area, and most copulate from time to time. I observe the woman whose mate has just seeded her. He is falling asleep, satisfied. She looks tired, but I stand tall and gesture for her to follow me. She hesitates for a moment and then decides to take her chances. I knock her out a few minutes later and drag her to the darkest corner. Her man's seed is still oozing from her.

I carefully collect it in a glass syringe I found in the lab. Anthem is still asleep on the floor of my section. I lift her leg and inject the contents of the syringe into her. She wakes up, but I distract her by connecting with her myself. She is pleased. I make sure that she is not treated roughly this time. I gently stroke her scarred face with my fingers and whisper words she does not understand. During the next few intervals, I will repeat this process. Hopefully, she will ovulate and conceive. I will try again if she doesn't get it this month.

Chapter 33. Prisoners

Zina did not have time to speak to the newly arrived prisoner because Napovni also entered the cave, angrily complaining that his attempt to catch Vist had not worked. At least he had Viola now and could use her as bait. When Zina saw the woman's face under the familiar headwrap, she could not help herself

"Vi ... Viola!" She shouted and pressed her hands to her lips.

Ramus walked around the cave and cursed in a shrill voice, "I will pluck every wire, every piece of plastic, every molecule of metal from his body. We will see what he is worth without all that technology inside him!"

Zina was terrified. She looked at her husband first, who was also pale with horror. But Tom stood up straight, adopted Vist's usual posture, and said calmly, "It would not be any different for Vist to removing any flesh organ. Imagine your heart or limbs or brain being removed. The origin of the body part does not matter. It works – and that is all."

"You want to see Vist helpless," added Zina. "Is that what this is all about? You can cut the man's legs off, and he will become just that. Vist's implants are much harder to get."

"Good advice. Thank you, doctor. But it is not his physical incapacitation I want to observe. I want him to forget all that knowledge the humans accumulated from the day they started recording it. I will delete Vist and everything with him."

"If there's any brain damage—" started Tom.

Ramus interrupted him with a punch, which broke his nose and forced him to the floor. Zina didn't wait for her turn and fell to her knees next to her husband.

"Shut up! Both of you. I know what I want. I want his blood, his screams and ..." Ramus kept talking, splashing saliva droplets over everyone he faced, and Zina glanced furtively at "Miss Viola." This very feminine and timid person was sitting on the floor. Her back was straight, but her head was lowered. Her expression could not be discerned. Her hands seemed small. They were clenched and lay on closed knees. Was she petrified? For Vist, such a trick would have been a trifle.

Their torturer, by this time, looked so angry and lost for words that he chose a victim. Who would he beat this time? Steven was already less interesting. Who had the most bruises was unclear – was it Steven from the beatings, or Ramus himself, whose arms and legs were badly bruised by the Australian's iron body. And in that precise moment, Viola raised her head. Her gaze met with the bloodshot, yellowish eyes of Ramus.

"You!" Ramus told her coldly, "Follow me. You can tell me in no time how to find your boss."

Tom and Zina both jumped up to stand between Viola and Ramus. Even Rod tried to get up, but Steven rattled the chain and yelled, "Hey, Goldilocks. Have you only the strength left to beat women?"

The horrible man ignored him, pushed Zina and Tom to the floor again, grabbed Viola by the arm, and dragged her towards the door. She resisted, gasped several times, and fainted. Ramus grunted, lifted her, and threw her over his shoulder. When he disappeared through the door and locked it, the others looked at each other in bewilderment.

"It can't be Vist? Secretary Miss Viola ... my arse! Ugh! A clone, I guess. Zina, does Vist have clones?" Steven asked.

"The secretaries Cesario Kats and Miss Viola Crystal are in the mansion. I spoke to them both on my amulet many times. I don't know about clones, but this person was definitely Vist," said Zina confidently and helped Tom up.

"Pretending to be a woman? He he, cough, he definitely had me," Steven said, wheezing.

"And why are you so sure we haven't seen the real Vist just now? The pretence was only in the swoon, and everything else was real. Even the smell of honey," said Rod, sinking into the leaves again and staring up at the stone ceiling.

"It would be too easy. When was anything easy with Vist? Although now she can find out what this primate did to Marta. If it's not too late. We did not hear her for two days," said Tom. He hissed then touched the lump on the back of his head.

***

Ramus entered a large room that must have been his living quarters. The walls were hidden behind heavy carpets and curtains made of a proper fabric. The furniture, including a large bed, revealed his taste for antique luxury in a vulgar chic style. There was too much golden paint, shimmering folds, tassels, jewelled vases on every cabinet, and recreations of famous paintings from both worlds. There was a bronze statue resembling a werewolf on the marble stand. In the middle of the massive wooden table was a huge candle holder. It imitated a birthday cake made of a yellow metal, with a circle of real candles on the top. An old twenty-three-centimetre ZPE ray-gun was displayed in a glass box on a velvet cushion.

Ramus threw Viola to the parquet floor as soon as he thought she was awake.

"Okay, let's see if I can get you to cooperate with me. Earthlings are much more fun than locals to hurt. You can take more before bleeding to death. Oh, if only you knew what I will do to you!"

He grabbed Viola by the forearm and forced her up on her feet.

She pulled free, but Ramus laughed and said, "Pathetic. What are you going to do? You better behave, silly girl, if you want to be introduced to my mother. She is right here, behind this cloth." Ramus swayed towards one of the brocade curtains and called out, "Mother dear? We have a sweet girl for dinner tonight. Would you like a piece?"

He laughed. There was no reply, but someone else's presence washed over the room like a draught. Ramus addressed Viola once again, "Hah, she has not been feeling well recently, poor darling,"

Viola shook like a leaf. Her eyes were full of tears and her lips trembled, but she stood up straight with her chin slightly raised.

"You are doing remarkably well, sweetheart. Do you like it rough? I love entering human flesh with my ... well ... anything. Especially with my teeth. You will tell me all you know about Vist. Oh dear. You look like you want to slap me in the face."

Viola looked terrified. She squealed and slowly lifted her shaking hand.

"Oh, please do," said Ramus mockingly. "Finally – a woman with balls. Hit me, I beg of you. As hard as you can. Don't hold back. I want to enjoy some decent resistance."

He leaned forwards and closed his eyes, smiling.

The next moment he felt like he had been hit by a cannonball. There was a bright flash under his eyelids. The strong blow threw him backwards, and he fell to the floor. First, he heard a crack in his lower jaw, then a crack as the back of his skull smashed against the small marble stand, then an excruciating pain somewhere in the vertebrae of his neck, and – finally – a ringing in his ears. The shock forced him to open his eyes, and he saw a face in front of him, doubling in the blur. It was still wet, but the eyes were far from crying. The small fist was preparing to strike again. The cruel smirk did not belong to the frightened woman he saw a second ago; instead, a male voice spoke through all that ringing.

"Oh, I know everything about Vist."

Ramus failed to conjure a single thought before unconsciousness claimed him.

***

Viola – or Vist, to be clear – examined Ramus briefly, confirming his quite-severe injuries. The loader was aware of her enemy's remarkable organism, which was so unpredictable even in this state, and so she decided to secure him. She took Ramus's boot off to fasten him by the ankle and stared at his bare feet with curiosity. The skin on the sole of his feet was thicker than the sole of his boots, which were custom-made to fit. This characteristic was unknown on Noverca, but Vist was not surprised. The nails were pedicured and painted gold. A thorough search, however, failed to locate Ramus's amulet. That wasn't good. To ensure that Ramus would not wander from his room, Vist dragged the curtain aside.

Marta was awake but didn't say anything, as she failed to recognise Vist in the first instance. It was clear to Vist that the brave pilot didn't have long, and it was too late to help her even if Vist found her hours ago.

The poor woman was only being kept alive by the numerous pieces of medical equipment that formed the temporary system preserver around her, and this was a very temporary arrangement. Her limbs had been stripped of flesh to the bone, most of her internal organs had been removed, and what was left was still alive only because of the air and blood pumping through artificial lungs, vessels and hundreds of tubes. It was obvious that she felt no pain, and Ramus had ensured she could speak.

Marta finally smiled and said in a weak voice, "What took you so long?"

Vist found it difficult to say a word, maybe for the first time in her life. The green eyes filled with real tears this time. The loader sat next to Marta on a tall stool and gently touched her face. It was cold and clammy. Vist realised there was little time and carefully placed outstretched fingers on Marta's crown.

"Untie me, Vist, I can't stand it here."

"I am so sorry, Marta, but you cannot leave this place."

"Why? Oh, I see. He cut my legs off, didn't he? I suspected as much."

Vist could not reply yet. "Marta. What do you remember?"

"Not much. This brute brought me here and tied me up to this bed. At first, I thought it was a hospital, but soon I figured he was here alone. I saw no doctors, no nurses. He drugged me or something ... and more than once. Vist, how long have I been here? Martin has probably gone mad with worry. Who was this maniac? The crazy bastard mistook me for his mother. I tried to tell him that he was wrong, but he was talking about the genetic match and other impossible things." Marta tried to laugh but didn't succeed.

Vist sat back and looked at Marta with pain and effort. "I don't know how to tell you, but you are his mother ... technically."

"Not you too. For the sake of ...!" Marta frowned, then said, "You know I have no children."

"To be brief, Selest did not dispose of the foetus. Your aborted son came with her to Noverca. While we sat in the loop, she brought him up."

Marta went quiet for a long time. She stared at Vist at first, then at the ceiling, then closed her eyes and said, "That would explain the colour of his hair and skin. Nothing else makes sense. Did Selest experiment on him or something? He is not a human."

"Neither was the man who raped you during the first trip."

Another long pause ensued.

"I see. And you decided not to tell—"

"Would you have done so in my shoes?"

"I thought you never lied."

"I didn't."

"I guess not. It was a 'colonist.' You just didn't mention what kind."

"Yes."

"Take me out of here. Carry me if you have to, I know you can."

"Marta, I don't know what is worse, so I will not choose."

"He cut off my hands too?"

"Marta, he cut off and cut out much more than that. You will die soon. This beeping you can hear isn't a good sign. This TSP is similar to the one on the *Wasp*. It's not meant to work for so long. I don't know how he managed to get more than twelve hours out of it, but there is no time to clone new organs even if we were in New Tokyo right now. You are breathing with artificial lungs and ... you have no heart."

"But I can feel, I can worry ... I feel my wrist itching. I still love ... Oh, Vist! I am truly done this time!"

"Your brain is still working, Marta. This is what makes you who you are. I am talking to my friend, Marta Brodsky. You still feel it in your mind. You are still here."

Surprisingly, Marta didn't respond emotionally this time. Instead, she almost whispered, "I thought it was a bit quiet there. Okay. How long?"

"I don't know?"

"Did you kill him?"

"Probably. Do you know by any chance where he wore his amulet?"

"No. I would not be surprised if this bastard hid it under his skin. I want to say a few words to everyone. Let's not waste any time. Are you ready to record?"

"Always."

"First, this is for you, Martin. You were a very special welcome gift to me when I came back. I love you so much. I never thought I had that much love left in me, but you are ... wonderful. I got my appetite back, thanks to you, and remember this, don't hold on to your grief. Move on as soon as you can. Let her be ... smarter and more grateful than I was. You deserve that much. Trust me, it's the only way. It's the right thing to do. Goodbye, my love. Now, to my three mighty warriors ... *moi bogatyri*. The three musketeers, heroes of my childhood. I was so lucky to meet you. Never separate and stay friends forever. This is what makes you so strong. You were born on the opposite sides of Earth, but this small continent mixed you into a reliable alloy. I wish you lots of great adventures and good fortunes. Rodion, you have a great mind. It can still produce millions of ideas that can speed up the colony's progress. People like you are responsible for the fact that we still exist as a civilisation. Never stop thinking. There is no such thing as thinking too much. I loved your sandies too ..."

Marta rested for a minute, then continued, "You see, I already recited all this when I was awake. Just in case. I'm so glad you are here. Now, where was I? Oh yes, Zinochka, my best friend. Captain Tom. I wish you both the same thing, the wish of a woman on her death bed. Look at each other carefully once more. It's time to love for real. You are great together, and there is no need for anyone else, unless you mean a kid or two. Nat! You can have my gears. That flying monster is all yours now. I love you, boy. Well, you are a man now. Remember my lessons, even my nagging. Now for Scarlett ... small girl, big heart! I have a gift for you ..."

There were a few more words for other friends who Marta had found here on Noverca among the new arrivals, and then she took another break. Vist waited and watched her.

"I was hoping to die before it would be your turn, but I have no such luck," Marta added sarcastically, "What sort of goodbye can I give you?"

"I don't expect anything."

"I don't believe you. And no, I don't care anymore what you have in your pants. There is one thing you can tell me, though. I promise I won't tell ..." Marta said, almost laughing at her own joke. "Your real name," she added seriously, "I think you owe me that much."

"My name is Vist."

"No ... it's not what your parents named you."

"My parents had twins. One of them – me – was called Ipsum. That baby and another, and those parents, don't exist anymore and haven't for a long time. I am what I have become, and I cannot be called Ipsum anymore. I am Vist."

"I see. What was the name of the other baby?"

"Aliquis. These names were never meant to be permanent."

"Unisex names ... Your whole family was a bunch of weird ... bastards," Marta laughed. Vist could not resist joining her and smiled.

Her laughter ceased suddenly.

"Thank you for holding my hand ... sort of," said Marta and stopped breathing.

She was still smiling, but her eyes turned to Vist, lost their light, and her full lips collapsed as the machine stopped pumping blood. The automated feedback device signalled for the whole system to stop, and the beeping gradually reduced to silence.

In this silence, Vist sat motionless for almost a minute. He removed his fingers from the top of the dead woman's head, wiped his eyes, and stood up. The loader approached Ramus, who was still alive but unconscious. Vist looked at this strange creature. Ramus might have been a monster, but he resulted from a human's journey through time and space. He was a half-breed. The older woman who raised him, Selest, tried to love him and make him a man in inhuman conditions. All she could offer him was knowledge of true values, but, unfortunately, she didn't teach him enough about how they should work. His mother was a real unaltered and good-natured human. His father – a mutant capable of thinking and communicating – chose not to use those skills for his development. And Ramus Napovni? He was different. Smart enough and cruel enough to become the worst of any possible hybrid type. He could have chosen to be the best, smart and kind like his mother, but as strong and resilient as the svoloch who fathered him. Instead, he inherited from his father enough to become a disaster.

Of course, there were plenty of historical examples of people who consumed, in one way or another, whatever gave them life, or those who brought them up or gave them a start. To what end would such an irrationally selfless act result in self-inflicted harm? Would you have to be him to understand it? Perhaps.

Vist looked around the room. It was a large chamber that resembled a storage room or a museum of ugly but expensive things. Ramus was good at using technology. In the cave, without surface radiation, he must have his amulet charging somewhere nearby – presumably with a file in which Ramus kept more than his official political offerings to O'Teka.

It looked like he had gathered all his important things in one cave instead of having a separate lab, bedroom and study. The loader raised his hand to his shaved temple and turned off his personal amulet. Then his olive eyes closed, his breathing ceased, and for a few seconds, his pulse also stopped. But in those seconds, the barely perceptible noise of the amulet on the charger reached Vist's ears. Behind another curtain, the loader found a charging shelf with a necklace of ruby beads, in which each stone was shaped like a stag beetle larva's head. Access to the amulet was protected. Hacking it might take time.

"Show me your amulet, and I will tell you who you are," Vist said bitterly aloud with a chuckle.

He returned to Marta and carefully disconnected what was left of her from the temporary system preserver. A few minutes later, he carefully wrapped Marta in a clean, silky sheet found on the rack. Her place on the modified system preserver was now taken by the modifier himself. Vist reprogrammed it and connected it to Ramus's vital organs, ensuring Ramus was well secured and immobilised. When, or if he were to wake up, he would feel no pain but would also be unable to move ... or die ... for some time.

Chapter 34. The Branch

Epigraphica, offering to temple of O'Teka AL-915778

I went out today to visit the lake. Usually, it is covered by a thin veil of mist that condenses in the cool air at this time of the day. As a kid, I thought it was a cloud that had descended from the sky, but I know better now. There is no mist today. There has been no fog, dew or cool air in these regions for over twenty years. Worst of all, there is no lake.

This lowered ground with cracks of dry silt at the bottom, empty snail shells and fish bones is the only evidence that a lake was here once upon a time. The rock I loved sitting on with my fishing rod is still here. It seems smaller than I remember, but that is because I was small, too. I bend the prosthetic leg, lower myself on the flat surface, shift closer to the edge, and close my eyes. If I try hard enough, I can almost hear the buzzing of the passing bees, the birds singing and water splashing against the pebbles. But the wind on my face is too strong and dry to keep the image alive for long.

They say there are places in the universe where liquid water still circulates freely on the planet's surface, in its air and underground. There are birds, bugs, and fish ... also, they may look very different. A couple of years ago, I longed to reach such a place and experience unity with the ecosystem ... any ecosystem ... even an alien one. To feel the circle of life happening around me. Now I would be happy just to know that these places exist. That is it.

Selvan Mendoza, memoirs of the last Object team on Earth – 02.05.3464

I was right. The southlands are hotter and lighter. They are covered in strange dark vegetation, with very rich fauna and evidence of other humans living here. I find these unbeharts not threatening at all. In fact, they are even weaker than the Irrean race.

From now on, Anthem will only be protected by her older sister. Since I have learned that these unbeharts – the locals with violet skin – are not a threat to us, I am sure that both women and the baby will make it home safely. I hate to admit it, but I feel an attachment to Anthem, yet I must leave her behind. Although there are plenty of slimy amphibian eggs in the nearby creek, so I shall bring them food. Why not? As that fisherman in the knitted dress didn't even try to run? I strip him naked and drag his body to our resting hide.

Old Tma was busy while I was gone. With her hands, she dug a shallow hole in the soft mud, and Anthem curled up in it like Bebia did in a bio-sleep tank a long time ago! How long ago? A wave of memories hit my mind like a wind. I suddenly remember my flight in the transport unit and her old terminal, which I used to read in between hibernations.

Tma expects me to cut the unbehart's corpse, but I tell her to get on with it. I want to use Anthem's body one last time before I go. Her huge round stomach makes her less fun, but her swollen mammary glands compensate greatly for this. She will go into labour today. I know that because Tma caught two horrible-looking bugs and fed them to her. Apparently, this helps with the pain. I look hard at the pregnant girl, turn, and quickly walk away.

I don't need primitive Irrean women here. I like these parts and will never go back to the crater. I'm not in danger of starvation or attack in these woods. Here I will find more people who look like the inhabitants of the station. Here my personal space will be the way I want it to be.

I return to the fisherman's possessions and try to get his campfire going again. I have no experience with an open fire, but I've read enough about it. After a few attempts, I have plenty of hot flames. This is going to hurt, but what else can I do? I have no shaving equipment, and I can't walk among humans with long hair and insects on most of my body. Talking about insects. Those flies ... Maybe I, too, should eat one, but I don't know how to catch them, and I have no desire to go back. I am afraid that if I do, I will stay with Anthem. I almost get up ... No. I feel as sick as I did when thinking of Bebia. I stretch my hairy arm over the flame. The hair sparkles and burns off immediately, leaving a strong smell behind. I pull my arm out quickly enough not to get burned, but my new sense, my almost doubled perception of the world via those tactile hairs, leaves my body with a sharp pain in my spine. It's okay. I will get used to not sensing much. It could be a disadvantage, but the hairs will grow back eventually.

I stand up, turn away from the fire, and face the dark north. I close my eyes, clench my teeth, and fall backwards into the flames.

Chapter 35. Victory

Vist was still studying the final paragraphs of Ramus Napovni's journal when Nat entered the room with his crossbow and Mik with a ZPE paralyser. They stopped, looking around the over-decorated chamber. Nat noticed Vist wearing Viola's dress with a red necklace in his hand. He approached, breathing hard as if after a battle.

"What happened out there?" asked Vist, still looking at the holo-screen, "It sounded like a sword fight."

"It was almost that," Nat answered. "The ordermen are not allowed to use zappers during an official arrest, but the environmentalists attacked us with rays and maces. Unlike these villagers' wooden weapons, these maces are made of metal. Mik and I disarmed them all. Would you believe it? Some were not afraid to be demobilised but surrendered when they saw this baby."

He waved the crossbow in the air.

"Any casualties?"

"Not among the ordermen. Our team have been saved. I believe they are on the way to New Tokyo already in med-conmots."

Vist deactivated Napovni's amulet, passed by Nat, and approached Mik. Mik was standing over Ramus, who was still stretched out on the temporary system preserver. Mik did not say a word, but his face clearly showed his thoughts.

"Don't, Mik. We must live by the colony's law," said the metallic voice softly.

"When I received your message about Marta, I thought I wouldn't be able to cope. Can't he die accidentally, though?" said Mik.

"No. Ramus has survived so far, and now we can't kill a disabled, unconscious man."

"Couldn't you strike a little harder?" asked Nat.

"Nat, would you be as kind as to carry Marta out of here? It is her body on the bed. I can't tell you how sorry I am. Mik, you and I must move the TSP outside so the medics can transfer Ramus to their vehicle."

"What will be done to him then?"

"His injuries will be treated, and when he regains mobility, he will be exiled. I doubt that he will be offered rehabilitation for what he has done."

"So he will be set free! That is not justice," said Nat. "He killed a person who was like a mother to me. He deserves to die!"

Nat lifted his crossbow and aimed it at Ramus's forehead. Vist turned to him and raised both hands, still holding the ruby necklace and inviting his friends to pay attention to the surroundings.

"Nat, put it down. Mik ... guys, just think for a moment. This creature tried very hard to re-enter our civilisation, so for him going back to square one would be worse than death, believe me. Look around you. Look at the kinds of things he valued. Shiny curtains, golden furniture ... he even hired artists to make a statue from a 3D book illustration and this fake cake. He would lose all this and return to the wilderness with nothing ... not even his knife or these gems. What do you think this would mean to him?"

"But the conniving bastard will think of something to get back, you will see," said Mik, bending over Ramus again.

"Most certainly. But now we know more about Ramus than he realises. Mik, you understand more than anyone else in this world how important it is for us to be true to our convictions and to be ready and less ... relaxed. Even in this colony, where survival itself was founded on reason and moral values, someone at some point has always tried to go back and poison people's minds, starting a new cult or new organisation to feed their whims. We have to be more aware of those dangers. Ramus is a threat and should always be at the edge of our consciousness. Like the rest of his kind."

"This guy didn't turn Novercians to a new religion," said Nat.

"No. He started a noble movement, but the principle is much the same."

Nat took a deep breath and walked towards the bed. He gasped with sorrow and froze for a moment. "I can't. Vist ... You take her. I can't ..."

Tears rushed down his cheeks. He swayed and pressed his fingers to his eyes.

"I will take her," said Mik. "Unless it's an order, I have no obligation to move a muscle to save this svoloch. Plus, you don't need any help."

He carefully picked an almost weightless bundle with Marta's remains and walked out of the room. Nat looked up at the loader with reddened eyes in silent defiance and followed Mik without a single glance at the temporary system preserver.

The loader sighed and squeezed Ramus's amulet in his fist. The device gave out a long, soft buzz, then went dead and fell on the floor as Vist briefly opened his hand. Ruby beads jumped and clattered on the parquet.

Vist slowly approached the statue. For some time, he looked at the full size beast standing on its hind legs. Then Vist reached out with both hands and pressed them all his might on the werewolf's nape. The loader's face flushed, contorted with effort and hatred, to the point where no one would have recognised the architexter in that moment. His dry, olive-green eyes darkened, and a cry of pain escaped the loader's throat, angry and desperate. This is how pressurised steam escapes, or a flame after a door to fresh air is opened. The statue's metal trembled and bent under Vist's hands. And a few moments later, the beast was no longer standing on its hind legs. It was crouched on the ground, its nose on the pedestal, where a few drops of Ramus's blood still glistened like red jasper in the poor light.

"How long have you been conscious?" Vist asked in a clear male voice, still looking at the statue.

There was a small movement on the bed of the temporary system preserver, followed by a cough.

"Long enough to know that you saved my life a minute ago." Ramus's voice was weak and hoarse.

"There are many reasons for saving a life. Including saving it for punishment." Vist turned and walked over to the bed. "Mik would have killed you in a second, but you don't deserve that."

"I perfectly understand your sentiments. I am sentimental and would also kill you slowly."

Vist's face did not change its now cold and apparently indifferent expression. "We have different sentiments. Here, no one but you has the wild desire to torture and devour the defenceless. No. Your crimes require a more instructive answer."

Ramus rocked his head again and said with frustration, "I know. I heard. You will strip me of my possessions and throw me out. And what for? For the mere fact that I am what I was meant to be?"

"You were not meant to be a rapist and a man-eater, Pilialy. And most definitely, you were not meant to be a mind poisoner, a manipulator of people's weaknesses and failures."

After a pause, Ramus spoke with pain in his voice. "You've read Bebia's diary."

"Yes. I know what Selest did to you. And I read your journal. I know what you did to her."

"Then you should also know that she has done something much worse and more sinister to your people. You are a loader, aren't you? I know probably as much about you as you know about me. Are you aware of how you were created? I am just a hybrid, but you are nothing but a construct, almost like those poor Irreans you call svolochs!"

Ramus's voice became higher-pitched and louder. Soon he did not speak but screamed with his inability to move a finger. "All of you were cloned. Brothers and sisters who received implants from the age of two. In those days, back on Earth, the technology of integrating living tissue with metal and synthetics was not perfect, was it? How many children were sacrificed for science and for the profit of their investors? You know better than anyone what they would have done to me if I had lived at that time. Alone, Bebia could do little. But in her past, when she was making loaders ... sometimes it worked, and sometimes it did not. One in three of you died during the procedure, and everyone had an implant rejection. Every survivor ended up with up to fifty per cent of their original body being replaced. Are you sure, Mr Architexter, that your arms are really yours?

Mmm? Do you know that your lungs or heart probably belonged to one of your siblings? What about the rest of you? Whose brain do you have inside your skull? You know that you are also full of wires and artificial data storage, but your brain ... your brain! Is it even a living tissue? Or is it nothing but self-perfecting neuroware? What are you without it? Nothing! You are nothing! You are not a human, and you are not a computer. You are an abomination of both worlds."

Ramus stopped and waited for a reply. Vist was listening with the same emotionless face. Only once did his eyelashes twitch when Ramus mentioned the word "sibling." Ramus did not notice that. He gasped for air, staring at Vist with light-brown eyes.

Vist spoke quietly. "You were wrong. We will not take *everything* of value from you when you leave the colony. Your mind will still be with you. I give you my word that you will move again. Then, what you are 'meant to be' will be up to you. You can't control what you are born with, but you can decide what to gain. What to be is not wholly the choice of the creator, whatever or whoever that was. You will have a chance to see for yourself. I am not sure how to arrange that yet, but I will think of something."

Vist then travelled back to the capital in the Grand's conmot, who had come to see the cave with her own eyes. The architexter was very quiet until Grand mentioned the remains and the wills of those who had died during the kidnapping in her attempts to involve Vist in conversation. Seven were Gera-environmentalists, including the former cadet Nikolaya Gil.

"According to their verified wills, only four of those seven wished to have their bodies disposed of. When the family members attended the bequest meeting, they revealed the last wills registered in the temple a few years ago. Two wanted to end up in the Cloning Institute of Genetic Expansion. One wanted his body to be donated for medical recycling – he was a genuine environmentalist, if you ask me. And one wished to be preserved in the cryochamber for possible future reanimation."

"Forgive me, Grand, but why are you telling me all this?" Vist said, still thinking about something else.

"Because the last request is extremely expensive and totally pointless. You can buy a whole farm for such money or your own air transport. This man has made a fortune working for Napovni. How much money does Napovni himself have? He has no business of his own anymore. His organisation existed on charity." Grand sounded surprised more than concerned.

Vist's green eyes suddenly sparkled with interest.

"Nothing like this has happened for a long time. People started to forget about their optional wills. What about the girl? Gil?"

"She is a former cadet. Unless she registered a new will, her internal organs still belong to her comrades in case of an accident. Of course, her criminal activity deprives her of any privileges unless somebody in the academy vouched for her."

"Why donate? The organs can be cloned."

"It goes way back. A tradition from the first cycles of the colony. Also, it depends on the type of injury. What if there is not enough time for cloning? It will be easy to grow new leg muscles for Mr McLeod, or a spinal cord for Mr Baker-Green, but ..."

"Wait, what about Tolyan?"

"You have to check with his husband. Anatoly Baker-Green is still alive. At least he was this morning, according to Officer Werner's hospital report."

"I need to go to New Tokyo," said Vist and activated the amulet looking for Mik's location. "Mik, can you arrange for everyone to meet at the hospital?"

"We are all on our way there right now," answered Mik from behind the screen. "Aren't you?"

"I had planned on uploading a few things to the temple, but that's not urgent anymore. I'll see you soon."

Chapter 36. The Branch

I haven't been to many worlds. I know about the worlds people lived in from books and records. There was an Earth with a history that made me deeply regret that I had not been born thousands of years ago. I would have flourished in the Middle Ages and during the Renaissance. I would have built empires, conquered continents and enslaved entire races; I would have won all the world wars, and I would have been able to start one even in those centuries when it seemed impossible. I would have established a new religion, and the most popular gods would have been forgotten, not because they became unnecessary, but because the new one, the only one truly invincible, would come and replace them all. And his name would be ... Well, I would have come up with a name for sure. The planet would have been repopulated with my cloned offspring.

And then there were lunar colonies and catacombs on Mars; the stations with vast infrastructures on board. Those were very different times. Soon after I was born, a handful of people slowly flocked to one station orbiting

Jupiter to be transported to a colony close to a red dwarf. I was too young. Not much for me to work on.

Upon my arrival, I may have made the mistake of not accepting the landing instructions. Who knows what the consequences of such a choice were? But I survived among the savages and not without some superior status. Am I not capable of finding my place in the new civilisation? My method is not much different from what helped me earlier. Once again, I am alone against the whole unknown world. I must be patient and attentive. These unbeharts – the purple people with fur and scales on their cheeks – must not see me as a danger. I will study them as I studied the Irreans. It's just, I had to intimidate the Irreans at first. Here, I arouse pity and sympathy in people. With these people, I have to be vulnerable and timid. It would be foolish not to find a weakness to exploit. The Irreans' weakness was fear. These people also have a weakness, their compassion. I discovered it almost immediately.

I wake up in the cool water of a river running south-west from the mountains. I sink into mud almost up to my shoulders, and ugly large flies buzz around my head. They seem to be irritated by the smell of burned hair. I feel scared. How long have I been lying like this, available to any carnivore, insects and people? The Irreans could have found and devoured me. And I know nothing yet about the locals' nature.

Not far from me, the remains of a campfire are still smoking, and the sweetish smell of oil that the old fisherman poured into the fire mingles with the smell of burned flesh. My flesh.

I groan and try to get out of the mud. Several hours have passed since all the hair on my body and head has burned, and the shock and unbearable pain have knocked me unconscious.

I can't describe that pain. I have never felt anything like this in my life. I expected a burning sensation on my skin, but it is as if all my peripheral nervous system is burning, and my spinal cord has exploded in agony. I might have been screaming. I don't know. Perhaps my instinct rather than reason threw me into the water before I passed out.

As the river current washes my body of silt, I think about the things I have forgotten while living among the savages in the crater. I learned about certain things when reading Bebia's diaries in the transport. I think about the woman who cut me out of her womb and left me on Earth. I think about the old woman who saved my life but only used me in her scientific experiments and then enslaved me for labour. I think of the strange man named Vist who arranged all this. This man thought he was a hero just because he knew too much. And it's so simple to fix. I remember how easily the fisherman's skull shattered yesterday. The more I think about Vist, the more I become filled with hatred. It's all his fault. His and his ancestors. He arranged the evacuation and the change of the human race for which my body was used. When Bebia cut out pieces of my liver and lungs, I was a child, and who knows what else. But she loved me. If it hadn't been for Vist's instructions, I would have had a childhood, and there would have been other children at the station who would come to me for birthdays and bring me gifts ... in boxes with golden ribbons, like in that flick.

I wonder where Vist is now. And where is my mother? I would love to find them both, but they disappeared from that unfortunate planet before my birth. They may not ever be seen now.

It takes me a long time to get up and recover. I don't feel pain, but I don't understand why right away. I am drinking water from the river when one of the flies lands on my arm and bites me. I slap it, and a yellow mark appears at the site of the bite. I notice the same spot on my shoulder and remember Tma's precautions before Anthem's childbirth. I put the dead fly in my mouth, but it doesn't taste of anything. I swallow it and want to catch more, but the rest of the flies scatter and disappear as if they had guessed my intentions.

However, one was enough. I feel completely fine a few minutes later, and my burns have already begun to heal. I look through the things belonging to the fisherman I killed. First of all, I dress my naked body in his clothes. It seems that in this society, I again indulge in wearing clothes. But it's not a bad thing because the clothes will hide the new hair and other differences in physique, so as not to be evidently alien. And although I know that among these people, there must be earthlings from the KOSI station, I also know that I differ from them, much more so than from the Irreans. And now I have a pretty good idea why.

In the fisherman's camp, I find some terrible food and a flask with a foul liquid that smells like antiseptic. I don't want to drink or eat any of it, but the fly venom prevents me from tasting anything, and my stomach is empty. I sit by an extinguished fire, wondering if I should go further south, when four people come out to the riverbank, dressed in the same tunics as mine. They speak to me in proper human language. And although many words are unknown to me, this is the speech of civilised people – unbeharts who live in houses, sleep in a bed, and don't have insects in their hair.

Chapter 37. Recovery

After surgery to replace damaged spinal tissue, Rod rested in a hospital bed with his arms above a corset full of supporting jelly-like fluid. Steven sat in a chair next to him. He only had his hands, and one leg free. His head had almost disappeared under the bandage, and the restored leg rested on the footstool. He couldn't speak, so Rod talked for both of them. Zina listened, standing by the window. It was a holo-window, so she could see the Earth's terrestrial landscape, which Steven chose. A bright yellow sun illuminated a green meadow with a few white sheep and a silvery river between the hills at its zenith. Zina's arm was in a proper sling; the long cut across her face was sealed with a dressing.

Rod said, "I haven't seen you in your usual ancient-mummy costume for yonks. I almost forgot how you look in your bandages. But you will be as good as new soon, and with new jaws, you'll be a keeper again. This is how I got my missing finger back. Be patient. It's good for you not to talk but to listen."

Steven tapped his finger on his new amulet, and the holo-screen shone with running words. "I will remind you about it, be ready."

"I am always ready. Zina, how is Tom doing?"

"He is fine. Compared to you, we didn't get as many beatings from Napovni. Tom's broken nose is fixed, but his head still hurts. Rod, have you seen Tolyan today?"

"No." Rod's wrinkle between his eyebrows deepened.

"Why not? You were looking forward to seeing him. But now, Doctor Fenallen is saying that you haven't even asked after him since last week."

"That man is not my Tolyan."

"But he is. He might not remember you, but he will get to know you again. And your girls. They still can hug him."

"About that. Zin, I will not let them see him like this. He is ... someone else. We shouldn't even call him that name. Tolyan is gone. We should have yanked him out of the TSP and buried him on the same cycle as his comrade, Marta Brodsky. Please, let's change the subject."

Rod's eyes looked down, avoiding Zina's gaze. His fingers moved in aimless circles as he tried to focus on the only thing he could do.

"Okay. We can talk once you are out of that corset. We have to decide what to do with him. You won't have to make all the decisions alone. Now tell me more about your book." Zina sat down and looked at Rod with expectation. "Tell us about those Cruisers. Tom mentioned that you found some strange decisions made on KOSI just before the launch."

"Yes," said Steven's amulet.

The bandaged Australian vigorously waved his hands in the air. Rod's forehead became smooth again, and he smiled.

"Steven is trying to tell you that some of the Gera-environmentalists that captured us for Napovni were former Cruisers and their descendants. Believe it or not, a few Cruisers made their way to the evacuation pods. That explains a lot, don't you think? Pass me my amulet. There's a good lass ... it's just over there. Ta."

"How? Why were they even allowed to come to the station?"

Rod activated the book notes for reference. "I have found this story and its versions in quite a few pods. It happened just a few days before the evacuation. At that time, the fathers of Cruisers were well in it and admitted that their Moon Project was a ruse, a simple tool of deception. They pleaded on behalf of the remaining group living beneath the Moon's surface to show mercy and evacuate them too. Unfortunately, there was literally no room for charity. After questioning their humanity, a few owners of private pods said they would take some young people who had been left on the Moon. They could leave some of their possessions behind and install an extra bio-sleep tank in their luggage compartment without threatening the whole project. The Cruisers said they had quite a few members under sixteen years old. But the number who could be saved was limited to fourteen. The only transport capable of a final trip to the Moon could not safely bring more people than that. The rest of the fleet had already been scrapped, as there were no plans to use it again. Object was really burning bridges. This last small ship was not equipped for passengers and was due for demolition, too, as its materials were in high demand by the station. The Moon group's answer was that "there will be fourteen children prepared to say goodbye to their families, who prefer their little darlings to live as orphans on another planet, rather than die in agony like their parents, left behind by heartless fellow men."

"That sounds a lot like the Cruisers. Fallacy, an appeal to the emotions – their usual tools," Zina said contemptuously.

"You are not wrong," said Rod and carried on. "When that transport had returned, instead of fourteen kids, there were only eight, aged from four to thirteen. The rest were three adult men. I say! What happened then made it into my *Summary of the Earth Evacuation* as a historical incident. The pilot of that transport deserved a whole chapter in my book. Karl Schulz-Lahmann was a loyal Object member who did not die on the Moon only because no Cruiser could fly or even start his old and capricious vessel. He did not make any radio communications apart from the usual acknowledgements of the docking instructions on his way back. People who came to the dock to receive children saw a man by the hatch, pushing Karl's body out and sealing himself in. The meds grabbed the body and took it to the preserver. He was stabbed in the heart seconds after he stopped the engine, so saving him was easy enough. The Cruiser's knowledge was greatly outdated, and they either did not know or had forgotten about Object's advanced surgery technology. There was a written note with the demands in his hand, saying that the children would die too if the 'true believers' who had arrived were not granted a pod each and transported to the colony immediately."

Zina listened with her mouth open.

"They received a reply from the speaker by the pilot seat, stating that they would all be ejected into space if they did not surrender. All they could hope for was that they would not be killed on the spot, so the children had better be unharmed. There was no answer for almost an hour. In the meantime, the pilot regained consciousness. Before med personnel took him to the operation theatre to save his life, Karl said the following:

When he arrived at one of the lunar ports, he was immediately boarded by sixteen adult men who demanded they go to Jupiter immediately. One glance at their zappers told Karl that they had not zapped anything for ages. He said they could kill him and try to fly this piece of junk themselves, but he had come for the children and would not leave without them. Also, he had no oxygen capacity for the extra two pairs of lungs nor space for stasis tanks with enough power to run them. The older man called himself Father Sebastian and said there were no children on the Moon. Then he pulled a very old pistol from his pocket and shot two of his followers. 'Now,' he said, 'you have fourteen. Let's go!' Our brave pilot replied that now he had no intention of bringing such danger to Object. Even if he did not return from this journey, his family had to have a chance to evacuate safely. He would rather die than put the people of Object at risk.

A young and strong man standing next to Father Sebastian grabbed the gun from his leader and promoted himself with a single shot. He said that eight young boys were under the surface, and he was the father of two. He was not alone in wanting the children to be safe, and after more shooting and fighting among the brothers, the ship was ready to go with the new party on board.

When the pilot was taken to surgery, the terrorists were given their ultimatum, 'We know that you are the parents of those kids … or at least some of you. Come out and surrender to our justice system. You will not be punished for his murder but for the attempt only. *The pilot is alive.* That is a serious mitigation. Accept it while you still can.'"

"Mmm-m-m!" said Steven.

"Exactly that!" replied Rod, "The Cruisers were bluffing like sharpers. It took just a few more minutes for them to give up their faith, plan and devotion to the Lord. When eight boys and their three birth fathers came out, they were asked why no mothers travelled with their children. Apparently, the inferior women were nothing but men's reward for good service. Due to the environmental conditions inside the Moon dwelling, these three were the only fertile men among the other brothers. Eight boys were the only people they cared for enough to take their chances with Object. Needless to say, neither of them, the boys included, comprehended any concern for their mothers or for the possible female children left on the Moon."

Zina started to breathe again, "I will read your book ... every word of it. I am sure."

"Now, how about a cup of tea? I would love—" Rod was interrupted by the door opening. Tom walked in and greeted everyone in the room. He still had a dressing over his nose bridge and dark bruises under his eyes. For a moment, he looked as if he had forgotten what he was going to say.

He asked his wife, "Zina, did you check your messages? We are all invited to the wedding."

"Yes, Tom. Scarlett and Harlow will look exactly the same in those bridal dresses. I need to talk to them about it," said Zina, only then noticing that Tom hadn't come to tell her about Scarlett and Harlow, "Tom, what is it?"

"We need to see Vist. It's about Marta. Right now!"

"Let's go, then."

"Hey, what about us? This sounds important," waved Rod.

"Mmm?" asked Steven.

"We can't all come here. You are still holding your amulets. You and Steve will have to be on the screen."

Tom and Zina went out into the street, where Vist, Mik and Nat were standing near a strange antique vehicle.

"What is it? Is it you, Mik, who brought this monster here?" Zina asked.

"It's not a monster. It's Victoria. Steven has probably forgotten about her, but he will be in for a pleasant surprise when he leaves the hospital. Scarlett has wedding plans for this car. I don't know what sort. Come on, Nat, tell us about Marta's will. He let it slip to me at the funeral, and I denounced him to Vist when she asked me about Nikolaya Gil's will."

Nat looked pretty confident. He waited for Rod and Steven's holograms to appear above Tom's amulet and told everyone about one conversation during the last rescue expedition.

"Marta? She wanted to become a loader?" Zina looked confused.

"But this isn't a formal wish. Mr Larsson uploaded her will from the temple. She wished to donate her remains to research for scientific purposes. There was almost nothing left of her to bury or donate," Tom said.

"That's right, this is not a will but more like a last request," Nat objected. "Don't you believe me? Mik, tell them."

"I believe you," said Rod from the screen, and Steven nodded. "I see no point in making it up, although you were drunk that evening. But Marta was always sober. That's what matters."

"Marta's last messages to us were played back by Vist at the funeral, and not a word was said about ..." Zina turned to the architexter, "Hey, Vist, why aren't you saying anything?"

The loader pulled her right hand from her sleeve and looked at her empty palm as if it was holding something.

"Now I have Selest's last volume. I can indeed make Marta into a loader. She would not be as complex as me but better than those made on Earth at the start of the project. I just need a body ... any well-preserved body. I also need a copy of her neuropath. I have it right here." Vist closed her hand into a fist. "I downloaded her just before her brain was completely gone. I was sure I would have to delete it anyway. I knew why I was doing it. I was clinging to her. It's the same as grabbing the hand of a dying person, knowing that soon you will have to let go. Only ... she had no hands."

"Are you saying you can download a person's memories, their consciousness?" asked Nat, rubbing his forehead as if trying to imagine his mind being copied elsewhere.

"I don't think so, not in the way you imagine. Her knowledge and a certain amount of self-awareness. Yes, that describes it better. You have to understand that this is a kind of intrusion or violation. During the resistance, we on Earth used this tool a few times for interrogation and information retention, but never for identity reconstruction."

"But what if she hates it and changes her mind?" Mik asked.

"She won't. It is a different type of existence. Things are still important, but it is a different type of importance. I don't know how to explain it. I think it is time to let you know some of my secrets," said Vist, looking into their faces. "When I was a kid, my sibling and I once performed the loaders' 'backup ritual' without telling anyone, not even our parents. We were nineteen, and both of us had to be sedated for twenty-nine hours to avoid overload. I called myself Whist when we discovered that we could not play the game whist together ever again for obvious reasons. Later my name turned into Vist. But after the rest of my family died, I wished I had backed up every one of them. At least my twin has been in my head ever since. I know you always were curious about which of the twins I am. The answer is – I am both. To some extent, of course. My twin is nineteen forever. And my body – that is another story. Zina, I am grateful that you never tried to take my DNA to discover the truth out of your respect for my wishes, but the thing is, it wouldn't have worked. Ramus once called me a construct, and he wasn't wrong. I am an artificial chimaera. I have DNA in different organs and the body parts of four – two females and two males. They were clones, just like my twin and I."

It was impossible to understand and accept this information immediately. Nobody said a word for some time. They all had to think about it later. It was too unexpected ... too cruel.

Then Steven hummed, lifted his hand, and pointed at Mik.

Mik shook his head, "If you're asking about our former cadet, she is out of the question. Her training mentors have looked into her finances. They confirmed that she made a new will two months ago. That was her ticket to Ramus's organisation. Some Gera-environmentalists younger than thirty, mostly women, stated in those agreements that their dead bodies would belong to Ramus Napovni for him to dispose of."

"I wonder if they knew about his cannibalism," Tom said.

"Why else do they call him a god of svoloch behind his back?" Zina frowned and winced from the pain in her face wound.

"We have to decide," Vist said, "about Marta's last wish. Are we carrying it out? We need another body if we do. Other dead Gera-environmentalists had wills. Their families would be happy to receive that money."

"I have more questions for you, Vist," said Rod, "Millions—"

"Me too," interrupted Zina, "I am sure we all have those. But shouldn't we ask Mr Larsson about Marta? He is her next of kin."

"Zina!" Rod almost shouted, "Let me finish! Martin has buried his wife, who is gone as far as he knows. But if we all agree to fulfil her last wishes, then ... Vist, you should have. You should use Tolyan. I could not pull the plug, but I don't mind if you wire him up. He is not coming back anyway."

"He is not dead," Mik frowned, and Steven waved his hand frantically.

"Guys, accept it. He is. Let me have a look at his will again."

It took a minute to access Tolyan's records. Mik looked very miserable, and Steven slowly shook his head in grief.

"This is not right," Nat said, "I feel it."

Tom said, "Feelings are ..."

"Are not a tool of cognition. I know," finished Nat.

Finally, on his screen, Rod's face was replaced with Tolyan's smiling face.

"Hi, darling," he said cheerfully, stroking his beard with both hands, "This so-called Legal Master is pretty annoying, but I agreed to record it, as apparently, it may leave you and the girls with a decent sum if I die. Plus, he won't leave me alone until ... okay, okay, Mr Covchun, I know I have time limitations. So, where can I sell myself? I looked into the options and saw that the Species Preservation Collection pays more than the university hospital. So here we are. The original human in good condition can also be sold at auction. Don't let them have me, Rod, unless they stuff your pockets well. Okay? Done."

Tolyan's face disappeared, and everyone saw Rod again. He was crying.

Chapter 38. The Branch

First, I was taken to the village of the salt spheres. It was a large village near the seashore. I was there for a short time, no more than two or three intervals or cycles, as they call it. But I remembered this moment many years later, and the idea of protecting the environment came to mind. The scrawny woman who looked after me and smeared herbal muck on my burns demanded that I spend a few minutes outside, exposed to Vitr (the name of the nearby star here) and fresh air during the "waken hours."

"It will speed up the recovery," she said, pushing aside the edge of the woven carpet that hung over the doorway.

I had just woke up, and for a moment, I almost believed I was back in my lab, in the old ship, as the light was poor and the smells of sweat and dry dirt were very similar. But instead of a dark ceiling, there was a salt vault above me. I lay on blankets and hides scattered on the earthen floor of a round room. There were bowls and jugs on a low table, with some rags and bunches of dry plants in piles. I must have had a good and long sleep because now I could see it all clearly and in detail. A few hours ago, I had a very cloudy head and couldn't understand why there were no corners in the room. Instead of a window, there was a hole that even a head couldn't get through.

I was fed something that looked like dry meat, but only when I woke up and put another piece in my mouth did I taste something that reminded me of ee.

Outside, the red light was brighter than in the forest at the foot of the mountains. Some garden beds had been dug up in front of the spherical house, and, sitting on a stone bench, I could not believe my eyes. Two huge hens were fussing and scratching the ground in the shade under the wall. They were black, with strange white eyes, and one of these would have lasted me for many hours. The last time I saw fried chicken at the station was when I was about sixteen. Bebia used to give me two or three from her skewer, and I couldn't get enough. I wonder what else they have here from the old world.

I looked up at the beds. Two young people with shiny faces and identical knitted tunics were making themselves comfortable near a bush with thorny trunks. I saw similar plants in pictures in books on the Earth's geography. Such plants grew in dry and hot areas and were covered with long needles. Beautiful large flowers spread an incomprehensibly sour smell over some of these trunks. Also, apparently, there were fruits – oblong, the size of a human head, and covered with either fluff or tangled fibres. A young boy and a girl sat down near one such fruit, and I saw the girl pull this fluff with her fingers and twist a thin thread from it. When the thread was long enough, the boy picked up the end and wound it around a jagged spool.

I sat under a grassy canopy and watched the spinners. After they had collected what they could from one bush, they moved on to the next, leaving finished spools of colourless yarn on the ground. It soon became clear that they were both hot, and that working in the heat was inconvenient. Malice rose in me, but I drove it away. I had to please these people and learn to be sympathetic. Like Bebia was.

"Hey," I called out to them, "What are these ... plants?"

The young people stopped their work and exchanged glances.

Apparently, they understood me because the boy answered, "It's a weaver's cactus. We are harvesting yarn from it."

"And why don't you pick up the fruits and take them into the shade? It's too hot here for you."

The boy laughed. I hardly suppressed the urge to bite off half of his face, but the girl herself hushed him, "Come on, he's an Earthman. How would he know?" She turned to me, "because there will be nothing to harvest after thirteen cycles. Not all flowers will bear fruit, and the fruit ripens for several weeks. The silk bugs try to nest around the fruit when the juice ferments. We must collect enough of their fibres to turn the yarn into our clothes, towels, covers and carpets. We must cherish the gifts of our Lord and not waste them for today only. The Lord said, 'I will give you a seed, and it will feed you today, but if I teach you how to sow it and care for it, you will always be full.'"

At the time, I didn't understand half of what she told me, but the girl's manner was similar to Bebia's when she played a school game with me. I caught myself thinking of Bebia again – something I had almost stopped doing when living in the crater.

"Now, the Lord at least approves of the cultivation of cacti in the village. Our predecessors had to look for them in the wildlands in the past. That was both difficult and dangerous," said the boy in the same manner. "Praise the Lord!"

I looked them both over. They were even more malnourished than the Irreans. While I could still enjoy the girl if I had the chance, I was better off waiting and learning a little longer before I started taking what I wanted.

That was a generation ago, or thirty-five Earth years. Over the first five years, I was gradually integrated into the colony. I was shocked to see a city with so many people! I thought this would never have been possible for Earth colonists to achieve. After two days in the village, I was taken to the modern hospital, which was more advanced than our medical facility at the station. Soon, I was approved as a healthy individual. I let them fix the scars on my face, but I strongly objected to a full examination. To my surprise, I was left to be and to think about it. They explained that being genetically mapped for possible transplants and surgery would benefit me. But I was always welcome to change my mind and agree to receive help adapting to the new climate. Of course, I did not reveal what they should not know.

After being accepted as an evacuee from Earth, I was granted certain privileges and opportunities. My first personal space was just a small room on the farm, where I was given my first assignment. Just as I was expected to work at the station, I was expected to earn my living here. I also felt that they expected me to enjoy working. That was strange and disappointing, but I decided to do something about it later. They asked me about my skills, and I told them I was a surgical assistant at KOSI. Unfortunately, my knowledge and experience were not efficient anymore, and I would have to study first to catch up.

I could do that. I am a fast learner. Bebia told me so.

Chapter 39. Loader

No one spoke a word for several long minutes. They knew each other well, and no comments were needed. Rod's pain at having lost his soulmate was indescribable. They all mourned the loss of their comrade deeply and painfully. Marta's death had been horrendous, and that mourning still roamed their subconscious even when they weren't thinking about her. And still alive, but at the same time, lost to them all, Tolyan had also become a responsibility. They felt the same bitterness and desire not to participate in all this.

The silence was broken by a conv-call to Zina's amulet. The troubled round face of the newly returned Scarlett was covered with stubble, but her delicate features had not yet disappeared under the silky strands.

The girl greeted everyone and said, "Dr Zina, I just received word from the secured med unit that there are changes in the detainee's condition. He was responding to a stimulant and wiggled his toes an hour ago. They have already relayed this information to the magistrate. You said you would inform the architexter yourself."

"Thank you, Scarlett. We'll be right there."

When Zina's holo-screen collapsed, Rod looked at Vist with still wet eyes and said with great effort, "I could never fully understand you, and it used to bug me, you will never know how much. But when we all came back to Earth from here and met again in the Oak in the Dead Forest, I had thought a lot about what it might mean – you know – being you. And so I decided ... I figured ... that it is better to be you than not at all. Damn you, woman! You are the most selfish person I know! You used to do ... crazy things! And you used to drive me nuts ... because I always expected you to do something terrible and nasty ... like trying to take over the world or something. But that was a good couple of generations ago. All this time, you took care of us. I mean all of us. All people. You are not even a god! You are some engineered organism that knows everything, does the right things ... and you always get what you want!" Rod looked down at his hands. "I guess it is all about what it was that you wanted."

"Rod," Vist answered in a soft female voice, "you are an inventor and engineer. You know better than anyone the purpose of all your inventions. Their main objective is to help people. The only difference is that I didn't do anything to my detriment. I was created for that."

"But you are not a thing. You are a living being. Enhanced but still living, and maybe more self-aware than the rest of us. I saw your eyes when you heard about Chang's death. You have a stubborn strand of hair that often falls on your face; your left eyebrow jumps up when you doubt something. Even your metallic voice has a hundred intonations, and I wouldn't be surprised if you are not spared from hangovers. Tell me, are you happy? I mean, usually. Not right this moment, of course. Honestly! Are you?" Rod looked into Vist's olive eyes again.

Vist did not hesitate a second, "Very much so. I have everything I want. And you are right. It is all about ... what to want and why."

"And Tolyan. I mean, will Marta be the same?"

"In this respect, yes. Yes. Knowing her ..."

"Then do it. Take Tolyan and turn him into a happy person. Make him or Marta a loader. It does not matter. Better to be like you than not at all. There are people in the world who I would suggest the opposite for. But not you."

The screen with Rod's face disappeared. Then Steven nodded and was gone too.

"I have to attend the case hearing and then meet with Napovni. He declined his participation but has to hear the result," said Vist. "Zina, am I allowed to use your conference room to attend it? Thank you. Tom, can you bring Tolyan to my house? I have everything I need there."

"How can we help?" asked Mik. "If you are going to check on the svoloch you might need an extra pair of hands."

"It's alright, Nat can come with me. As for you, Mik, I have a favour to ask."

When Vist explained to Mik what was required of him, he frowned indignantly at first as if he wanted to say something but immediately clenched his fist and burst out laughing. It was not a happy laugh but a bitter and malicious one.

"It wouldn't have crossed my mind," he said as he climbed into the driver's seat of his vehicle, Victoria, then started the engine and drove off towards the city morgue.

***

Vist, Tom, Zina and Nat returned to the main hospital building. Tom was still thinking about Vist's origin. He thought the new information should disgust him. Instead, Tom felt that other negative feelings, such as guilt, were clouding his marriage. His chagrin about his life's imperfections somehow evaporated with every thought. He walked behind everyone and watched as Vist walked steadily and calmly in front of him in her long robe. Her gait had not changed in so many years. This is how a man might walk if carrying something heavy, or a woman if she had to put on someone else's shoes. On Vist's left, Nat walked broadly like a soldier, young and reckless. Tom used to stride like this at his age too. And Zina walked on the right, feminine and elegant, clasping her bad arm in the sling. Tom thought his love for Zina had long existed separately from his feelings for

Vist. For him, the loader had become an object of adoration, reminiscent of a love, if not for Tom's mother, then for home, for the world, or for life and beauty itself. Tom's desire to wrap his arms around Vist became something more: a desire to protect, unite, warm up his own reality, existence and even his wife, Zina, with that embrace. How strange! He was sure it used to be the other way around. Tom wondered what Zina felt about Vist now and, to his surprise, recognised a small sting of jealousy of a completely new and different vector.

"Vist," Zina said, "what did you mean when you said you can now create a loader? What does Selest have to do with all this?"

"She was the one to assemble us soon after birth. She never was sure which one of us ended up growing up here," Vist said, pointing to his head.

"What about you?" Tom asked. "Are you sure you know who you are?"

"Yes, I am sure," answered Vist. "I guess that makes me more of a Frankenstein monster than Ramus. What she did to Ramus was the opposite. She took his body parts for other people, as he could grow the missing organs back."

"What?" Nat turned and looked at Vist with disbelief. "This creature can grow his appendix back if you remove it?"

"He never had one, but he can grow things back. Unlike Steven, who needed a cloned muscle to replace the eaten one, Ramus would just need time to regenerate."

"But where did he learn to do that?" Nat asked.

"He inherited this ability from his father." Vist stopped and turned to face his friends, "I understand how shocking that might sound, but the creature we called the svoloch has this ability. Samantha, in her time, found starfish genes in Abraham's samples but could not explain them. I, too, was wondering, since there were no starfish on Noverca, apart from the ones the colonists brought. I first suspected that *Ark-8* and *Noah-8* were not the first ships to land here. Unfortunately, we had to leave for Earth, and the rest of the study had to be completed by Selest."

"And she has blueprints for loaders," Zina said, "something Samantha didn't have."

"Yes, but I would not repeat the initial project here on Noverca. It was not very merciful, as you now know. But the svoloch's regeneration ability can prevent the tissue rejections that killed many subjects on Earth. Selest found a new and safe way to integrate the human brain with neuroware but never had a chance to test it."

"She found that trait in Ramus, right?" asked Tom.

"You see, Selest decided to allow the svoloch–human hybrid to live so that her source lasted a little longer. She was sure that the incompatibility would destroy it, but on the contrary, she ended up with a little boy who could heal his cuts and bruises within hours. At first, she just took genes from him, which helped speed up the evacuees' preparations. She was already attached to him but still decided to experiment with his organs after he started growing back broken teeth, a finger bitten off by a dog on the station, and an ear he lost in a haircut accident. But then she was forced to use him repeatedly as a donor for those who needed a transplant."

"That is horrible!" Zina said, "I can't believe she could do that to a baby. It's inhumane."

"No wonder he is a bit pissed off," Nat added.

"Let me guess. You will test this regeneration mechanism out on Tolyan," said Tom. "What if it doesn't work?"

"Tolyan's brain is new, healthy and blank. Like the brain of the newborn. The cloning technology on Noverca is another factor that contributes to my plan. What they have achieved here would have also spared countless lives on Earth."

"If the church had not stopped us a few hundred years ago, we would have that too," Nat grunted, "Hey, Vist! How about going out there and finding the other ships? The ones that brought the other svoloch here? Let's have another expedition when all this is over."

Vist checked the time, "We will see. Napovni's hearing starts in a few minutes. You,

Mr Alloyway, should come with me to see the detainee when this is over. We will also ask him about what he found there – in the northern ice." The loader smiled and turned to Tom and Zina, "I will meet with you and Tolyan later tonight. Bring him to my laboratory and make him comfortable."

Vist and Nat went to the secured ward, while Tom and Zina went to the opposite wing. In the light room with colourful walls, they found Nurse Matthew and Tolyan. Matthew was reading something on his amulet, and Tolyan sat in front of the holo-window. The screen showed a farmyard with swans and ducks. The big guy's lips were stretched into the smile of the sleeping man, who was having a good dream. A small drop of saliva shone on his green shirt collar like a diamond pin. His eyes followed every movement of the tiny yellow duckling on the simulated windowsill.

Zina stood in front of him and said, "Hello, my friend. How are you today?"

Tolyan leaned to the side, trying to look around the sudden obstacle. He whined indistinctly and struck his elbow out. Zina fell to the floor and screamed in pain. Her arm still hurt from the dislocation. Tom rushed to pick her up, and Nurse Matthew dropped the amulet and grabbed the syringe from the bedside table.

"Do it!" Zina said forcefully, hissing at him, "Rod is right. This is not Tolyan anymore."

Chapter 40. The Branch

I am well settled down in the city. I like living here more than in the crater, yet at the same time, I feel more restricted. Yes, I have clean sheets and plenty of meat, cooked or raw, but rules and laws bind me worse than a cage. Breaking them might lead to me being kicked out and returned to the village. That is, if I am caught.

I have my own amulet now, a smaller form of the personal terminal and much more advanced. It gives me access to plenty of information in the library they call the Temple of O'Teka.

My career has changed dramatically too. After a couple of years as an apprentice, I got a job in the veterinary clinic. I was paid for my work. I learned how to use the local electronic currency, but instead of purchasing larger apartments, I buy and order things that make me feel good, although just for a short time. It took almost ten years before I opened my own business. I took on many apprentices and finally have some free time. They complain that I do not pay them much, but I always find something wrong with their work, so they will have to put up with me a little longer. I get away with being different, but only just. My excuse is that I am an alien. I am glad to say that I am more successful than many of the other earthlings who came from KOSI.

I am still studying the colonists. I find them extremely difficult to manipulate. They keep questioning everything I suggest. They do not believe me when I try to mislead them. They check the facts, compare notes and refer to O'Teka when they have the tiniest of doubts. This society has a very unique system of leadership. It will be hard to get to the top. Elections happen at different times. Being a Grand means you can't be anything else. You can't use your name, live at home, or do what you love most. You just have no time for that. Every Grand keeps their post for between three and five years and then retires when they feel they have achieved or failed what they planned. It takes a year to prepare the ideas for improving the colony, and there are no more than two or three candidates every time. Since everyone can become a candidate, I am trying this year myself. Why not? I have a few ideas for improving this world, but I doubt they will like them. I have to find out what they want first. Haven't I learned enough about them? I have been watching them for a generation.

Almost thirty-five years! This is also an age when the colonists can apply for a licence to have children. The Irreans – or the svolochs as the unbeharts call them here – did nothing but reproduce, yet their population was much smaller than that of the colonists. Spiritual villages do not care to prove to anyone that they can raise a child. They are lucky if the kid survives childhood. But the purple people behind the walls have to ensure they can afford to raise a family, even if they have been married for decades. They calculate their genetic compatibility and carefully select their children's future traits.

Taking a female without disturbing the peace is also hard. You don't just take whichever one you want. They have to choose you too, but I am less popular here. My height, strength or intelligence do not appeal to these purple bitches. They are not afraid of me for some reason, although they should be. They don't expect me to do anything, and they are right. I do not dare yet. In my frustration, I was so close to roaring and ripping them apart a few times, especially when they smirked at me with contempt. I truly don't understand what they want. More studying is needed, but I am on my way to the village of god believers in the meantime. Female mystics are less capricious there. They allow you to do anything with them if you bring them a gift. You can even hurt them, but not too much. I don't want any complications. Those villagers can be useful to me in one cycle. Gosh, I hate that word!

My business allows me to leave the city at any time. I have a conmot for transporting sick animals to and from the farms. The woman I am about to enjoy is called Lilla, and she is sitting beside me, squealing with delight. Before, I picked her up from the village for a ride, and we had gone far enough already. She is one of the few born in exile and has never been to the city. This is her first time in a conmot. She is about twenty years old, and it is easy to impress her. There is no road here, but the ground is dense, and the rocks on the left side are well lit; they look like huge chunks of raw meat in the red light. Suddenly, Lilla points her finger at a mountain fold and squeaks.

"What's the matter?" I ask.

"I know this place," she says, "we took kiln clay here. It was very sticky and better than coastal clay. But the mine was deployed here, so we scraped everything we could and found a new one near the peninsula."

I stop my conmot, "A cave? Show me. Is it big?"

"Very big, it has corridors. Sometimes the svolochs come from the mountains and hide in the caves, but this is not their season, so it should be safe."

We get out of the vehicle, and she leads me to a wide crack in the rock. I take off, raise the activated amulet above my head, and light the way. The cave is vast. Nothing grows here. It's dry and has enough room for all the old spaceship dwellers. The entrance can be broadened so that even a conmot will fit inside it. Two ideas come to my mind at once.

"What is it that your Great Martyr Jeremos says? We didn't find this place by ourselves?"

Lilla thinks for a moment and then understands.

"No, no. It goes like this ... by the will of the Lord, all our finds are from him – our food and shelter, our well-being and security."

"What does your Lord say about procreation?"

"Children are a great gift from the Lord; therefore, do not deny them, but having received them, take care of them. Submit to the will of the Lord and your man because the first gives you a womb, and the second gives you seed."

"Yes. Yes," I think out loud. "How do you like the idea that men choose and take their wives in the colony, and children can be born from the age of twenty-five Earth years instead of thirty-five? At least half the citizen population may be happy to support me. If that does not work, I will try to come up with an idea that sounds even more benevolent. I will move my things into this cave and bring people here. Anyone who fails to fulfil their purpose will find a new purpose with me. I don't think I can recruit any svoloch. Still, villagers, earthlings or even colonists who struggle ... they could be much easier to persuade here, with no ordermen to protect them. And the women here, I am sure they will have no choice but to show me respect, love and lust!"

"He he ... You are funny when you say strange things like that."

I look at her stupid face and feel the familiar thirst for celebration and the appetite for my preference.

"Listen, Lilla. Did you tell anyone where you were going today?"

Chapter 41. Mik

Mik slowly walked along the morgue corridor, looking with surprise at the pictures and diagrams on the walls. They were part of the training props for trainees choosing physiological research as their purpose. Besides a rather young professor who owned the establishment, several anatomist trainees and five apprentices worked there.

After reading about how much it costs a private person to maintain a body in a pre-animated state per cycle, Mik was shocked. But later, he saw that if the deceased voluntarily donated their remains for scientific research, then the relatives would receive much greater compensation.

"Why do the relatives need the organs to remain alive? Their loved one is no more," Mik asked the apprentice, leading him towards the office.

"This is a chance to extend the farewell and funeral service for relatives, but the body can't be preserved for more than a couple of weeks, even in the physio-suspension system.

From a legal standpoint, this allows time to study or challenge the will. And it is useful for us to reanimate living tissue and not a corpse. You see, sir, I have studied the architexter's new offering about the loaders' history. Is it true, sir, that we will have loaders here on Gera one day?"

The apprentice turned his beautiful transparent eyes to the famous hero. He was a young Uzhan with sparse bronze scales on lavender cheeks.

"No," Mik replied firmly. "For Vist, such an option can only be an emergency, an extreme measure. At least for now."

"It's a pity. I would have asked him for an apprenticeship. It sounds like a new direction in progressive medicine. An excellent purpose for people like me."

"Not in my lifetime, I hope ..."

Mik found that he had never thought much about what more loaders might mean for Noverca. If they were all like Vist, then that would probably be nothing but good. But what if they turned out to be a new race, dominant in every way? In principle, this should not be possible in the colony's society. However, cannibals and mystics lived on this planet. Why couldn't some crazy dictator show up in one of the most unexpected places? What if that dictator is a loader? Who knows what the colony would then turn into?

Mik's thoughts were interrupted by another mortuary worker. At least this one wore a uniform like Uzhan's, but this man was short and hairy, like a character from ancient legends and myths. His ears seemed longer because of the stiff tassels at the ends.

"Valeriy, that guy you let in is not leaving."

"Did you remind him of the visiting hours?"

"I did, and he showed me his fist. I don't know what that means, but now I'm afraid to approach him."

Upon hearing this, Mik intervened. "Is this visitor an earthling?"

"I didn't ask, but maybe. He has very uneven pigmentation."

"Lead the way. I will talk to him."

Valeriy lifted his long finger in protest, "But you have a meeting with the manager in ten minutes."

"It won't take that long."

The suspended corpses section looked different from the more familiar parts of the mortuary. The bodies were suspended in a jelly-like liquid. They looked covered in silver because of the gaseous layer on the skin. They were wrapped in wires and tubes that kept the organs alive, but unlike the temporary system preserver, the equipment to which they were connected could not support a living person. Each reservoir was tilted at a forty-five-degree angle. The upper part of some of the reservoirs was made of thick glass, and you could see the face and shoulders of the deceased. A young man was standing, practically hugging one of the reservoirs. He stroked the glass with his fingers and whispered something. A female anatomist was standing at the equipment control panel and, judging by her face, she did not know what to do. Mik walked up to the guy and said, "Buddy, you have to go."

The young man did not react, and when Mik repeated the request, the man said, "I told you, leave me alone if you don't want me to break your nose."

At the same time, he continued to touch the glass, which was illuminated from the inside, and he did not turn his head.

Mik used two fingers to grab the guy's wrist. The young man barked indignantly and turned around, but his hand was trapped as if held by pincers. He twitched a couple of times and stared in surprise at the dark face. He looked about twenty-five years old. His face bore two characteristic scars on his cheekbones, indicating that he had recently removed implants that allowed him to use oxygen dissolved in seawater and dive for up to twenty-three minutes. Furthermore, he was dressed in civilian clothes that resembled the Novercian scout uniform in its colour, cut and accessories.

"Master King?" His voice went from sluggish to respectful.

"Yes, you know me. Do I know you?"

"Most likely, no. You retired the year I entered."

"Are you a land-scout academy cadet?"

"Not anymore. My name is Orpheus Shivka."

Mik let go of his wrist. Orpheus began to rub it but stood straight before his former master. His face was tear-stained, like a child's.

"Have you left the academy to join the Gera-environmentalists?"

"I went to join her." Orpheus turned his eyes towards the glass top of the reservoir, "to the academy and the True One. I would have followed her to oblivion itself."

Mik stepped closer to the reservoir and regarded the deceased's face. Despite the silvery layer of gas, the absence of hair and the removed vibrissae, he recognised Nikolaya Gil. Without turning around, asked, "And why did *she* need it?"

"I don't know." Orpheus sobbed softly, "Nikky regretted it two weeks after the initiation, but he knows how to convince people at the start."

"Who? Napovni?"

"You know the True One? Yes. She was almost in love with him, and at the same time, she was terribly afraid of him."

"What about you, and how do you know this girl?"

Orpheus did not answer right away, "Our parents are from the last batch of Grounders. We grew up together. We've always been together. Starting a family together was our goal from the age of eleven. She was a great scout, better than all of us."

"What changed?"

"Last year, she won the annual Breakthrough competition and was invited along with the other sixteen winners to the presentation. The presentation was attended by several politicians and veteran land explorers."

"I remember that presentation. I attended the first part."

"But after the ceremony, she didn't return but instead went to the True One's residence. I don't know how he did it, but she was a completely different person the next cycle. And a month later, she dropped out. She often went to him and said that some meetings were held there. She started talking about protecting nature."

"I see. Why is she in suspension? Are you paying for this?"

"I don't have such funds. The True One always paid for us as members. We had to change our wills, leaving everything to his organisation – our belongings, valuables and ... bodies. I'm not sure why, though."

Mik grimaced and asked, "How many of you are left in his organisation?"

"The apprentices and active members? Sixty-two. Most of us are already in rehab ... since few days ago."

"What about the inactive members?"

"You mean our sponsors and supporters? There are hundreds, maybe thousands."

The morgue's apprentices, who had patiently waited at the end of the hall, now approached slowly but surely.

"Let's get out of here, son," said Mik.

Together, they walked out of the mortuary building into a sunny avenue of real green acacias, unusually bright in Vitr's crimson light.

Orpheus, whose head was lowered during the conversation, looked up and asked, "Are you here for me? I have already been arrested after the conservationists' dissolution. The ordermen let me go because I didn't participate in the recruiting."

Mik pulled Nikolaya's amulet out of his pocket and looked at it. Then he put it into Orpheus's hand.

"I brought this here. I intended to leave it at the office to be handed over to Gil's family. But it's better if you do that."

The young man recognised it immediately, "This was lost! Where did you get it from?"

"She dropped it when she tried to poison me."

Mik turned and walked towards his car, Victoria, at the end of the avenue. A few passers-by were inspecting the car with curiosity and taking pictures of it.

After getting in, Mik activated his own amulet fitted into his sunglasses. He sent the message to Vist, *Found her. You have a couple of cycles left.* Then he put the glasses on, and instead of the trees in front of him, he saw the Sun on the holo-screen.

The Sun was swollen, dimmed by the filter and an incomprehensible colour on the screen, but it was the Sun. A star that can no longer be called by that name because it has gobbled up its own system of planets and destroyed all that once relied on its warmth and caress. Then he heard a voice. The voice of a man Mik loved like his father coughed for a long time before speaking. Mik had already listened to this recording, which Vist had recently uploaded, several times. But now he felt an especially acute unease and needed to hear it again.

"Here it is, my boys. Look at it one last time. Hear me for the last time too. Selest says I won't make it to see the launch. She did her best, trust me. I just ran out of fuel. I'm an old wreck who hoped until now to see your faces. I thought I would die in an armchair under some black tree, on the shore of that green brine that you call the Equatorial Ocean. I thought you would hold my hands then. Cough! I knew people who cared where they died. It was important for someone to die under this treacherous sun. Or on that unfortunate planet, Earth, which already looked like a ball of shit when we moved to Mars. Mars was also home to some other people, and they decided to stay there. Only Selest talks about staying on KOSI. We all orbit Jupiter now, and she will probably stay here with this monster she raised to be a pain in the arse for everyone. I don't know what she leans more towards, saving this roach eater from disaster or saving the evacuees from him. I know what I would have done. Actually, no. I don't think I am that cruel.

Boys, if you have children of your own, do one thing for me, will you? Teach them not to be desperate motherfuckers. Teach them what I would have taught my kids if I had any ... to absorb love and multiply it. Teach them to know what is truly good for them. Let them find a proper way of taking care of themselves. The human way. As soon as we turn into animals – and I am not talking about growing scales and gills. As soon as we forget that we are a civilised society, and we forget our most important values, which we must look after, then we will devour ourselves, just as this sun devoured my home.

My home. It is with you now, and I can't get to it. Vist promised me that she would take care of you. Remind her of that word she gave an old man many years ago. And I, Alan Lillypond, I'm going to burn in the hell you see on the screen. My dry, useless body will lie in my cabin and wait for cremation, which the devil himself in the underworld could not dream of."

The sun's circle darted to the side, and pale, kind eyes appeared on the full screen under white eyebrows and surrounded by wrinkles.

"I love you, Steve, Mik and Tolik. I have always loved you."

That was the end of the recording, but Mik didn't immediately take off his glasses. Suddenly, he started the engine, turned Victoria around and quickly overtook Orpheus, who was walking along the avenue in the opposite direction.

"Hey, Shivka. I'm going to open a new anti-fallacy academy. Will your comrades be interested?"

Orpheus frowned. "It was harder to get to your school before. Call, and they will come. Especially after rehab. Where else would they go? Can I come, Master King?"

"I will consider your candidacy first."

Chapter 42. The Branch

Ramus lifted his head, craned his neck, and tried to see his feet, which were covered in white hospital sheets. He focused, ignoring the sharp pain in his neck, although it was good to feel something there. His left leg swung a couple of centimetres to the side, and Ramus leaned back against the pillow, sweating and panting. He was as tired as if he had lifted and carried a huge boulder.

His gaze wandered around the room again and settled on the face of a strong guard. This Earthman had kept an eye on him since the start of his shift.

"Why are there no screens on the wall in this room?" Ramus asked petulantly, "I will die of boredom. I get it. You can't get enough of looking at me, but you won't even hang a picture on my wall. All I have to look at is your ugly mug."

The guard didn't reply but narrowed his eyes and pursed his lips. An expression that Novercians were apparently incapable of appeared on his face. Ramus decided that he had nothing to lose if he tried.

"Is this your holy purpose in this world? Standing by the door? Are you going to impress women with this? Or your grandchildren in the future? Or is this your apprenticeship? You will have to serve long before you rank as first officer. Shame. You are an earthling. You are stronger and more enduring than these violets and cornflowers. You can make your way to respect and prosperity much faster if you work for me. What do you say, um ...?" Ramus scrutinised the name on the black-and-silver uniform, "Peter?"

The guard looked about thirty years old. His eyes were equipped with an enhanced retina, and his head was shaved and protected by a radiation-reflecting shell. This meant he often worked in the wilds. Peter looked at the door and moved closer to the bed, where the paralysed Ramus was tied down with broad straps.

"Sir," he said, "I am not really supposed to talk to you."

Ramus took a deep breath, "I won't tell anyone. It will be our first secret. Do you have an amulet with you? I can make a generous transfer right now. An advance! Most of my followers were earthlings, and I have always been pleased with their work. I know that I can trust you with my bank codes."

Peter smiled. "Thank you, sir, but all I wanted to say is that you can't afford me. You don't have what I want, and my conscience is not for sale."

Ramus swallowed and snorted contemptuously. "Moron, you could have taken your advance first and then turned me down."

Peter returned to his post. "Yes, I am an earthling. The origin of my parents is one of my legacies. But you are mistaken in your belief that all earthlings can be corrupted. My advice to you is not to try and recruit any of us. Another attempt could cost you dearly."

After that, the young guard fell silent, and all attempts to talk to him again were in vain. He still followed Ramus's every move, but his face was now calm and confident.

An hour or two later, another young earthling replaced him. This one had red curls and bright, carefree blue eyes. He took his place at the door and also stared at Ramus, but it was clear he was thinking about something of his own, something probably very pleasant. He looked like a man who had just returned from an exciting date or had finally found a solution to a personal challenge.

Ramus remembered Peter's words and didn't dare offer this guard anything. The former politician felt completely helpless for the first time since he had been immobilised. He even regretted having refused remote participation for his case's hearing. He lowered his eyelids and lifted them again only when he heard the door opening and closing. Vist was standing by the bed, and behind him was a very easy-to-read face. Ramus thought to himself with plain horror, this man wants to kill me.

He closed his eyes again and groaned as if in pain. The metallic voice spoke softly, but without this useful sympathy that Mr Napovni could evoke when he needed it.

"I just listened to the verdict, and it's final. You have been sentenced to exile and oblivion. The magistrates' decision states that you will be removed from this city with limited possessions. Your personal amulet and your terminals will be destroyed, and your data will be deleted. The same goes for your essays and other offerings to O'Teka. They will be erased. As the architexter, it is my duty to carry out the sentence of oblivion. I can't change it, but the time of its execution is completely up to me. What does this mean for you?"

"You came to gloat," said Ramus with closed eyes.

He could not stand the sight of Vist. What everyone saw as content, Ramus saw as smugness. The loader's face was the only one that had shown no emotions towards Ramus since his capture. No fear, no hate, no compassion, not even contempt. Viola's crying face been an act, and Vist's real, calm face was a constant reminder of that one single time that Ramus had been fooled.

"I came to trade."

"What can the great architexter possibly want from a vile svoloch like me?"

"The most valuable thing on this planet. Information."

"If it's so valuable, are you offering much in return?"

"Value is a subjective matter," said Vist and turned around. "Nat, tell Mr Napovni what oblivion would mean to you, please."

After a short hesitation, the young man stepped forwards in surprise.

Ramus lifted his eyelids and looked warily at Nat who said, "If I had been working for forty years on something of use to the colony, I would feel that my life was wasted if no one ever benefited from my efforts and time. I am not an artist or a writer. I did not make scientific discoveries or develop ideas for a better society or a prosperous economy. I can offer only the results of direct physical actions and ways to improve them. The first is useful now, and the second will benefit those who inherit my profession. Being condemned to oblivion means that my contribution to the present will be forgotten, and my contribution to the future ... well, someone else will eventually develop and make those improvements. My descendants will not even remember my name after two or three generations. I will be truly erased."

Every muscle on Ramus's face tightened, and he said with rather forced mockery, "Nat? I heard this name before. Oh, yes. From that delicious-looking girl. And what is it you do here? Save people and their transport for scrap? Scout the eastern and western islands for colonisation purposes? And do people pay a lot for that? For risking your life? How much is your life, Nat? Can I buy it?"

"They do pay a lot, and you could probably offer more. But can you offer me that feeling I get when I fly my avion over unknown areas, that thrill and the sense of adventure? I doubt that you even understand what I am talking about. Finding a treasure and owning it is by no means the same feeling. And the things I value, you would not take for a treasure. Tell us, Mr Napovni, how much you don't want to be forgotten?"

Ramus did not give a direct answer. He thought for a moment and then said to Nat, as he still did not want to meet Vist's eyes, "Your construct here said the sentence can't be revoked. I will be erased anyway. What is the point of this trade?"

Vist replied in the same voice, "It will be erased from the temple, but it can be stored elsewhere. And that will be completely legal. Oblivion is all about the temple, nothing else. Nobody will find you in the temple, but if someone wants to find you, they will be able to."

"Where will you store my work?" Ramus was forced to look at Vist.

Vist took a hand out of his sleeve and pointed at his head, "Here."

"Oh yeah, a walking, talking database. Until you die?"

"Nope. After I die, the information will still be accessible."

Ramus's eyes suddenly sparkled viciously.

"I want something else too. I will be thrown out, but I hope to return in due course. I also want you to store my belongings and hope you have a spare room for them in your mansion."

Vist shrugged.

"I doubt you will come back, but if you manage somehow to be the first to do so, and for a good reason, you will never care about those shiny things again."

"Do we have a deal or not?"

"Yes."

"And how do you know what I tell you is the truth?"

Nat let out short laughter, "I would like to see you try and trick the loader."

Ramus looked at Vist with hateful eyes, "What do you want to know?"

"According to the law, before deletion your personal journals are to be psychologically studied, with fact-filtering by the architexter ... by me. I want a more detailed account of that ship you found on the northern ice and of its occupants. I also want to learn more about Selest. Now... try to keep your head perfectly still please..."

Chapter 43. Obydva

Epigraphica, offering to temple of O'Teka K-4183351

I'm used to doing everything one hundred per cent. When it was physically impossible, I approached the highest level of perfection that I could. Therefore, when I listened to the preacher's words, I also achieved a perfect level of attention and honestly believed in the creator. Thanks to those annoying contradictions that religious ideas carry, I still failed to believe one hundred per cent. There has always been a doubt in my mind that the Lord exists. Only under the influence of Bliss did this recede, as did the ability to think, so I gave up the drug. I needed mental clarity to study loaders. We have destroyed hundreds of these creatures that are closer to the Lord than mere mortals. I delved into their work and became increasingly convinced that we needlessly exterminated this result of human genius. I know this is blasphemous, but now it matters no longer.

After all, we dishonestly told everyone and even each other that the loaders are just an abomination, objectionable to the Lord. In fact, we feared that one loader with such remarkable abilities might eventually take over the world's leadership. But in the end, I came to an unexpected conclusion.

There is no God, at least not the one I believed in. I am sure he could be a loader, but not a god. We were worried about nothing. That's why they are loaders, not leaders. The simplest desire to seize power over all humanity is just as inaccessible to them as it was to the Lord. It could not be ...

should not be ... considering you believe in him one hundred per cent, as I tried to. The Lord is supposed to be omnipotent. An entity that can do anything can satisfy any of its needs. Our faith is useless to him, just as public recognition is useless to loaders.

Of course, a loader is not a Lord and is not omnipotent; he is subject to weaknesses, like any of us, but he differs from us in his values. None of the loaders we killed had even the foundations of a thirst for prominence. (Just like my donkey Hodzha has no desire for meaty snacks). They appreciated beauty and enjoyed pleasures even more than we do. Still, the most important joy for them was the process of reasoning, acquiring information, admiration for achievements, and the result of their work and art. None of them felt envy or a haughty pride. Satisfaction – yes, but not hubris. You have to understand the difference if you are committed to the true a hundred per cent, like I was.

Former Father Klaoos, from a suicide note. Cruisers archives, Folder 912

The head that had once been Tolyan's was now clean-shaven. Without these lovely curls or a beard, and with strongly sagging cheeks, his pale face became alien. Even Rod did not recognise the former Russian warrior in him. Instead of brown eyes, he now had one completely black pearl, and the other glowed with the white light of a dual camera. His body had lost half its weight. Because of the additional two vertebrae, he became a little taller, and his voice became hoarse and quiet. He sat in the large chair in Vist's house.

"Have you thought of a name yet?" asked Vist, removing the wire from the new loader's thumb and clicking the dark nail back into place. "You understand that you no longer resemble Marta, and you don't look like Tolyan either."

"I'm not only like, and I'm not that at all anymore. Marta didn't know this much. You've uploaded a lot, haven't you?" said a low voice – still Tolyan's, but duller and more raucous.

"You now have great data capacity – much greater than mine when I was ten. The living axons in your brain integrate nicely with the neuropath of Marta's memories. So, I thought I would add a few implants for storage and to test your conduits. You should remember more every cycle, but do not stop taking medication to avoid the shock."

"I now understand why you didn't leave the name Ipsum for yourself. How much metal and synthetics is there in my body? Apart from skeletal implants?"

"Together with wires – 14.6 grams of metal, a little plastic and 22.9 grams of nanopolymers. Compared to me, you are wireless. In your skull – no more than 4 grams of the PNS. The rest is in the spinal column and in your new ribs."

"What about the backup? Surely that is heavier."

"It is too early to install. I shall wait for a year or so. See how you do and how much you can memorise."

"Will I remember Tolyan's life at all?"

"Some ... yes. Not much. Tolyan was very healthy and was rarely scanned at routine medical check-ups. Also, he did not visit the temple regularly enough. My own records contained very little of his neural pathways. That is why my first attempts to reload him on my return failed. Perhaps you will sometimes experience flashes of his memories. It will affect your perception no more than Marta's mind. You are now a completely new person with residuals of my friends' memories. So ... what shall I call you?"

"Obydva. Call me Obydva."

"I know that word! Is that in your mother tongue? Ukrainian? Not bad!"

"Yes. Tolyan was a nice man, a lovely person in every way, and a great father too. He loved Rod so much! And if he had not lost his mind ... so stupidly ... oh, shit!" Tolyan's head dropped for a second, but then he looked up again, "I don't want to forget him. I should be grateful for his body, but I can't stop feeling guilty. So I want to let Marta go and focus on Tolyan. He became my vessel so that I will become his mind."

"You know you can't do that. And if you try to be one or the other, you will fail."

"I know I can't be him. But I can be Obydva. I can become a friend to Tolyan's friends and maybe some comfort for his girls. Right?"

"I don't have an answer for you. Let's see how everybody accepts you first," Vist turned the laboratory screens off and helped Obydva to get up. "Let's walk some more. Viola, please open the door."

The tall double door opened, and Obydva stepped onto the balcony, leaning on Vist's shoulder.

"It's so high up here. I am almost dizzy like in the temple. I've never been to this part of your house. I haven't been ..."

"Not to worry. You'll get used to it."

"I thought Ramus was the only freak on Noverca who liked beautiful ... by his standards ... things. Can we stop for a moment? Phew, Tolyan's lungs are great, but I guess you can have too much of a good thing."

"Just go with it. It's part of the adjustment. Weren't you dropping a hint about the things in my house a minute ago?"

"I was. They are unusual but beautiful and luxurious. You are too rich, even for a loader. Martin would love to decorate his hotel in the same style, but in our house, he preferred simple wooden furniture."

"That's still expensive. Real wood is not in abundance on Gera. My material is much cheaper, and the furniture ... well, don't forget I made it all with my own hands."

"And this patterned balcony, too? You carved it from salt spheres?"

"Took me a while, but yes. I had to use a zapper to cut it."

They walked in silence for a minute. The south side of the house was sunny and exposed to the mild wind. The temple's spire was visible in the west and was divided into a ruby-coloured half that faced Vitr, and a deep black side that faced the north. The whole city was beneath them, swimming in the unusually green gardens inside the protective dome.

"Don't tell Martin who I am, please," said Obydva. "I love him too much to hurt him again."

"We won't tell him."

"Did Rod say anything after the integration?"

"Yes, he came to see you a couple of cycles ago when you were still in a coma. He cried and said goodbye once again. He also said he is still happy about Tolyan's donorship and can't wait to meet *you*."

"That is comforting to know. What about the others?"

"Looks like it was much harder on Mik and Steven. They are very unsettled, but I am sure it is only a matter of time. Tom and Zina have accepted the entire thing much more easily. Scarlett wants you to be one of her bridesmaids. Nat is not saying much, but he is strong. He will get there."

"I must talk to him."

"Wait until you are all levelled. It will be better when you don't have to lean on people all the time to walk."

"Are you making fun of an old woman?"

"You are neither a woman nor old anymore."

Obydva almost laughed but had to press both hands to his chest and sit on the floor.

"Is his heart too big for me?"

"No. Your mind is adjusting to a new body. The neuroware works fast. You will feel very different tomorrow and every day after," said Vist, sitting next to Obydva, "I will tell you a secret if you want."

"That you also have a pair of balls?"

"You wish I just told you that! No. It's about your mind's adjustment. You are going to love it. Do you remember our last conversation in Ramus's cave?"

"How can I forget?"

"How does that make you feel?"

"It makes me want to visit him in the hospital and take a bite of *his* liver."

"Angry, huh?" Vist smiled at the frowning face. "Soon you will stop feeling that."

"What? Are you saying I will not feel hate for that svoloch again?"

"You will ... a lot. Enough for both of you. But what you will want to do about it will change. This is my gift to you. You will feel everything you should. You might get upset when you have to, but it will not hurt anymore. You will learn how to love a man again ... or even a woman – Obydva may be full of surprises – but it will give you nothing but joy even when you are apart. All your feelings are going to be stronger and more intense. They will stay fresh for a longer time, but how you manage them will be the best thing that has ever happened to you."

Obydva turned to look at Vist's smiling face. Vist's eyes, which now looked different, were full of tears.

"Sounds good to me. How old are you, Vist? Really?"

"Ah, it is so rude to ask a loader ... Well, my mind is much older than me. My body is much younger because I fully regenerate every seven years. You, too, can now live as long as you choose."

"Listen, Tolyan was in his prime, right?"

"Yes. He is not yet sixty."

"Do you think I can have a child of my own? One day?"

"I can't see why not."

"What will I feel then?" Obydva almost frowned.

"What do you mean?"

"Will I feel what a ... parent should?"

"You will feel even more."

"How is that possible?"

"Because your mind can perceive things at a much deeper level, and your reasoning abilities are now enhanced. The greater your understanding of things, the more you appreciate them."

Vist watched Obydva with delight. The creature sitting on the balcony floor looked like a big man recovering from a few serious surgical procedures. But the expression on the tired face was of a very emotional and tearful woman full of happiness and hope. Obydva was sobbing.

"Oh, Vist. If that is true ... then I don't know why—"

Vist winked with a grin.

"Hush, my friend. Don't tell the others. Yet!"

Obydva was now laughing and crying quietly at the same time. He grabbed Vist with both arms, pressed his face to Vist's robe, and shook in the mixture of sensations. Vist hugged

Obydva and put her head on Tolyan's broad shoulder.

"You will be alright. It is all part of the adjustment. It will get better."

The red sun shone through the holes in the balcony pattern. It sparkled in a tiny drop on Vist's eyelashes. Obydva's shoulders soon stopped shaking, but they sat like that for a long time, embracing. Each was thinking of something, but Vist felt that what had once been Marta was gaining some new, inexpressible peace. The loader knew from his experience that past anxieties and worries were slipping from Obydva's soul like an old snakeskin. Memories would remain, but they would not disturb this almost newly born human being. A new life and new perceptions, tasks, and concerns would soon emerge, and a balance would also be restored.

A deep sigh escaped Vist's lips.

"Oh, Tolyan! Too bad you can't rejoice with us, my sweet old friend," Vist whispered, but Obydva did not hear her. He fell asleep naturally for the first time in his new life, still hugging Vist like a child embracing a stuffed toy.

Chapter 44. The Branch

I was told I would be sedated for almost a week, but I remember waking up several times. For short periods, perhaps no more than an hour each time. It was enough for them to test the basic functions of my body, to ask about what I felt in my fingers and toes, but not enough to answer my questions. I didn't have many of them, but there were natural anxieties. I remember times they offered me some food and water to check if my body had accepted it. I'm not exactly a doctor, but I knew that wasn't necessary. I was able to eat and drink before the procedure. But I couldn't move, and that is what they should really have been checking. They did a little, although my memory of it was very hazy. I definitely stood on my feet and slowly moved along the wall, and the unusually tall nurse led me by the arm. This only seemed to last about a minute, but I can't be sure of my perception of time under the influence of the goon-fly's venom.

I also remember sitting in an armchair, and they tried to shine a light into my eyes. This caused unbearable pain, and I heard a piercing scream. I am sure it was not I who was screaming, but I protested too, and the lights went out, and I fell unconscious again.

At one point, a woman sat by my bedside. At first, I thought it was Bebia, but after blinking, I saw a man clearly. I didn't recognise his face, although it looked familiar. He reminded me of one of my captives; he was just as huge.

Today I woke up with incredible clarity. Now, I distinctly see the screen of a holo-window on which a small creature covered with feathers is stirring and squeaking. For the first time since talking to that awful loader, I close my eyes and listen, examining all the sensations in my body. Yes. It's fixed. I know this for two reasons. First, I can feel my limbs. I am aware of my chest breathing. I enjoy twisting my feet and wrists. I flex my fingers and rotate my hip slightly, feeling the movement in my spine. The damn loader kept his word, and I'll be able to walk on my feet again. When the time comes, I'll tear him apart with these very hands.

Second, they are afraid of me. Why else would the nurses restrain my fully functioning body with straps? I feel my bed slowly turn on the mechanism and assume an upright position. I find myself face to face with the magistrate. So he is about to read out the verdict. I'm ready. I know what's next. Fools. They should have killed me. They had the sense not to rehabilitate me, but even in exile, I am more dangerous to them than all the populations of village mystics and Irreans combined. It will take me time, but I will return to the colony. I'll be back for my valuables, for retribution, and for the Grand's title. I will return with an army that I will raise under my leadership. I now know what to do.

The magistrate reads the conditions from his amulet's screen. They have already brought me to the northern bank of the river Thanile. This is the same place where the inhabitants of the salty village found me, helpless and burned, almost forty years ago. The magistrate and his two escorts step aside, and the wall in front of me collapses into folds to reveal a clearing of cerise skies and inky bushes. One of the attendants carries out a linen luggage bag and drops it into the grass. It contains provisions for several cycles, medicines prescribed to me for a month, and some simple clothes. There are no weapons or electronic gadgets. At best, there will be a small folding knife, a pink wax lighter, a simple trowel and a skein of twine. I have been deprived of my large handzap blade.

The last words of the magistrate state that I am forbidden to enter the territory of the colony, including its cities, farms, training grounds and research sites, which are all marked with a security power fence. Never mind, I'll find a way to cross that barrier too.

One of the attendants unfastens the white belts, freeing my hands. I raise my long, wide sleeves in front of me. I felt determined to grab him by the throat a second ago, but now I know it won't do any good. My arms are still weak and heavy. I have to get stronger first. My strength will return to me as I heal quickly. After the procedure, my body is hairless and inadequate. Eventually, it will, once again, be covered with sensitive hair, replete with its former robustness and speed.

Now my legs are free too. I look down. I am wearing some kind of long grey robe, which stinks of some spice to repel insects. I take unsteady steps, but I'm in no hurry to get off the transport platform and onto the ground. One of the escorts impatiently pushes me in the back. I take an involuntary step, and my weak legs buckle. I lower myself to the grass. Behind me, the transport's white door folds and slams shut. It silently takes off and flies away over the tops of the trees and hills. I look up. The sun seems to be shining a little too bright today, but it is not as hot as usual. Dark-bluish leaves above my head look black against the cloudy sky.

I check the contents of my bag. The first thing I see looks like an object from another life. It's a piece of synthetic paper. Not only that. It could be a page torn from a notebook and glued over the hand mirror in the thin frame. I have not seen anything like this in a long time. There is writing on it – another old-fashioned thing. I read it. It is a message from someone who knows I can read in this language:

I gave you my word that you will move again. I also told you that you will keep your mind. Unfortunately, your body turned out to be too dangerous to the people of Gera. It is a weapon. I can't let you keep and use your biological advantages against us. I have copied your neuropaths into an integrated semiartificial brain and installed them into a body, which, according to legal documents, also belongs to you. You have been reborn. You can achieve great things with your memories, intelligence, medical skills and ability to learn. Look after yourself. You still have a chance to be a good person.

Don't waste it.

Vist.

My eyes shift from those words to my hands. I can see thin dark fingers holding the paper, partially covered with a sleeve.

I drop the mirror and pull the sleeve back; this is not my hand. It is small and covered in dark-purple, smooth, thin skin. I look at both of my hands with horror. I touch my face – it feels wrong! I run those strange insect-like fingers over my body. I find no broad chest, no strong legs. I kick off the walking boots and look at my feet. They are also small and purple. The sole is thin and fragile. And what is this on my front? Mammary glands? This is the body of a woman. I find the dropped mirror on the ground and tear the paper off the glass surface.

The face in the mirror looks familiar. It was a girl who failed to complete her mission. She died and was preserved for the inquest. No, no ... this is not me. This is a fragile creature, a weak woman, an inferior who is incapable of bringing me my desired status. Reality shows the difference between who I was and who I am as I roar and smash the mirror with my fist. In the past, the glass would have shattered to smithereens. Small cuts on my knuckles would start healing almost before my eyes. Now I scream in pain in a voice that is not mine, but pitiful, much higher.

The mirror is smashed. Something crunches in my wrist, and a wave of pain rolls over my arm. The back of my hand is covered with deep cuts, from which blood flows in streams. I lick it out of habit, but it doesn't taste the same. My stomach cramps and turns inside out. I fall on my back in despair, eyes wide open. I see clouds running across the sky – yellow wisps against a burgundy background. And even higher, above the dirty clouds, I see a thin and perfectly straight strip of white vapour. It isn't natural. It has been left behind by a flying craft that the colony never had. My consciousness does not register this fact.

Hot and suffocating darkness claims my mind.

Chapter 45. Easter Egg.

Epigraphica, offering to temple of O'Teka F-857113

Even broken in spirit as he is, no one can feel more deeply than he does the beauties of nature. The starry sky, the sea and every sight afforded by these wonderful regions, seems still to have the power of elevating his soul from Earth. Such a man has a double existence: he may suffer misery, and be overwhelmed by disappointments; yet, when he has retired into himself, he will be like a celestial spirit that has a halo around him, within whose circle no grief or folly ventures.

Mary Shelley, Frankenstein (personal library S. Dvali)

"If Vist is not in the temple and not at home, then where is he? Viola, today is the wedding cycle. The brides will not start the ceremony without the architexter."

The face on the screen smiled with understanding and said, "I know, but the boss did not leave any instructions today about his whereabouts. Try Paradise, Doctor Zina."

"The city garden? Okay, but please, let me know if Vist comes home in the meantime.

And remind him about the wedding if you could be so kind."

"You have my word."

Zina deactivated and returned the amulet, which also served as a large moonstone brooch, to her dress shoulder. She was wearing an evening dress made of dark-blue velvet. Her wedding band and this brooch were the only accessories she was wearing. Her black-and-silver hair fell on her back and covered her like a cloak. Her hand had long since recovered from the dislocation, and it now held two stems of orchids entwined with white ribbons. She wanted Vist to see her like this.

It took Zina a good ten minutes to find the loader. Paradise was the oldest garden in the colony, and it was now overtaking the biggest part of the White Capital's old town. Vist was there, sitting by the fountain and staring at the large oak with green leaves. Or at least that was what Zina thought. Vist's eyes were open and even blinked from time to time, but his olive-green irises were tightly closed. His pupils had almost disappeared, and the eyelashes were half down. His handsome face was slightly tense, making him seem especially masculine and wise. Zina could smell the honey wax over the smell of flowers.

"Vist, what are you doing here?"

Vist blinked twice and turned to Zina. Two very ordinary green eyes looked at the woman in front of him.

"I am reading. Well, I was reading. You look lovely, Zina. As beautiful as on your own wedding cycle. Is this *sponsa cymbidium*?"

The architexter nodded at the flowers, and Zina could not help a broad smile. "Yes, it is. Vist, you don't forget things. Do you have any intention of coming to Scarlett's wedding?"

"Of course. I planned to be there for the less intense part to congratulate the girls," answered the metallic voice.

"But the ceremony is the most important moment. All of us want you there."

"At that moment, I will be the last thing both girls will be thinking of. I am sure you know that."

"Vist! Come on, you have twenty minutes to get home and ready yourself. It is not about what they are thinking in that moment, but about them knowing that you are there."

"Okay, if that matters. I did not realise. But then again, I can't expect girls to share my judgement of their situation."

Vist got up, and they both walked towards the gate.

"What are you going to wear this time? A dress or suit?"

Vist laughed, "Which do you prefer?"

"I am not sure. You looked like a theatre actor at both weddings many years ago, professionally prepared for the role. Or for a masquerade, especially at Rod and Tolyan's wedding. You looked pretty convincing in that frock of the same colour as your eyes, but when you walked in wearing that tuxedo a week later at the special ceremony for Tom and me, everything returned to normal. So, we still don't know."

"Good. I would never have done this if I hadn't lost the bet to Rod and Steven. You will have to wait until *my* wedding cycle. But today, I will be in my best robe. How is Mr Baker?"

Vist and Zina left the garden and turned towards the temple.

"He is alright, I think. Yesterday he allowed Obydva to see the girls. Phoebe rushed to wrap her arms around him, but Groonya took her time. I reckon they are treating the situation the same way as kids whose parents are divorced do. They accept that Papa will not be living with them anymore. Marta and Tolyan both loved those girls, and Obydva remembers that. Nobody cried this time."

"Yes, Obydva is gaining control over his intensified emotions. He hasn't cried since he listened to the last message from Général two weeks ago."

"Does he still live in your house?"

"For another month, maybe. Obydva wants to live and work in Pettogreco. He is an excellent chef, after all. I bought him a house there."

"Why don't you persuade him to stay?"

"Obydva is his own person now. Or will be soon. He wants to find his purpose, but we will see him often, don't you worry."

"Vist." Zina stopped just before they approached the mansion by the temple. "You have been living alone all your life, in your huge house and inside your broad robes. Still hiding your true self from everyone. Viola and Cesario are both not real people but computer programs. Obydva is moving out. I don't know if you will ever have a wedding."

Zina did not expect this from herself. She was sure that she was also coming to terms with her feelings, but now she was suddenly very upset. She bit her lip and commanded herself not to start sobbing like a little girl.

"Zina, what are you talking about?"

"I am pregnant, Vist. My new ovaries work. Tom and I will have children. Rod has children. Nat and Andrea will marry next year and apply for a licence. Now Scarlett is planning to have at least four kids. Even Obydva wants to meet someone and have a child and a new life. We all have our clones living in the colony, including nine of Chang and six of General Lillypond. But you, you are only joking about it. Damn you, Vist! We know now that you were sewn together from the pieces of your brothers and sisters. At least five people are uploaded into your head full of platinum wires. So what? After all, you, too, like Obydva, have become someone ... a person. An individual. We all love you, Vist, and we worry about you. Why don't you come out and live among us, with people. Men or women, Novercians or earthlings, or even loaders, if you make more of them. I can tell you are lonely. I am afraid you will always be alone." Zina paused, adjusted her flowers, then without looking at Vist, she added, "I will see you in the temple. We will all be waiting for you."

She turned around and walked towards the spire.

Vist looked after her in surprise and shrugged.

"Alone?" he said softly, "But I'm never alone."

Vist entered the house. As he passed by the laboratory inside, he looked in briefly.

A large apparatus was built into a niche in the wall. It was similar to both the suspension reservoir in the morgue and the huge artificial womb in the hospital's incubator. The support system worked properly, judging by the indicator lights and the quiet clicking of the computer. Besides the turbid liquid, a strand of floating long hair similar to yellow filiform algae was visible in the round window, illuminated from within.

Vist nodded in satisfaction and went into the wardrobe room to change. He unfastened the metal disc from his shaved temple and placed it on the vanity table. After thinking for a minute, Vist turned away and pulled his robe over his head, when suddenly ... the loader froze.

The amulet on the table squeaked its usual conv-call twice, and the holo-screen turned itself on, demanding permission to communicate. The inscription *Object and Vist* appeared on the screen.

Vist stood there like a statue for a whole minute. His handsome features suddenly hardened, and his green eyes shone incredibly brightly. The architexter almost stopped breathing.

Many years ago, in another life on Noverca, a loader had left her notebook to a young man. The key to this particular cypher was hidden among the quotes and poems in that book. In that same year, among all the other information that the loader uploaded to the Temple of O'Teka was a secret – an easter egg. The message was coded in so complex a manner that it looked like attempts to decipher it had long since been abandoned. And now Vist heard a signal that could only mean one thing. Someone had been smart enough to access the message and reach the architexter's special channel.

The loader caught himself worrying for a second, but then pulled herself together, let go of the robe's hem, returned to the table and answered the call.

"You?" Vist exclaimed with surprise, "You are so ... young."

"Architexter?" On the screen, the face of young Timofey stopped smiling, and he nodded respectfully in greeting, speechless.

"You solved the unsolvable mathematical task! I see that my hopes were not in vain!" Vist said happily.

"I'm sorry, I didn't know it was your conv-call sign. I found some strange virus in the program and ..."

But Vist just laughed.

Your name is Timofey Hesley. Andrea's brother? Right? Are you free right now?"

"Well, yes. I could only deal with this riddle after work. The master permitted it."

"Don't leave the temple. Meet me there in the Hall of Solemn Ceremonies in ten minutes."

Once again, as Vist passed the lab, the loader stopped to check the reservoir that contained the suspended body of Ramus.

Walking away, Vist said out loud in her – or his – metallic voice, "To be alone in a world full of such different people? Impossible."

To be continued.

Book 3   Act and Vist, an Official Trailer:

Well, fancy that! What a surprise! The target took the bait and turned up.

And they say that this is the smartest person on the planet.

A figure in a dark robe stepped out of the four-seater conmot. The hot wind immediately lifted the long copper hair off one side. The person in the robe walked a few steps forward and stopped at a wide shield with a coast map. It appeared as if he ... or she was looking for something.

In the dense shade of black foliage, the sniper sat down with his feet in the direction of the target and rested his toes on the stone ledges. He carefully put both feet into the piercer's stirrups and pulled the bowstring towards his chin, slowly lying on his back.

He squinted at the tiny weather display showing the strength and direction of the wind and aimed at the person's head, adjusted accordingly.

In the last forty-six years, he had never missed a hunt. Never!

Focusing for a second on the tip of the screw arrow, he imagined it taking all that ancient technology out of that skull and the loader's brains. The sniper shifted his eyes to the reddish hair a couple of hundred meters in front of him and unclenched his fingers.

ABOUT THE AUTHOR

Author Anka B. Troitsky was born in the USSR in 1968, grew up in Kazakhstan and left for the UK in 1993, not believing that Russia would become a European country during her lifetime. Her greatest hope lies in human progress in science and life through reason, not a whim.

Printed in Great Britain
by Amazon